The Union Trilogy

Book 2

Light the Way

Joe Kipling

Cillian Press

First published in Great Britain in 2015
by Cillian Press Limited. 83 Ducie Street, Manchester M1 2JQ
www.cillianpress.co.uk

British Library Cataloguing in Publication Data.
A catalogue record for this book is available from the British Library.

Paperback ISBN: 978-1-909776-12-8
eBook ISBN: 978-1-909776-13-5

Published by
Cillian Press – Manchester - 2015
www.cillianpress.co.uk

To my sister Pippy Kippers
There ain't no hill or mountain we can't climb

In *Blinded by the Light* we are introduced to MaryAnn Hunter. MaryAnn lives in the Manchester Neighbourhood, one of three Boundary towns constructed by the Light pharmaceutical company to protect the rich (Alpha) and the skilled (Bravo) from the Sandman Virus that decimated the UK 20 years previously.

MaryAnn's father is the Legislator and responsible for maintaining law and order within the Neighbourhood. This affords her a position of privilege as an Alpha.

MaryAnn's life changes after her parents are killed in an explosion at the Building of Light. Not only does this incident rob MaryAnn of her parents, but it also leaves her permanently scarred. With no other family, MaryAnn is sent to live with the Director of the Light and his daughter Maud in their claustrophobic home.

The death of her parents reunites MaryAnn with her long lost brother Daryl, who is now a member of the Union, a rebel organisation fighting for the rights of the Echo living on the Outside. When her brother is captured and held prisoner by the Light MaryAnn is recruited by her uncle, Patrick Hunter, the leader of the Union, and Peter Mallory, Daryl's best friend, to rescue him. The rescue exposes MaryAnn as a traitor to the Light and she is later captured and tortured by the Director.

MaryAnn is rescued by an unlikely ally; Mr Murray, the Director's chauffeur, who is a Union spy. She flees the Neighbourhood and hides out with Peter on his family's farm until it's safe to travel to the Union headquarters.

After recuperating from her injuries MaryAnn is issued with an ultimatum by Uncle Patrick; either join the Union and fight for the Echo or leave her newfound family behind.

What will she decide?

CHAPTER 1

Collection Day

CHARLOTTE:

The thick black night slipped effortlessly into a thin grey dawn as we finished the milking and cleaned up the sheds. Dad and I strolled home across the scrubby fields in companionable silence, neither of us feeling the need to speak. We'd finished the first chore of the day and we were both looking forward to breakfast.

I climbed the stairs to my room and slid into the seat at my desk. I could hear the sound of clattering pots in the kitchen below. It was mail day and if I hurried I could finish my letter to Uncle Ethan before Mum called me to breakfast.

The knock at the front door was unexpected and I paused mid-sentence. It was too early for the post truck.

I listened to the sound of heavy footsteps in the hall and the familiar creak of the front door. I stiffened at the cry of surprise that followed.

'Run, Charlotte, run,' Dad yelled up the stairs. A warning meant for me! I froze, a rabbit caught in the headlights. 'Charlotte, get out now,' he hollered.

Terrified, I leapt up from the desk. In my panic the chair tipped over and as I sprinted out of the room I heard it clatter noisily to the floor. I bounded across the hall and pushed my way into the bathroom. Once inside I ran to the window. As I fumbled with the clasp I heard footsteps outside. This wasn't one of Dad's drills. This was for real.

The door flew open with such force that I thought it would be torn from its hinges. A Watch entered, his starched grey uniform clashing uncomfortably with the cosy interior of our family bathroom.

I was confused. My collection date was still a week away. Mum and Dad were packing up the farm, planning to run to the Union.

The Watch grabbed me roughly around the shoulders. As he hauled me away from the window I could feel the paunch of his stomach press invitingly against my back. Panicked, I thrust my elbow into his fleshy middle, muscle memory making the action easy. Mum and Dad had trained me well. "*The world is dangerous,*" they had cautioned. "*You have to learn to look after yourself.*"

The Watch let out a grunt of surprise and for a brief moment I felt the arm around my shoulders relax. It was the opportunity I needed. I tore away from his grasp and sprinted down the stairs.

My heart pounded wildly as I darted across the yard. I had to get to the hideout, an abandoned shepherd's hut hidden deep in the hills. We'd practised this drill so many times that I knew the route by heart.

I steered away from the Watch stationed by the garden gate, avoiding her grasp and racing to the perimeter of the yard. I climbed the fence that bounded the yard, feeling the splintered wood bite into my thighs. I paused for a moment, distracted by a cry of pain. As I glanced back towards the house my throat went dry. The Watch had followed me out of the house; his gun was trained on the slumped body of my dad, as he lay sprawled out across the porch.

Dad hollered at me, his voice hoarse, demanding that I keep on running. I stared in horror as the Watch raised his gun and slammed the butt down hard. There was a sickening crunch as it made contact with bone. Blood poured down my dad's cheek, trickling through his beard and pooling onto the collar of his shirt. If I ran the Watch would kill him, wanting to send a message to the rest of the Community, *"You will not disobey the Light. You cannot escape the Watch. You belong to us."*

Miserably I clambered down from the fence and stumbled back towards the house. Dad tried to catch my eye but I refused to meet his gaze, not wanting to acknowledge his look of defeat. He shook his head and a trail of blood splattered across the white painted porch. He wanted me to run, but I couldn't leave him to die.

The Watch grabbed my upper arm. 'Don't hurt her,' Mum pleaded. Her face was scrunched up as if she was trying not to cry. The Watch squeezed my arm tightly in response. I pressed my lips together, determined not to make a sound.

'Identity card,' the Watch barked.

'Can I say goodbye to my family?' I begged.

'Let her say goodbye,' Dad called hoarsely from the porch.

'I asked for your identity card,' the Watch replied.

Using my free hand I pulled my card from the pocket of my cardigan and handed it to her. She studied it for a moment and then tucked it into her belt before firmly steering me across the farmyard and out through the garden gate.

'Please,' Mum begged. 'Please, let her say goodbye.'

The Watch gave no response as she hauled me towards a dark grey bus parked in the lane. She yanked open the rear doors and as she pushed me inside I lost my footing, skinning my knee on the rough metal floor. I scrambled to my feet, conscious that I was being watched. I ignored the curious eyes and crawled into the nearest seat, cradling my throbbing knee with my hand.

I peered out of the window. My family were framed in the porch. Mum was holding onto my little brother Matty; he must have been hiding in the living room. He looked terrified as he gripped tightly at her dress. Mum stroked Matty's hair as she stared at the bus, grim faced and silent. My dad, normally stoic and strong, was slumped against the wall of the porch, his head buried in his hands. As the bus pulled away from the yard I craned my neck, watching my family until finally we rounded a corner and the farmhouse, my home for thirteen years, slid painfully out of view.

I could feel the other Immunes watching me curiously. As I peered around the bus I counted five of them in total. Three I recognised from the Community. Malcolm - Mally Mould - was hard to miss, with his mop of ginger hair and skin so white it was almost blue. I hadn't spoken to Mally in a long time, we'd been friends when were younger but for some reason we'd drifted apart.

Robyn Chesterfield was seated beside Mally. We'd both attended the same Community school, but we hadn't been friends; she was a year older and way too popular to hang around with someone like me.

The boy slouching across the seat opposite me was Eric Castle. I'd recognise his insolent expression anywhere. He was sixteen and had twin sisters who were my age. Everyone in our Community knew about the Castles. Eric's dad was a drunk; a loud crazy man with a red puffy face and swollen bloodshot eyes.

The other two people were strangers. A dark-haired athletic looking boy and a small girl dressed in a colourful rainbow jumper that contrasted harshly with her bright pink hair. The girl leant towards me, her hoop earrings jangling brightly. I watched fascinated by the light as it played across her skin, giving it a shimmering quality. 'Hi,' she whispered softly, 'I'm Flo; Flo Perkins.'

'Charlotte Swift,' I replied quietly.

The athletic looking boy introduced himself as Dale Trafford, but any further conversation was interrupted by a hiss from Eric. 'Hey Mouldy Pants.'

Mally reddened.

'Hey Mouldy, I'm talking to you.'

Mally didn't respond.

'Are you ignoring me Mouldy Pants?'

Robyn exhaled loudly and tossed white blonde curls out of her eyes. A malicious grin spread across Eric's face as she became his next target.

'It's Robyn isn't it?' he queried. When the blonde-haired girl didn't respond he continued. 'Well, Robyn Chesterton. I'm going to call you Chesty,' he said. 'Chesty Chesterton on account of your...your massive you-know-whats.'

Robin scowled and clasped her hands across her chest.

'Hey Mouldy, do you think Chesty looks good?'

A crimson flush spread across Mally's cheeks as he feigned a sudden interest in his hands. 'Hey Chesty! I think Mouldy likes you...but it's not your face he's interested in,' Eric sniggered.

I caught Mally's eye. Eric was a bully and well known in the Community for his unpredictable behaviour. Unfortunately Eric caught the look and I cringed.

'Charlotte isn't it?' he enquired.

I pretended to ignore him.

'Or maybe you prefer Charlie?'

'Charlotte's fine,' I replied as I chewed anxiously on my thumbnail. I hated being called Charlie. It was a boy's name.

'Was that your mummy and daddy bawling their eyes out because the mean old Watch took precious little Charlie away?'

At the mention of my parents I choked back a knot of misery and blinked furiously to keep my eyes from watering.

'You're not going to cry are you?' Eric sneered.

'Just because your dad threw you onto the bus and asked the Watch for money doesn't mean you have to make Charlotte feel bad because her parents wanted to keep her.' Flo ended her outburst with a fierce glare. I cast her an admiring glance; she had to be very brave to stand up to Eric. All the kids in the Community were terrified of him.

Eric studied Flo thoughtfully.

'You got something else you want to say?' she questioned. 'Maybe you have a cute nickname for me too?'

'Quiet back there,' a voice called from the front of the bus.

Flo raised her eyebrows at Eric. It was an obvious challenge.

Eric clasped his hands behind his head, and leant back casually in his seat, his lips drawn into a silent mocking smile.

Finally the bus was quiet.

My eyes flew open as my head slammed painfully against the bus window. I moaned and rubbed at the spot where I'd made contact with the glass. I could already feel a lump beginning to grow.

The air in the bus was stale; too many people crammed into a small space. Sweat trickled down my back, soaking my dress and adding to the already pungent air.

The other occupants of the bus seemed to be sleeping, heads nodding slowly to the rhythm of the road. I peered out of the window and with a sinking heart I watched the countryside fly by. Unlike the roads in my Community this one was well maintained, with no potholes or abandoned rusting wrecks of old cars. It must be the North Road. My dad said you needed a special permit from the Light to use it.

At the thought of my dad a fresh wave of misery engulfed me. I was terrified, more frightened than I'd ever been in my life. Even more afraid than the time I'd been chased by a wild dog on the farm and had to hide up a tree all morning until Dad came looking for me and shot it.

I'd tested Immune a week ago and Mum and Dad had said we'd have to leave the farm and go and live with my Uncle Ethan. He was in the Union and could protect me. Usually Immunes were given two weeks to say our goodbyes and to prepare for the journey to the LightHouse, but the Watch had arrived early.

The Light taught us that it was an honour to test Immune and to be given the opportunity to become part of the Select Neighbourhoods Project. Every Echo knew that it was just a matter of immunity, not honour. I belonged to the Light and from now on my life was no longer my own. After I'd completed my re-education at the LightHouse I would be reassigned Delta and forced to work in the Neighbourhood. I would never see my family again.

Lost in my own misery it was a moment before I realised that Flo was awake and trying to attract my attention. She leant across the aisle until her pink head was only inches from mine. She kept her voice low as she spoke and I had to strain to catch each word. She fascinated me. I'd never seen anyone with such beautiful shimmering skin. Her hair was cut short, like a boy's, and pulled into stiff pink spikes. I ran a hand through my own coarse dark hair. It must look so dull in comparison.

'Are you alright?' she asked, her tone friendly.

I smothered an unexpected giggle with my hand. What a stupid question. Of course I wasn't all right.

Flo returned my grin as if she'd gotten the joke too.

I unbuttoned my cardigan and fanned my face with my hands.

'Hot?' she queried.

'There's no air,' I gasped.

'Do you know how far it is to the LightHouse?' she asked.

I shook my head. 'No, but I think it's a fair way.'

'My mum said that it's somewhere in the North,' Mally interrupted. His eyes were bleary with sleep and he followed his comment with a wide yawn.

'No talking in the back,' a female voice barked from the front of the bus. Mally's eyes widened in terror.

Flo ignored the order. 'You hungry?' she whispered as she pulled a sticky sweet from her pocket and offered it to me.

I glanced nervously towards the front of the bus.

'Go on,' Flo encouraged. 'I expect there won't be many sweets at the LightHouse. We might as well enjoy them while we can.'

I shook my head.

'I have enough for both of us,' she urged, her voice a little louder.

'I told you to be quiet,' the Watch appeared from the front of the bus. I caught a flash of wood as she brought down her baton, striking Flo across the shoulder. Flo let out a painful cry. Eric, who had been fast asleep, jumped to his feet with a startled yell. He surveyed the occupants of the bus, his face a mask of panic. His eyes narrowed as he caught sight of Flo bent double and moaning softly. The panic left his eyes, only to be replaced by a cold hard stare.

'Did you hit her?' Eric challenged the Watch.

'Sit down,' the Watch barked.

Indecision played across the contours of Eric's face and for a brief moment I thought he was going to attack the Watch. I held my breath.

'I said sit down,' the Watch growled savagely.

Eric slowly retook his seat, but he kept his eyes firmly fixed on the Watch.

'You will all be quiet.' The Watch's features were pulled into a wolfish snarl. She turned on her heel and without another word disappeared into the front of the bus.

A shiver ran down my spine. I felt cold all over. I'd seen fights between kids in the Community, but I'd never seen a grown up hit a child before. At home Mum and Dad had punished me when I did something naughty, but they never hit me. I felt the sting of tears and as I cowered in my seat I gave in to the full misery of my situation.

CHAPTER 2

To the LightHouse

CHARLOTTE:

The bus came to a juddering halt and the Watch re-appeared. I tensed nervously and was relieved when she ordered us off the bus, her baton remaining safely in her belt.

I staggered to my feet, my body clumsy with fatigue. It was already getting dark outside and the sun was beginning to dip below the horizon. We'd been driving all day and this was the farthest I'd ever been from home. The thought brought with it a hollow feeling of despair. I was completely alone. No-one could help me now.

The Watch escorted us to a squat wooden building. Once inside we were led to a long table and ordered to sit down. My stomach growled hungrily as bowls of soup were placed in front of us. I hadn't eaten all day.

Ignoring the spoon that had been provided, Eric picked up his bowl and swallowed the contents in a few noisy gulps. He caught me staring and pointed at my bowl. 'If you don't want it, I'll have it.'

'Leave her alone,' Flo replied. She picked up my spoon and handed it to me. I took it from her with a grateful smile. The soup was thin and tasteless but I was so hungry I wolfed it down.

As soon as we'd all finished eating the Watch ordered us out of the building. The bus had disappeared and we were told to climb into a small truck. Once inside I found myself squashed onto the back seat between Mally and Flo.

The road was no longer well maintained, its surface pitted with so many potholes that the truck pitched and dived across its uneven surface. As I peered into the dark night the horizon looked as if it was on fire. The light radiated so brightly that it had to be a Neighbourhood. Dad had told me that each of the Neighbourhoods had electrical lights that could stay on all night. I felt strangely drawn to the luminous glow.

We drove through the night until the sky began to lighten and the truck came to a halt along a jagged curve of coastline. At the request of the Watch we all clambered out onto a gravel path. The morning air was crisp, bringing with it the distinct smell of wet grass that reminded me of home. I spotted a large blue and white boat moored at the end of a wooden jetty, its cabin protruding precariously from the deck. Beyond the jetty I could make out a small grey island sitting a few miles off the shore.

'Move.' The Watch shepherded us towards the jetty and onto the waiting boat. She led us below deck to a small cramped seating area, where she ordered us to sit down and be quiet.

As the engine roared to life I noticed that Mally had turned a startling shade of green.

'You don't look very well,' I whispered.

'Boats make me sick.' He clasped a hand over his mouth.

Dale, who was sitting in the seat opposite Mally, jumped to his feet and moved further down the cabin.

The Watch arrived a few moments later carrying a tray of sand-wiches and drinks. After handing them out she left us to eat our meal alone. I hungrily unwrapped my sandwich and took a bite. The cheese tasted funny, definitely not as nice as the goats' cheese my mum made on the farm. Mally's sandwich lay untouched on his lap. 'You want that?' Eric asked as he made a grab for it. Mally shook his head and Eric ripped open the packaging and stuffed the sandwich into his mouth before anyone could protest.

A short time later the Watch returned and we followed her up onto the deck of the boat. We were heading towards the island I'd seen from the shore. It was a forbidding place bordered by steep cliffs topped with green foliage that slipped precariously down its sheer rocky face.

After the boat docked we disembarked onto a rock-strewn beach. We crunched across the beach and along a path that rose steeply around the face of the cliff. Soon I was out of breath and sweating with the effort. I unbuttoned my cardigan and tied it around my waist.

'That's a good idea,' Flo said as she pulled the rainbow jumper over her head to reveal a thin strappy vest underneath. I was surprised to find that her arms and shoulders were covered in a web of tattoos.

'Are those real?' I asked.

'Yeah, my mam drew then. She's a tattoo artist.'

'Are they all flowers?' I questioned as I admired a string of white daisies.

'That's my mam's speciality. She's good at birds too, but mainly she tattoos flowers.'

'I'd never be allowed a tattoo,' I said as I tried to imagine the look on my mum's face if I'd ever got one.

'Mam made me wait until I was fifteen before she'd let me have my first one,' Flo said. 'That was two years ago. She was teaching me to tattoo...before...' she trailed off uncertainly and then shrugged. 'I suppose it doesn't matter anymore does it?' She turned her attention back to the path and we finished the remainder of the climb in silence.

'This way,' the Watch barked as we arrived puffing and panting at the top of the cliff. We followed the Watch along a rough track bordered by dense shrubs. A short time later we rounded a bend and came face to face with a stone wall topped with a coil of lethal looking wire.

The Watch led us through a metal gate into an ugly square courtyard that housed an even uglier grey stone building. It was a house from one of the old horror films that Matty loved to watch. They always gave him nightmares but no-one could persuade him to turn them off.

Chiselled into the stone above the building entrance were the words, *'With humility and respect. Let us Light the way'*. A chill ran through me. We'd arrived at the LightHouse. It was a name that struck terror into the hearts of all Echo children. It was the monster that hid under our beds and tormented our dreams.

The door to the building swung open with an eerie creak and the Watch ordered us to enter one at a time. As I stepped tentatively over the threshold I was held by an invisible force. There was a flicker of green light and I was released into the interior of the LightHouse. Feeling a little queasy I joined Flo and Mally inside the gloomy entrance hall.

'What was that?' I asked.

'I think it's called a HealthScan,' Mally replied. 'All of the buildings in the Neighbourhood have them. They're supposed to check for disease…at least that's what my mum said.'

'Your mum seems to know a lot about the Neighbourhood,' Flo queried.

Mally shrugged, 'She reads a lot. Always picking up those community bulletins and pamphlets the Union hand out.'

The remainder of the group entered the building and as we gathered together in the draughty hall a door opened, splicing the gloom with a shaft of weak light.

A woman entered. Every aspect of the woman was pointy and angular; her collarbone jutted out starkly from the neck of her blouse and her cheekbones cut sharp grooves across the surface of her skin. Her black hair was pulled into a tight bun, drawing her cream skin taut across her face. When she spoke her voice was low and clipped and I had to strain to catch each word.

'Residents, welcome to your new home. I am the Warden and I'm responsible for this facility.' The Warden's eyes were as black as marble as she surveyed each of us in turn. 'The LightHouse will be your home for the next 18 months. I expect each of you to take advantage of the great opportunity that the Light is offering you. When you leave this facility you will be eagerly welcomed into our glorious Neighbourhood.' She clapped her hands briskly. 'Follow me. Its time for your orientation tour.'

We followed the Warden into a wide corridor to be greeted by a line of people clad in a shapeless brown uniform. Each person had a shaved head, making it difficult to tell if they were boys or girls.

In the Community a shaved head meant head lice. I scratched absent-mindedly hoping that there hadn't been an outbreak in the LightHouse.

'These are our Trustees,' the Warden advised. 'They will be responsible for your care during your stay with us at the LightHouse.'

'Are they men or women?' I heard Dale whisper.

The Warden swung around to face him. 'The Trustees are here to teach, there is no need for gender,' she replied.

Eric smirked at this, he nudged Dale. 'Well I don't know about you but I like my girls to be girls,' he said as he belligerently traced out a female form in the air. Dale took a step backwards, distancing himself from Eric.

The Warden fixed Eric with a stern glare. 'There are severe penalties for Residents who disrespect the authority of our Trustees.' With this warning ringing in our ears she directed us along the corridor and through a door that read, *Processing*. Once inside we were each searched by a Trustee. My necklace was confiscated. The wooden pendant had been a present from my dad and I was reluctant to part with it. The Trustee informed me in an officious tone that personal items were not allowed in the LightHouse and I could have it back after my graduation if I still wanted it.

When the body search was over we were instructed to take a seat on a low wooden bench where we waited to be called over to a Trustee seated behind a desk.

Finally it was my turn to approach the desk and answer the Trustee's questions.

I confirmed that my name was Charlotte Swift, that I was thirteen and lived with my father, mother and my brother Matty at Little Elm Meadows.

The Trustee asked about educational achievements and I told her that I'd received some basic schooling. Seemingly satisfied with my responses she handed me over to another Trustee who escorted me to a machine in the corner of the room. The Trustee ordered me to step onto a wide metal plate. I climbed onto it tentatively and was surprised to find that the machine was able to calculate my weight.

As I stepped off the plate the Trustee whipped out a tape measure. This I recognised. Mum was hardly ever seen without one. She worked as a seamstress, sewing clothes for people in the Community.

As the tape measure encircled my waist I noticed that the Trustee's hands were covered by a pair of gloves. They were so thin they almost appeared transparent. I peered at them curiously. They didn't seem to serve any purpose. It certainly wasn't cold enough in the room to require gloves. The Trustee measured my thigh and upper arm and then pulled out a handheld electronic device. I watched fascinated as the Trustee tapped the device with a short stubby finger. I craned my neck to get a better look, but the Trustee discreetly shielded the screen from view.

Next the Trustee ordered me to stand in front of a whitewashed wall. There was a blinding flash of light and the pronounced click of a camera as my photograph was taken.

With the group *processed* we were marched along the corridor to a door that read '*Decontamination*'. It didn't sound very welcoming. Once inside the boys were ordered to follow one of the Trustees while Flo, Robyn and I were escorted into a different room. The interior was sterile, decorated from floor to ceiling with glossy white tiles. It was icy cold and I shivered.

'Take off your clothes,' the Trustee ordered.

Startled, I glanced at the other girls. No-one moved.

The Trustee took a threatening step towards us. 'You're filthy. Now take off your clothes or I'll do it for you.'

We quickly did as we were told. I pulled off my cardigan and with shaking hands I clumsily undid the buttons down the front of my dress.

'Onto the floor,' the Trustee ordered.

I placed my clothes carefully onto the floor and with an air of disgust the Trustee picked them up and stuffed them into an orange bag. As soon as we were undressed the Trustee ordered us to a row of showers. There were no cubicles to hide our modesty.

As I positioned myself under a showerhead I heard the hollow clanking of pipes. I let out an involuntary squeal as razor-like droplets of cold water drilled into my body like a thousand tiny needles. The water warmed up quickly and the Trustee ordered us to wash.

When the stream of water stopped I was about to step out of the shower and was startled when the Trustee barked an order not to move. I remained rooted to the spot.

Again I heard the rattle of pipes, followed by a loud hiss. This time I was drenched in a cloud of feather-light liquid. The air filled with the pungent aroma of antiseptic. The smell was suffocating and I gasped for breath. Liquid spilled into my mouth and I spat it out in disgust, it tasted vile. My eyes were stinging and I rubbed at them furiously. I could hear Robyn and Flo, and from the sounds they were making it was obvious that they were suffering the same discomfort. I struggled to stay under the shower until the hissing noise ceased and the liquid torture came to an end.

The Trustee ordered us into a changing area where we were handed towels and clean clothes.

'What about our old clothes?' Flo enquired.

'They'll be burnt.' The Trustee's lip curled in disgust.

Flo turned to me with a look of annoyance. 'I loved that jumper. My mam knitted it for my birthday.'

I detected a sliver of movement as the Trustee took a threatening step towards Flo.

'Shush,' I whispered, unable to hide my panic.

Flo's eyes widened as she touched her shoulder. Without another word she shook out the red trousers and quickly pulled them on.

The Trustee handed us each a pair of gloves, 'Put these on.'

The gloves were the same as I'd seen the Trustees wearing. They were made of a weird transparent material. I pulled them on and found that they fitted almost like a second skin. 'You must wear the gloves at all times,' the Trustee warned. 'Anyone found breaking this rule will be severely punished.'

We were herded back into the corridor and found the Warden waiting for us. The boys were outside too and dressed in matching red uniforms. I noticed that Eric was finding it difficult to maintain his tough image without his battered jacket and spiky hair.

The Warden handed each of us a red badge. I took mine from her outstretched hand and peered at it with interest. It was a new identity card. The first thing I noticed was my picture. I looked slightly startled, my dark eyes wide, my forehead creased into a deep frown. I also noticed that my status had changed. I was no longer an Echo. My new designation was Delta.

'You must wear your badge at all times,' the Warden advised. 'Anyone found without a badge will be severely punished.'

We continued the tour of the LightHouse and with each step my heart sank a little further. The Warden led us to a bleak dining room that contained rows of wooden tables. Each table was fitted with a single narrow bench, all facing the front of the room. The Warden pointed to a serving hatch from which she told us we would collect our food. She indicated a grey box. 'Before you can collect your meal you must scan your badge. You will receive three meals a day and each will be calculated to provide the exact nutrition you need based on your height, weight and level of daily physical activity.' I peered at the scanner with interest, but the Warden was already heading towards the door and I had to hurry to catch up.

The next stop on the tour was the 'common room'. This room contained grey sofas and a number of round metal tables and chairs. There was a pile of board games stacked neatly on one of the tables. I noticed a bookshelf and I wandered over to take a look. I scrutinised some of the titles: *A Biography of the Directorship; A History of the Select Neighbourhood Project; Alpha, Bravo, Delta, Echo: A Code of Conduct.* "Propaganda literature", my mum would have called it.

The most disturbing part of the tour was *Detention*. This was a long narrow room that contained a large number of windowless brick cells. Each cell was identical and fitted with a toilet, sink and a bed topped with a thin mattress. The Warden warned us that Detention was used as punishment for Residents who disobeyed the LightHouse rules. 'I expect some of you will become very well acquainted with these cells,' she said as she cast her eye over Eric. I was relieved to leave Detention and head towards a large hall that the Warden referred to as *assembly*. This room contained rows of metal chairs facing a podium on a raised wooden stage. The Warden ordered us to take a seat and then climbed onto the podium.

From the podium she gave us what she called the *welcome briefing*. First she asked the Trustees to give us our *daily schedule*. I took the paper from the Trustee and read it with interest: *Shower, breakfast, assembly, cleaning detail, orientation, lunch, work detail, dinner, leisure, lights out.*

'The beginning and end of each activity will be indicated by a siren,' the Warden informed us. She clicked her fingers and I jumped as the air was filled with a loud wailing noise. 'As soon as you hear the siren you will immediately move on to your next activity. Anyone who does not obey will be severely punished.'

'Any questions?' the Warden asked as she came to the end of the briefing.

'What does assembly mean?' Flo called out.

The Warden frowned. 'Resident, at the LightHouse we put our hand up when we want to ask a question.'

Flo raised her hand.

The Warden nodded approvingly. 'Resident, you have a question?'

'I don't understand all of the words on the schedule,' Flo said. 'What do assembly and orientation mean?'

'At the daily assembly we will ask you to reaffirm your commitment to the leadership of the Light. You will also receive your daily cleaning and work detail. In addition to the daily assemblies we sometimes hold evening assemblies. These are specifically designed for contemplation and exploration to strengthen our devotion to the Light.'

'...and what about orientation?' Flo asked.

There was a protracted silence during which the Warden pursed her lips.

Flo slowly raised her hand in the air.

'Resident, you have a question?'

'Yes, I wanted to know what orientation is.' I detected a slightly impatient tone to Flo's voice.

'Orientation is a specially formulated programme designed to teach the Residents about the Neighbourhoods. At the LightHouse we must ensure that all Residents attain a certain level of educational achievement before they cross the Boundary.'

Flo raised her hand again.

'Yes Resident.' The Warden's voice sounded a little weary.

'I can already read and write. My mam taught me.'

'Excellent,' the Warden replied briskly. 'Then you have a head start over some of our less skilled Residents. But you'll find there's a lot more to the orientation sessions than just learning to read and write. Although for those of you who are illiterate,' her eyes rested on Eric for a moment, 'there will be the opportunity to learn the necessary basic skills.'

'It all sounds like a lot of hard work to me,' Eric muttered a little too loudly. The Warden turned to him. 'Resident, do you have a question?'

Eric studied her for a moment and then leant back casually in his seat, his hands clasped behind his head.

'As I've already explained, the respectful way to ask a question is to raise your hand,' the Warden continued.

'Yes ma'am,' Eric growled.

The Warden frowned. 'Resident, as this is your first day I'm prepared to be lenient, but I've already told you that we don't tolerate disrespectful behaviour at the LightHouse. I expect you to follow this rule. Is that clear?' When Eric didn't reply the Warden repeated, 'Is that clear?'

Eric responded with a curt nod.

'Excellent,' the Warden said. 'Now it is time for you to go to your dormitories.'

When we arrived at the dormitories we were separated from the boys and taken to a room on the opposite side of the corridor. The dormitories were grim-looking rooms with beds for eight people. They were sparsely decorated with grey curtains and bare walls desperate for a bright poster or picture. The Trustee allocated each of us a bed and a wooden truck. On my bed I found a small bag containing a pair of red pyjamas, a toothbrush, toothpaste and soap. I sniffed at the soap and recoiled in disgust. It reminded me of a doctor's surgery.

I stowed my meagre possessions in the wooden trunk and climbed onto my bed. It had been little more than a day since I'd left the farm but I already missed my family so much. Everything seemed so hopeless and miserable.

CHAPTER 3

Into the Lions Den

CHARLOTTE:

I heard a clamour in the corridor and I watched fearfully as the door to the dormitory flew open and four girls entered. They came to a standstill when they caught sight of us.

'Newbies!' a blonde girl observed. Her short hair was cut into a blunt bob that finished just below her chin. 'You just arrived?' she asked as she blew her fringe out of her eyes.

'Yeah, this afternoon,' Flo replied.

'What are your names?'

After we'd introduced ourselves the blonde-haired girl announced that she was called Clara, Clara Holmes. She introduced the other girls; 'Megan and Marissa are twins,' she said as she pointed to two chubby girls standing by the closed door. The girls were completely identical with dark eyes and long black hair that fell in thick corkscrew curls.

'I'm Bekka, with two k's,' a ginger-haired girl said as she threw herself across one of the beds. Her face was streaked with grime, her hair caught up in an untidy ponytail.

'Where have you all been?' Flo asked.

'We just finished work detail,' Clara replied.

'Yeah as I was saying a minute ago,' Bekka interrupted, her ginger ponytail swinging from side to side as she raised herself up on her elbows. 'I was rock breaking again today. That's twice in one week. Either it's plain bad luck or someone really has it in for me. I'm knackered.'

'Rock breaking?' Flo queried.

'One of the nastier work duties,' Clara responded. 'If you're lucky you'll get put in the laundry or the sewing room. They're the best jobs.'

'Yeah,' Bekka said. 'Rock breaking is horrible. Especially twice in one week.'

'Also try and steer clear of farm duties,' Clara continued. 'You have to clean out the animals. It's disgusting.'

'Sounds like home,' I replied feeling a little wistful. Farm duties sounded perfect.

'You lived on a farm?' the question came from one of the twins - Megan or Marissa, I wasn't sure which.

I nodded shyly, a little embarrassed at being the centre of attention.

'Some of the other Residents come from farms too,' the twin responded. 'Our dad was a healer. Self-taught so the Neighbourhood wasn't interested. We lived in a really nice Community, not one of those backwards ones. We had shops and a community centre and an amazing milk bar.'

'I'd kill for a strawberry milkshake right now,' her twin sighed.

'Not many milk bars around here,' the other twin continued. 'Although it does mean we've lost a few pounds,' she patted her rounded stomach. 'Dad would be happy. He always complained that having fat daughters was bad for the health business.'

'Yeah there's definitely no milk bars in this hellhole,' Bekka replied, the vehemence clear in her voice.

Clara and the twins visibly cringed. 'Bekka, keep your voice down,' Clara shushed as her eyes darted towards the door.

'Stop worrying Clara. The Trustees aren't standing outside the door listening to us. They're too busy thinking up some sadistic punishment for the next person who breaks the rules.'

'Is it really that bad in here?' Flo asked.

Bekka crinkled her nose in disgust. 'It really is. The Trustees are monsters and the food sucks. They make us do pointless jobs like picking up rocks on the beach and hammering them into pieces so they can use the crushed stones to fill in the roads in the Neighbourhood. It's ridiculous.'

Her outburst was followed by an awkward silence. 'I don't know why you're always complaining. There's nothing we can do about it. We just have to make the best of it,' Clara responded.

Bekka threw her a poisonous look. 'Yeah well, maybe I don't want to make the best of it.'

The twins looked scandalised.

'It's that type of talk that gets you put on rock breaking duty so often,' Clara warned.

'You all sound like you've been here a long time?' Robyn observed.

Bekka rolled over and pulled up the edge of her mattress. I could make out a number of deep grooves cut along the edge of the wooden bed frame. 'We've been trying to keep track of the days. We think we've been here about four weeks. There aren't any clocks in the LightHouse,' she continued, 'so it's difficult to measure time. We also think that the Trustees mess with our schedules, getting us up at different times.'

'Why would the Trustees mess with your schedules?' Flo queried.

'To control us. Why else?' Bekka replied, matter of fact.

Clara rolled her eyes. 'Bekka, you shouldn't say things like that.'

Bekka ignored Clara, 'In the LightHouse the Warden and the Trustees control everything. They tell us when to get up, when to eat, when to sleep. If we don't know what day it is, or even what time it is, then it keeps us disorientated.' She turned to Flo, 'What day did they collect you?'

'It was yesterday, the 24th April.'

'They collected us on the 22nd March so we've been here just over a month. My system works.' She was interrupted by the blast of a siren.

'That's dinner,' one of the twins announced eagerly.

'Come on,' Clara said as she headed towards the door. 'We don't want to be late.'

I caught sight of Mally in the corridor and hurried to catch up with him. There was an angry red mark on his cheek. 'What happened?' I asked.

Eric appeared from behind and placed a casual arm around Mally's shoulder. 'Nothing for you to worry about Charlie! Mouldy and I were just messing around weren't we?'

There was a vivid flash of pink. 'Come with me,' Flo hissed as she took hold of Eric's arm. He tried to shrug her off, but despite her small size she propelled him away from us down the corridor.

'What was that all about?' I asked Mally.

'It's nothing. I'm fine,' he replied.

'You don't look fine,' I indicated his cheek. 'You should keep away from Eric.'

'Easy for you to say,' he replied as we entered the dining hall. 'You don't have to share a room with him.'

We joined the queue at the serving hatch and as I touched my badge to the scanner it flashed green. I wanted to take a look at it to investigate how it worked but the woman behind the counter clicked her tongue impatiently and I hurried to pick up a tray. I was served a spoonful of a stew and a lump of grey mashed potato. This was topped with a hunk of dry looking bread.

I waited for Mally to collect his food and then we went in search of an empty seat. I caught sight of Flo's pink head in the midst of a sea of people and I steered Mally towards her. As we approached the table I faltered. Eric was in the seat beside Flo. I glanced questioningly at Mally.

'It's not as if I can escape,' he replied miserably. 'I have to share a dorm with him.'

I placed my tray on the table and sat down beside Flo. As I picked up a forkful of stew I noticed that it was already starting to congeal. My stomach churned queasily.

'You like the gourmet food?' Flo held up a spoonful of the greasy stew.

'Just like Mother used to make,' Eric replied. His plateful of food was substantially larger than mine and I watched as he crammed a huge forkful into his mouth. When no-one responded he pointed his fork in my direction. 'What's the matter? Is no-one talking to me?' he asked.

'I think you owe Mally an apology,' Flo said.

'An apology for what?' Eric replied. 'I was only messing around. I wrestle with my friends all the time and I never have to apologise to them.'

'Just say you're sorry,' Flo urged.

Eric shrugged, 'Mally, I'm sorry if I hurt you. I didn't realise you were so delicate.'

Flo glared at him.

'What?' Eric asked defensively.

'It's not very nice to call Mally delicate.'

'I was trying to apologise,' he protested.

'Well try harder,' she growled.

Eric turned to Mally again, 'I'm sorry,' he said. 'I really didn't mean to hurt you.'

Mally picked up a piece of bread and pulled it apart. Eric frowned as he watched him quietly crumble it over his stew. 'See, I knew it would be a waste of time apologising.'

'Mally, Eric didn't mean to hurt you. He's just a stupid lump who doesn't realise his own strength,' Flo said. Eric accepted this comment without complaint.

Mally shrugged in response.

'Does that mean you accept my apology?' Eric asked.

When Mally nodded, Flo smiled brightly. 'See, I knew we could all be best friends.'

I admired Flo's optimism, but I wasn't sure whether Mally or I were ready to be best friends with Eric. I think an uneasy truce was the best we could hope for.

Mally took a mouthful of food and immediately spat it back onto his plate. He wiped his mouth with the back of his hand. 'What is this? It's disgusting.'

'It's got a unique flavour hasn't it?' Bekka called from further down the table.

'I've never tasted anything like it,' Mally said.

'It's not even real meat,' Bekka said. 'They make it out of those soya beans that they force the Communities to grow.'

'It looks like meat,' Flo said as she eyed her forkful of food a little dubiously.

'Try it and see,' Bekka urged.

Flo nibbled at the corner of a meat chunk and grimaced. 'Why would they even eat this?' she said as she placed her fork on her plate.

'Who knows! The Neighbourhood's crazy.'

'Bekka,' Clara hissed. 'You'll get us into trouble.'

I tried to force down some of the food, but it was so horrible I could barely swallow it. I was relieved when the siren indicated the end of the meal and we filed out of the dining room and followed the other Residents to the common room for *leisure time*. The room was busy when we arrived and Mally and I paused awkwardly in the doorway. New people always made me feel uncomfortable. The girls from my dorm were already sprawled out on one of the sofas. Robyn had joined them and was playing cards with the twins.

Flo linked her arm through both of ours. 'Into the lion's den,' she muttered with a grimace and pulled us after her. Eric joined us a few moments later and the four of us played a game of cards until we heard the siren blast that indicated bedtime.

CHAPTER 4

Under Observation

MARYANN:

I threw my book across the bed in frustration and watched as it bounced off the metal bedframe and clattered noisily to the floor. My throat was raw and my head was throbbing horribly from another cold. Dr Lee said that after living in isolation in the Neighbourhood I was vulnerable to infection and he needed to keep me under observation. This was my third trip to hospital in two months and I was growing tired of his tests and examinations.

On a positive note spending so much time in hospital meant that I was still living with the Union. Uncle Patrick couldn't force me to make a decision about my future while I was ill.

'Little sister, you want some intelligent company?' Daryl appeared in the doorway.

'That would be great. If you can find some then send them in.'

'Ha ha ha, funny girl.' Daryl flopped down heavily on the edge of my bed. 'Here, I stole this for you.' He rummaged in his waistcoat pocket and pulled out a squashed bundle of napkins. 'Sorry it's slightly squished,' he said as he handed it to me.

My mouth watered at the sight of the chocolate cake inside.

'You'd better eat it quickly before Dr Lee gets back. Otherwise he'll confiscate it and force you to eat something healthy instead.' My mouth was too full of cake to give a coherent response.

'I spoke to Dr Lee this morning,' he said. 'He's going to discharge you in a couple of days.'

I smiled widely through a mouthful of cake.

'Delightful,' Daryl responded with a grimace. 'What would Granny Hunter say if she could see you now?'

I started to laugh but choked on the cake and the laughter became a coughing fit. Daryl slapped me hard across the back. 'I haven't thought about Granny Hunter for years. Do you remember my eighth birthday when she bought me deportment lessons?'

Daryl guffawed loudly. 'We didn't even know what deportment lessons were. You thought it was something fun and teased me about it for days.'

'Imagine how horrified I was when I found out I had to spend every Saturday with that scary *plastic face* lady and learn how to eat soup properly. She used to force me to walk up and down her lounge with a book on my head.'

'Heads up, back straight, stomach in,' we both chorused and burst out laughing.

'Hey! You do know this is a hospital don't you? How is anyone supposed to get better with all this racket going on?' Peter was framed in the doorway. Flash Gordon danced excitedly around his feet.

'Why does Flash have a stethoscope around his neck?' I questioned.

'He's Doctor Flash today,' Peter explained as he gave the dog's head an affectionate pat.

'Come in mate,' Daryl said, 'and bring your furry doctor friend with you.'

Peter flopped into a vacant chair by the door while Flash leapt onto my bed. He tunnelled deep under the covers until I felt his cold nose snuffling against my leg.

'Looks like you're feeling better today,' Peter said. 'The last time

I visited, you were all red nosed and miserable.'

'We were just reminiscing about the good old days,' Daryl said. 'When all we had to worry about was scary plastic faced ladies forcing MaryAnn to parade around the lounge with a book on her head.'

I burst into another fit of giggles as Peter gave us both a quizzical look.

'I guess you had to be there,' Daryl shrugged.

'If you're feeling better does it mean you'll be out in time for the May Day party?' Peter asked.

'Yes. Dr Lee said he's releasing me in a couple of days.'

'The May Day party is amazing,' Daryl enthused. 'You'll love it.'

'Is it better than Easter?' I enquired as I remembered the boiled eggs we'd painted and raced down the hill outside the cave.

'Yeah, much better than Easter because we have a circus,' Peter said.

'A circus?'

'Yeah the circus is part of the Union. The leader is a Union Steward,' Peter explained. 'They visit every year for the May Day party.'

'They have fire-eaters and jugglers and acrobats. I've been waiting all year to see it,' Daryl said.

Peter smirked. 'Yeah I bet you have.'

Daryl's brow furrowed.

'What's the matter?' I asked as I glanced first at Peter and then Daryl.

'It's nothing,' Daryl replied. 'Peter's being an idiot.'

'Daryl made a special friend the last time the circus visited,' Peter continued.

'Shut up,' Daryl said.

'She had lovely pink hair.'

'She! Your friend is a girl?' I queried. Daryl's cheeks had turned pink with embarrassment.

'Yeah Daryl has a girlfriend.'

'I do not have a girlfriend,' Daryl protested.

'They made quite the couple,' Peter winked at me.

'We are not a couple,' Daryl hissed. 'We're friends, that's all.' He turned to me. 'If you want to talk about girlfriends then what about Peter? He's been out with every girl under the age of 30 in the Union.'

'Well that's a bit insulting,' Peter replied. 'I don't impose an age restriction. The Mallory charm is something women of all ages should be allowed to experience.'

I pretended to gag.

Peter smirked again. 'Anyway don't try and change the subject Daryl, we were talking about your girlfriend.'

'She is not my girlfriend.'

'The last time she visited you both seemed very *close*,' Peter emphasised the word *close*.

Daryl fidgeted uncomfortably. 'We're just friends that's all,' he mumbled.

'If you say so,' Peter replied as he gave me a sly wink.

I took pity on Daryl. 'So tell me what else happens on May Day apart from the circus?'

'There's loads of other stuff,' Daryl replied. 'Lots of eating and drinking and dancing. We also have competitions: hay bale throwing, archery, wood chopping. Last year I judged the baking competition… best two hours of my life.' He pushed out his stomach and patted it contentedly before turning to Peter with a quizzical look. 'Peter, didn't you judge one of the competitions last year too?'

Peter's responded with a scowl. 'You know very well that I was a judge last year.'

'What competition did you judge?' He rapped his knuckles against the side of his head. 'My memory must be failing me because I seem to have forgotten…maybe you can enlighten us.'

Peter exhaled loudly. 'Well Daryl, as you seem to have so conveniently forgotten I was fortunate enough to judge the fancy dress parade.'

'Sounds amazing,' Daryl murmured appreciatively.

'The animal fancy dress parade.'

'Fun!' Daryl responded with a wicked grin.

Peter shook his head. 'It poured down with rain and I got absolutely soaked. So no it wasn't fun!'

'Wasn't there some type of incident with a dog?' Daryl queried.

'As Daryl very well knows,' Peter addressed me. 'One of the dogs dressed as an Ewok escaped from its owner and peed on my boot.'

Daryl's eyes widened with a look of mock innocence. 'I remember now, that was awful. So remind me who was the winner of the competition?'

'It was a pig dressed as the Director.'

I burst out laughing. 'Someone dressed a pig up as the Director?'

'Yeah he was very popular. Especially wearing the blonde wig and tie.'

'Didn't you have some bad luck with the pig as well?' Daryl asked.

Peter continued to address me. 'As Daryl very well knows, in all the excitement of the competition the pig managed to escape from its owner.'

'Not again,' Daryl said, 'that was a bit of bad luck, especially after the incident with the dog. So, remind me what happened next?' Daryl didn't even try to hide the grin on his face.

'I tried to catch the pig, I grabbed it by its tie, but it managed to break free…'

'Slippery little pig,' Daryl interjected.

Peter threw him a poisonous look.

'The pig dragged me into the mud.'

'It wasn't just normal mud though was it?' Daryl was choking back laughter.

'Thank you for reminding me Daryl. No it wasn't normal mud, because unfortunately the cow dressed as Thor…'

Daryl rolled off the side of the bed as tears streamed down his cheeks. 'Ha ha ha ha, a cow dressed as Thor. Can you imagine it?'

'You had to be there,' Peter responded dryly.

'So you were telling us about the cow?' Daryl spluttered as he clambered back onto the bed.

Peter sighed. 'Unfortunately the cow had done a poo in the mud and...'

'And!' Daryl urged.

'And I fell face down in it.'

'So while I was toasty warm inside the cave eating cake...'

'I was eating cow poo in the pouring rain,' Peter finished for him.

'That was such bad luck,' I said as I laughed loudly.

'What was really interesting is that when I confronted Patrick and warned him that if he ever asked me to judge the fancy dress competition again I would leave the Union he seemed really surprised. He said that he'd heard that animals in fancy dress made me laugh and that I'd been desperate to judge the competition for years.'

'I wonder where Patrick could have gotten that idea from?' Daryl replied.

'Yeah I wonder,' Peter replied wryly. 'A little advice my friend. If I were you I'd sleep with one eye open, because you never know when it might be time for a little payback.'

CHAPTER 5

Red, Amber, Green

CHARLOTTE:

The sun shimmered brightly as we sprawled out on blankets enjoying a picnic by the river. Matty climbed a tree, hanging upside down from a branch making a noise like a monkey. My dad roared with laughter. The laughter grew louder, filling my head until the sound made me clasp my hands over my ears.

I bolted upright. A siren shrieked loudly above my head shattering my happy memories and leaving me to face a different more frightening reality.

'What's happening?' Flo cried out, her voice shrill above the wail of the siren.

'It's evening assembly,' Bekka mumbled sleepily as she clambered out of bed.

'What does that mean?' Flo queried.

'It means we have to go and listen to a lecture about the Neighbourhoods. How we should feel privileged that we've been selected to serve them, blah blah boring blah.'

'It usually lasts for a couple of hours,' Clara said as she glared at Bekka, 'and we don't get to sleep late tomorrow morning either.'

A Trustee threw open the door and ordered us to hurry up. I

jumped out of bed immediately.

'What about getting changed?' I whispered to Bekka as we followed the Trustee out of the room.

'We go in our pyjamas,' she replied.

Outside in the corridor I picked my way through the sea of red bodies until I'd located Mally. His pale face was crumpled with sleep, his ginger hair sticking out at right angles. 'What's going on?' he yawned.

'An assembly,' I replied.

'In the middle of the night?'

'Seems like it,' I shrugged.

'This place is nuts,' he muttered.

Someone crashed into me from behind and taken by surprise I pitched forward. Mally made a grab for my arm, holding me upright.

'I'm sorry,' I heard Eric mutter. 'I didn't mean to knock into you. It was an accident.'

Eric was pale faced and there was a thin sheen of sweat on his forehead.

'Eric, are you alright?' Mally asked. I was surprised to hear real concern in his voice. I was even more surprised by the hostile glare from Eric. I thought that last night we'd agreed to be friends!

'Leave me alone,' Eric hissed before disappearing into the throng of Residents.

I raised a questioning eyebrow at Mally.

'Nothing to worry about,' he replied.

As we filed into assembly we were ordered to sit at the back of the hall. I took a seat beside Bekka as a group of people entered wearing orange pyjamas.

'That's Amber population,' Bekka explained in a low whisper. 'Once you've been in Red population for six months you graduate to Amber population and then after that to Green. See! Here they are now!' A group of people in apple green pyjamas filed into the room and filled the rows in front of Amber population.

'I thought we were the only people here,' I whispered.

'They live in another part of the LightHouse. They have a different schedule so we only see them at evening assembly.'

I examined the newcomers with interest. In contrast to Red population, who fidgeted impatiently in their seats, Amber and Green population were composed, backs rigid, hands placed loosely in their laps.

The Warden entered the hall and in a few graceful steps she climbed to the podium. With a clap of her hands she immediately commanded everyone's full attention.

'Good health and happiness,' she called out across the hall.

'In the Light we Trust,' the audience chorused in unison.

The Warden paused and surveyed her audience over the top of black-rimmed glasses. 'Before we begin our assembly I want you to stand so that we can reaffirm our commitment to the Light.'

Chairs scraped noisily as we all climbed to our feet. An electric screen flickered into life behind the Warden and I recited the unfamiliar words.

I pledge my allegiance to the Light, to obey the Directorship who lead with wisdom and compassion.

I pledge my commitment to the Neighbourhoods, to serve with humility and respect.

The Light is Right. The Light is Might.'

The screen faded to black as the Warden ordered us to retake our seats.

'Today I want to talk to you about the Select Neighbourhoods Project so that you understand the important role you have to play in the survival of our people…your people.'

I tried hard to focus on the lecture, but I was so tired that soon the Warden's voice became nothing more than an irritating buzz. My eyes were heavy and I couldn't keep them open. I felt a sharp dig in the ribs and jerked upright.

'Don't go to sleep,' Bekka's voice hissed in my ear, 'or you'll end up in Detention.' I shuddered at the thought of the horrible windowless cells and blinked frantically. I fought desperately to stay awake for the rest of the assembly until finally the Warden dismissed us and we returned to our dorms.

The following morning I woke with eyes gritty from sleep. I dragged myself out of bed and joined the others for another miserable experience in the showers.

After breakfast we filed into morning assembly. Flo, Eric, Mally and I were allocated rock collecting work detail. 'Bad luck,' Bekka whispered with undisguised cheerfulness. She'd been given kitchen duties.

Flo and I spent the morning cleaning the dormitories under the watchful eye of a Trustee. I was exhausted by the time the siren blared to signal orientation.

Flo and I followed a group of red uniforms until we arrived at a classroom. As we entered, a squat looking Trustee ordered us into a separate room. Mally, Eric, Dale and Robyn were already seated at a table.

The Trustee placed a piece of paper in front of each of us. 'Before you join the rest of the class we must assess your learning level. You have one hour to complete the exercises on this paper. You will remain seated until the test is over...and no talking.' The Trustee clumped out of the room.

I picked up my paper. The questions were pretty easy. Some basic maths and grammar questions and an essay about the skills we thought we could bring to the Neighbourhood. I was distracted by the scrape of a chair. I glanced up to find Eric on his feet, prowling restlessly around the room.

'Eric,' Flo hissed. 'Sit down.'

Our test papers were forgotten for the moment as Eric commanded everyone's attention.

'If the Trustee comes back you'll get into trouble,' Mally warned.

'Eric!' Flo barked. 'Sit down before the Trustee comes back.'

'Too late for that.' The Trustee was scowling by the open door. 'I told you to remain in your seat.'

No-one made a sound.

'So what are you doing?'

'Well I'm not doing your stupid test am I?' Eric said.

The Trustee's green eyes narrowed. 'Sit down.'

Eric ignored the command.

'Sit down,' the Trustee repeated, carefully enunciating each word.

When Eric still didn't respond, the Trustee silently turned and left the room.

'Eric!' Flo hissed. She sounded worried. 'Sit down and do as you're told.'

Eric shook his head, 'I'm not taking their stupid *lack of intelligence* test.'

The door to the room flew open and four Trustees entered. Without a word they grabbed Eric and slammed him hard against the wall. Eric struggled as a Trustee grasped his arm and pinned it behind his back. I winced as the bone cracked painfully. Eric grunted loudly as he was forced down to his knees.

'You're hurting him,' Mally was on his feet.

'Sit down Resident.'

'But you're hurting him,' Mally protested.

'I said sit down Resident,' the Trustee snapped. Mally didn't move. He was shaking, his eyes wide and fearful. I wanted to jump up and force him back into his seat but I was too afraid. Time seemed to slow down as a Trustee let go of Eric and strode across the room towards Mally. One moment Mally was on his feet, red faced and uncertain, the next he was on the floor, face down with a knee thrust into his back.

We all watched in horrified silence as the boys were dragged from the room. 'Finish your papers,' the Trustee barked as the door slammed closed behind them.

I peered down at my paper but the words swam before my eyes as I tried to make sense of what had happened – why would Mally defend Eric?

At the end of orientation as I handed my test paper back to the Trustee I asked about Mally, but I was dismissed without a response.

After Flo and I had eaten dinner we were directed to a cloakroom and handed a pair of boots and a waterproof jacket. The boys hadn't returned and my stomach knotted with anxiety every time I thought about Mally. I'd just seen how scary life in the LightHouse could be.

We arrived at the beach and the Trustees ordered us to collect rocks and store them at the base of the cliff. Relay teams were positioned along the path to carry the rocks to the top of the cliff where a wagon waited to transport them to the LightHouse.

Flo and I worked as a team, sharing the burden of the heavier rocks. It was exhausting work and by the time the Trustee ordered us back to the LightHouse my arms were burning with fatigue. In the dining hall I devoured every bit of slop from my plate. I was so hungry I didn't care how bad it tasted. As I ate I kept a watchful eye out for Mally.

'Do you think he'll come back this evening?' I asked as Flo and I sprawled out on one of the sofas in the common room.

'Eric?' Flo queried.

'No! I was talking about Mally. I don't care about Eric. He was the one that caused all of the trouble in the first place.'

Flo gave me a strange look. 'Eric didn't ask Mally to stick up for him.'

'Eric should have just done the test,' I replied.

'I don't think Eric can read or write,' Flo said. 'He was embarrassed.'

I didn't think that Eric was embarrassed. He was just a trouble-maker. Thankfully, I was saved from having to reply by the sound of the siren that signalled bedtime.

Mally didn't make an appearance until the following morning when he arrived at breakfast looking tired and drawn.

'What happened to you?' I asked as he slipped into the seat beside me.

'I was sent to Detention...I'm absolutely starved,' he replied as he shovelled porridge into his mouth.

'Where's Eric?' Flo interrupted anxiously. 'Have you seen him?'

Mally shook his head. 'They split us up when they took us out of orientation. He might have been in one of the other cells but they played music all night so I couldn't hear anything.'

'He'll be fine,' I reassured her. 'They'll probably let him out later today.'

The following morning Eric still hadn't returned. At breakfast Flo searched the dining hall for him, but he was nowhere to be found.

'Are you sure you didn't see him in Detention?' she quizzed Mally.

'I told you, I was on my own the whole time and the music was so loud that I couldn't hear anything.'

'They have to let him out sometime,' Flo protested. 'They can't keep him in Detention forever.' She fixed Mally and me with a stare. 'Can they?'

'I don't know,' I replied uncertainly. 'Maybe he'll be in assembly?'

When Eric wasn't in assembly Flo grew increasingly agitated. At one point she lost her head altogether and suggested that we speak to one of the Trustees.

Mally regarded her with horror. 'Flo you know you can't question the Trustees, you'll end up in Detention too.'

Flo was allocated cleaning duty in the dorms with Bekka. She radiated such an air of misery as we left her that I was compelled to give her hand a brief squeeze before Mally and I headed to the dining hall. 'Eric will be fine,' I said with as much confidence as I could muster. 'He can look after himself.' His ability to take care of himself was something I was certain of.

Mally and I collected large buckets of soapy water. 'I wonder where Eric is?' he said as he scrubbed a brush across the floor of the dining hall. 'I really thought he'd be back for breakfast.'

'Maybe he won't behave,' I said, 'so they won't let him out?'

'He never did like being told what to do. Do you remember what he was like at school? He was always in trouble.'

'That's why I don't understand how you could stand up for him. You know he's a trouble causer. He's not even nice to you.'

'I didn't plan to do it... It just happened.' Mally paused thoughtfully. 'I don't know whether I can explain it.'

'Why don't you try?'

'It's just...well have you ever seen his back?'

I was puzzled by the question. 'No of course not.'

'It's covered in scars. The first night in the dorm he had a nightmare. When I asked him about it he got really angry and threatened to punch me. You remember how weird he was in the corridor afterwards?'

I nodded as I remembered the look he'd given Mally for asking if he was all right.

'When the Trustees grabbed him and slammed him into the wall I just thought that they shouldn't be allowed to hurt him like that.'

'They wouldn't have hurt him if he'd just done as he was told. He's a bully. My mum says that bullies are just cowards and if you stand up to them they'll back down.'

Mally cocked an eyebrow. 'You've met Eric right? You think that if I stand up to him we'll become friends...or do you think he'll tear my head off and use it as a football?'

I studied Mally's wiry frame. He wasn't built for fighting. 'Maybe you have a point,' I admitted reluctantly.

'This isn't one of those cheesy stories where the weakling challenges the bully and triumphs against all odds. The best I could hope for is that I keep my head attached to my shoulders,' he said.

'Oh poor Mally,' I whispered sympathetically. 'If it isn't horrible enough being in the LightHouse, you also have to deal with Eric too.'

Mally turned his attention to the door where Eric was framed in the entrance. He was watching us carefully. I wasn't sure how long he'd been there, or how much of our conversation he'd overheard. As he caught my eye he sauntered towards us, an irritating cockiness to his gait.

'Hey, it's Mally and his girlfriend Charlie. Were you talking about me?' Eric asked.

I could feel my face flush red.

Eric peered at me curiously. 'You were talking about me!' he said. 'I hope you were saying nice things.'

'You think we'd say anything nice about you after you got Mally locked up in Detention?'

'Charlotte…' Mally warned. 'Leave it alone.'

'Well Charlie I thought you were just a quiet little mouse but it looks like you do have a bite after all,' Eric sneered. He turned to Mally. 'They locked you up in Detention too?'

Mally nodded, 'I got out yesterday.'

A series of emotions played across Eric's face then he surprised me by slapping Mally across the back. 'Thanks buddy,' he said as he turned on his heel and walked away.

Mally and I stared after him, mouths agape. 'Am I dreaming or did that really just happen?' Mally breathed.

CHAPTER 6

Family Ties Part 1

MARYANN:

I arrived in the bustling market place to find Daryl and Peter tucking into large plates of scrambled eggs and toast. I'd been given a clean bill of health and Dr Lee had released me from the hospital.

'Come and join the Breakfast Club,' Daryl cried as he pushed a plate of food towards me.

'Bet you're glad to be out of the hospital,' Peter said.

'You have no idea,' I sighed as I buttered a slice of toast.

'Peter's a bit disappointed though,' Daryl said.

Peter raised a questioning eyebrow. 'I am?'

Daryl grinned. 'Yeah, you don't have an excuse to chat up the nurses anymore.'

Peter scowled, 'I wasn't chatting them up. They do a difficult job. I was just being friendly.'

'Ah! That's my buddy,' Daryl said as he slapped Peter across the back, 'always such a good friend to the nurses…'

Peter jerked away from him. 'One time,' he protested. 'I went out with a nurse one time.'

'She was a bit of a nut job though,' Daryl laughed. 'Do you remember, she wouldn't leave you alone? *Petey what you doing tonight? Petey will you buy me some flowers? Petey let's braid my hair,'* Daryl fluttered his eyelashes.

Peter scowled, 'She didn't call me Petey and I don't braid hair.'

'She was crazy though. She might have been cute, but she was certifiably insane.'

'That's the dilemma, isn't it,' Peter replied sagely. 'How cute does a girl have to be before you cancel out the crazy?'

'Oh my god,' I exclaimed through a mouthful of toast. 'You're both disgusting.'

'It doesn't stop Peter being a bit of a hit with the ladies,' Daryl laughed.

Peter grinned. 'Well I don't want to sound immodest but I do have a certain boyish charm.'

I clasped my hands over my ears. 'Please stop it both of you.'

Daryl nudged me. 'You should be careful MaryAnn. Peter's always had a soft spot for brunettes.'

Peter winked at me as I pretended to gag. 'I would rather poke my eyes out with this spoon.'

Peter burst out laughing. 'MaryAnn did you just make a funny?' He turned to Daryl. 'Finally! There might be some hope for your sister after all.'

Still brandishing the spoon I waved it under Peter's nose. 'If you don't stop being so disgusting I'm moving to another table,' I threatened.

'If you don't like our company you can always join your friend Brandon,' Daryl sniggered.

Brandon had taken a seat at a table close by. He caught my eye and raised a hand in greeting. I flashed an embarrassed smile as Daryl let out an amused snort.

'What!' I poked my spoon at him.

'He's too old for you.'

'What do you mean too old?' I stammered.

'To be your boyfriend.'

'I…I…I don't want him to be my boyfriend. I don't even like him,' I said a little too defensively.

'Really!' Daryl laughed again. 'Then why have you gone red?'

'Stop embarrassing me,' I hissed.

'Peter and I think you love him.'

'What! No I do not. Why would you even think that?'

'Because you act like an idiot whenever he's around,' Daryl replied.

'I do not…' I paused, considering him for a moment. 'Do I?'

'I'm afraid so.'

'Oh no,' the flush of embarrassment had turned to shame. 'He must think I'm so stupid,' I said self-consciously as I twirled a strand of hair around my finger.

'What on earth are you doing?' Peter asked.

'What do you mean?'

'That thing with your hair,' he peered at me quizzically.

Embarrassed, I quickly tucked the hair behind my ear. 'Nothing,' I mumbled.

'How come he manages to get all the girls?' Daryl grumbled to Peter. 'What does he have that I don't?'

I was shocked at the question and forgot myself for a moment. 'Are you crazy?! Brandon's beautiful,' I breathed. 'His hair, those ice blue eyes, and he has the nicest…' I paused, aware that they were both staring at me in astonishment. 'Well, that's what I assume that other girls see in him. Obviously I'm not interested.'

'Obviously not,' Peter replied, his voice heavy with sarcasm.

'You seemed very interested in him the other night,' Daryl teased, 'when you were talking in your sleep.'

'Brandon I luurve you,' Peter simpered.

'I did not say that in my sleep,' I paused uncertainly, '…did I?'

Daryl burst out laughing and as he took a sip from his coffee, he started to choke. Peter slapped him hard across the back. 'Take it easy mate. MaryAnn looks like she's about to implode.'

Daryl continued to laugh, tears streaming down his face. Then he made a series of loud kissing noises on the back of his hand.

I slammed my spoon down on the table, 'You're an idiot Daryl,' I snapped. When he continued to laugh I jumped to my feet. 'I'm going to find Uncle Patrick and let him know I'm out of hospital.'

Daryl's laughter was still ringing in my ears as I stomped out of the market.

I made my way through the intersecting tunnels towards the small cave that Uncle Patrick used as an office. As I thundered around a corner I collided with something small and soft; papers scattered into the air. I groaned inwardly. It was Leah Carter; she was a Steward and for some unknown reason had taken a real dislike to me.

'Sorry,' I mumbled as I stooped to gather the papers strewn across the floor.

She slapped my hand away, 'Leave it alone. I can do it myself.'

'If that's what you want.' I dropped the papers I'd collected and stalked away. If she didn't want my help then I wasn't going to offer twice.

The door to Uncle Patrick's office was ajar and as I approached I could hear voices coming from inside. I hesitated. I didn't want to interrupt if he was busy. I was about to turn away when I heard Mr Murray.

'It's my niece,' he said. 'The Watch took her to the LightHouse.'

'She tested Immune?' I heard Uncle Patrick reply. I paused, curious.

'Yes. The Watch raided the farm a few days ago. Jenn's here with Matty. She's frantic.'

'I'm really sorry to hear that,' Uncle Patrick said. 'Tell her she's welcome to stay as long as she wants.'

There was a long pause. 'Was there something else?' Uncle Patrick asked.

'What about Charlotte?'

'You know there's nothing we can do for her now. She'll be re-educated and reassigned to Delta and then sent to the Neighbourhood to work.'

'She's my niece. I have to help her,' Mr Murray sounded angry.

'Murray, we don't even know where the LightHouse is. How can you help her?'

'You've heard the rumours about it being up north. We could investigate.'

'We don't have the resources to do that.'

'I can't abandon her,' Mr Murray protested.

'You're not the first person to ask for my help with a relative who's tested Immune, but there's nothing I can do. We can't risk another high profile operation. Not after Boundary Day.'

'WE can't risk an operation - or YOU can't?' Mr Murray startled me by shouting. 'If it was a member of your family in danger I suspect it would be a different story.'

'That's not fair. MaryAnn was important…'

'And my niece, she's not important?' Murray sounded furious.

'You're twisting my words. You know every member of the Union is important to me, particularly your family. If I could help I would.'

'Really!' Mr Murray's tone held a hint of disbelief.

'Murray, the only chance we have is that her re-education fails and she leaves the LightHouse intact. We have operatives who might be able to reach her when she's taken to one of the Neighbourhoods to work.'

'You know that doesn't happen anymore. I worked with Delta in the Manchester Neighbourhood remember! It's not like the old days when some of them could resist the process.'

'I'm sorry but that's all I can offer.'

'How can it be so easy for you to abandon my niece after everything I've done for you and the Union? I risked my life watching over

MaryAnn. I rescued her from the Director.'

'Maybe we should talk about this when you've had a chance to calm down.'

'Calm down, you want me to calm down?' Mr Murray's deep voice had risen an octave.

'Murray, there's nothing more to say. I can't help you.'

'Well if you won't help me then I'm going to find her on my own.'

'I suppose I can't stop you if that's what you want to do. But I can't give you any resources,' Uncle Patrick warned.

'That's fine by me.' Mr Murray stormed out of the office. He didn't even seem to notice that I was there as he charged past me.

I turned away from Uncle Patrick's office and went in search of Daryl and Peter. I thought they'd want to hear about Mr Murray.

The table in the market was empty when I entered so I tried the boat. I found them both in the galley.

Daryl stood up as I entered. 'You back already? Does that mean we're friends again?'

I sat down heavily at the table.

'What's wrong?' Peter asked.

'Mr. Murray's niece tested Immune.'

I gained their attention immediately. Peter's expression was grim. 'Has she been taken to the LightHouse?'

'That's what Mr Murray said. He asked Uncle Patrick for help, but he refused.'

Peter appeared outraged. 'We have to help him.'

'I dunno,' Daryl replied. 'Patrick thinks we should keep a low profile for the moment.'

'A low profile!' Peter exclaimed. 'Murray's risked his life for us more times than I can remember.' He pointed a finger at me, 'He saved MaryAnn.'

'Mr Murray's going to look for her on his own,' I said.

'He'll get himself killed,' Peter turned to Daryl. 'We have to help him.'

'No-one even knows where the LightHouse is,' Daryl protested.

'I don't care,' Peter said.

'Peter's right,' I agreed. 'We have to help him.'

Daryl shook his head. 'You're not getting involved. It's too dangerous.'

'I wasn't asking for permission,' I responded coolly.

'You'll just get in the way. You haven't had any training.'

I was outraged. 'I helped rescue you when you were captured by the Director.'

'She has a point,' Peter agreed.

Daryl scowled. 'She does not have a point. She's not coming with us. Have you forgotten what the Director did to her?'

I flinched at his comment. Following my escape from the Neighbourhood I'd tried to keep those memories tightly locked away. 'That's not fair. It wasn't my fault the Director captured me,' I argued. 'It was Peter who forgot to log out of the security system.' The instant the words were out of my mouth I wanted to force them back inside.

Peter gaped at me in horror.

'I didn't mean…I was just making a point…' I trailed off uncertainly.

There was a tense silence as Peter clambered to his feet. 'I have…I have to go…there's something I need to . . .' he stammered as he backed out of the cabin door and disappeared.

Daryl turned to me. 'What did you say that for?'

I shook my head miserably. 'I didn't mean to,' I swallowed.

'Do you have you any idea how bad he feels about what happened to you? He blames himself and now you've just made it a million times worse.'

'I didn't realise,' I whispered. I hadn't even considered that Peter might feel guilty.

'Of course you didn't realise,' Daryl sighed. 'MaryAnn, I know what happened to you was horrible, but you can't go around saying things like that.'

'I just wanted to help Mr Murray.'

Daryl ran a hand irritably through his hair. 'There's no point in arguing with you. You always get your own way anyway.' He got to his feet.

'Where are you going?' I asked.

'To find Peter.'

When I stood up to follow, he shook his head. 'No, you stay here.'

CHAPTER 7

The Rescue Mission

MARYANN:

Daryl returned a few hours later. 'We're going to speak to Mr Murray. I thought you'd want to come with us,' he said as he entered the bunkroom. I'd spent a miserable afternoon sprawled across my bed replaying the conversation over and over in my head and desperately wishing I could take back what I'd said to Peter.

Peter was waiting for us on the dock, his expression emotionless, hands clenched tightly by his side. I wanted to tell him that I didn't blame him, but the coward in me hung back as he turned away and strode purposefully towards the tunnels.

As we navigated our way through a dimly lit passageway I caught the sound of voices in the distance. We rounded a corner and I found myself face to face with Uncle Patrick. Leah followed at his heel clutching a stack of files to her chest.

'MaryAnn, it's so good to see you out of the hospital. You're looking a lot better,' Uncle Patrick exclaimed. I glanced at Leah, who gave me a venomous look.

'Where are you three off to?' Uncle Patrick asked.

'We're going to get something to eat,' Daryl replied in a casual tone.

Uncle Patrick glanced down at his watch. 'Maybe I'll come with you. It would be good to catch up with MaryAnn.' Daryl's shoulders stiffened for an instant and then relaxed. 'Are you sure you have the time?' he asked.

'No he doesn't have the time,' Leah interrupted, her tone sharp. 'We have a finance meeting to prepare for.'

Uncle Patrick pulled a face. 'Oh yes, the finance meeting. How could I possibly forget that?'

He touched my shoulder. 'Looks like we might have to postpone lunch.'

I arranged my features into an expression of disappointment. 'That's a shame. Maybe we can catch up later?' I suggested.

'Not today,' Leah took a firm grip of Uncle Patrick's arm. 'We have too much work to do.'

Uncle Patrick sighed loudly and waved his goodbyes as he followed Leah down the tunnel.

When they were out of earshot I turned to Daryl. 'What is her problem?'

'She's just jealous.'

'Jealous of what?'

'Of you!'

'Me!' I exclaimed. 'Why would she be jealous of me? I barely know her.'

'She has a thing for Patrick. Everyone knows about it. It's just Patrick who's totally oblivious.'

'She likes Uncle Patrick?' I was a little shocked. 'Then why would she be jealous of me? I'm no threat to her. He's my uncle!'

Daryl laughed. 'She definitely sees you as a threat. Do you know how much planning it took to get you across the Boundary? To rescue you from the Director? Patrick's barely had time to focus on anything else, especially Leah.'

I was a little shocked. 'I'm that important to him?'

Daryl nodded, 'It's not just your knowledge of the Neighbourhood that's important. You're also his family and he wants us to be together.'

I considered this as we entered the market. I'd had no idea that Uncle Patrick had used so many of the Union's resources to rescue me from the Director.

'Murray's over there,' Peter said.

We headed to the table where Mr Murray was staring gloomily into a mug of beer.

'We heard about your niece,' Peter said as he sat down opposite him.

Mr Murray slowly sipped his drink. 'News travels fast in this place,' he muttered.

'We want to help,' I said.

Mr Murray shook his head. 'Patrick doesn't want the Union involved.'

'That's not going to stop you is it?' Peter replied.

Mr Murray glanced up from his mug. 'I can't leave her in that place.'

'Then we're coming with you,' Peter said.

'It's too dangerous,' Mr Murray replied.

'We've already decided.' Peter held up a hand as Mr Murray continued to protest. 'We're coming with you,' he repeated firmly.

Mr Murray glanced at Daryl. 'Are you coming too?' he asked. 'Patrick's not going to like it.'

When Daryl didn't respond Peter gave him a sharp nudge, 'Daryl?'

To my surprise Daryl still didn't reply.

'Daryl I know this is difficult,' Peter began.

'Patrick's my family,' Daryl interrupted.

'But Uncle Patrick doesn't want to go,' I protested, 'and we owe Mr Murray for everything he's done for us.'

'You don't owe me anything,' Mr Murray's tone was brusque. 'I was just doing my job.'

Peter turned to Daryl. 'I understand how you must feel. Patrick took us in and trained us…but I think he's wrong. We're the Union. We should help Murray. We should be helping all the families that have had kids taken away from them.'

'He could throw us out of the Union,' Daryl whispered.

'I know,' Peter said quietly. 'That's why this has to be your decision.'

'Whatever I decide, you're going with Murray, aren't you?'

'I have to,' Peter replied determinedly. 'I can't sit by and do nothing.'

Daryl considered Peter for a moment and then shrugged. 'If I let you go on your own you'll just do something stupid and get yourself into trouble. I don't really have a choice do I?'

Peter responded with a curt nod before turning to Mr Murray. 'Do you have a plan?'

'I'm working on it,' he said. 'Charlotte was taken to the LightHouse a few days ago. Dan, my brother-in-law, went after her.'

Peter frowned, 'I thought the location of the LightHouse was secret.'

'Dan used to be in the army before the virus. He was Special Forces,' He's a great tracker. If he thinks he's found the LightHouse then I'm inclined to believe him.'

Peter and Daryl exchanged a glance. 'Where is it?' Peter asked.

'It's in the far north,' Mr Murray replied.

'I've heard rumours about it being in the north,' Peter said. 'It's going to be a long trip. When were you planning to leave?'

'I need a week to make the arrangements.'

'A week!' Daryl exclaimed. 'That doesn't give us a lot of time.'

Mr Murray shrugged. 'The longer we wait, the more time Charlotte has to spend in the LightHouse.'

'So any idea how we do this without Patrick finding out?' Peter asked.

The table was quiet as everyone considered the problem. I raised a tentative hand.

'You have an idea MaryAnn?' Mr Murray asked. When I nodded he flashed a brief smile. 'You don't have to put your hand up,' he said. 'We're not in school.'

Embarrassed, I dropped my hand into my lap. 'We could leave during the May Day party. Everyone will be busy and they probably won't realise we're missing until the following morning.' I waited uncertainly for his response and was pleased when he nodded. 'Good idea. I like it.'

I felt myself blush. Now there was no reason for Daryl to leave me behind. I'd had the best idea so far.

'What about transport?' Peter queried.

'That's going to be tricky,' Mr Murray frowned. 'We need a four wheel drive and you know how hard it is to find one that isn't falling apart.'

'Does your sister have a truck?' Peter asked.

'Dan dropped her off at a safe house and then took their truck north.'

'Can't we take one of the Union trucks?' I asked.

'We can't steal a truck from the Union,' Daryl said. 'I'm not doing anything that will put them in danger,' he wore a defiant look.

'It's okay Daryl,' Peter put a placating hand on his shoulder. 'We're not going to steal a truck. No-one wants to put the Union in danger.'

'What about your truck?' I asked, remembering the vehicle we'd used to escape from Peter's farm a few months earlier.

'It runs on diesel. We had enough fuel to get us here, but there's not enough to take us north and we'll never find diesel on the road. It's in the garage waiting to be converted to biofuel.'

I nodded even though I wasn't quite sure what biofuel was.

'Could you convert it?' Mr Murray asked.

Peter chewed his bottom lip thoughtfully, 'I suppose so. It'll take a bit of time though.'

'What about the biofuel?' Mr Murray asked.

'We had a bumper seed crop last year. So we can take as much fuel as we want. No-one's going to miss it,' Peter replied.

'Dan and I agreed a rendezvous,' Mr Murray explained. 'So we need to make sure we have enough fuel to make it there and back.'

'Does Dan have a PortPad so we can contact him?' I asked.

Mr Murray shook his head. 'PortPads don't work very well on the Outside. Patrick has a few in his office to contact our operatives in the Neighbourhood, but he has to use a booster to piggyback off the wireless signal in the Neighbourhood. The range isn't very good and there's always the danger that the Watch are tracking messages.'

'Then how do we contact him?' I queried.

'Dan will be at the rendezvous from midday for three hours. If we don't make contact he'll go back to camp and try again the following day.'

I considered Mr Murray's plan. It didn't seem like a very reliable method of communication to me.

'So we have to convert a truck, sort out supplies and plan our escape without Patrick finding out and we have a week to pull it all together?' Daryl questioned.

'When you say it like that you make it sound so easy,' Peter replied.

The following afternoon Daryl and I were eating lunch in the market when Mr Murray joined us at our table. He was accompanied by a petite woman who shared his dark features and jaded expression. He introduced her as his sister Jenn.

'Where's Peter?' Mr Murray asked as he fed Flash a piece of sausage from his plate.

'He's in the garage working on the truck,' Daryl replied. 'I'm looking after Flash for him.'

'How's it going? Will the truck be ready on time?' Mr Murray said.

'I hope so,' Daryl said. 'Peter's been working on it all morning.'

'It's got to be ready,' Jenn exclaimed. 'You have to rescue Charlotte. I can't bear to think of her living in the Neighbourhood with those monsters,' she finished helplessly.

'Not everyone in the Neighbourhood is a monster,' I replied.

'Alpha treat Delta really well. They work in nice homes and get enough food to eat.' I trailed off uncertainly as Jenn glowered at me.

'You make them sound like pets,' she almost spat. 'Delta are people, not animals.' There was a feverish pitch to her tone.

'It's okay, Jenn. Calm down,' Mr Murray clasped an arm around her shoulders.

I was confused by Jenn's response. My comment was meant to make her feel better. The Delta had a good life in the Neighbourhood, they were submissive and compliant, which is why they made such good servants. 'I'm sorry,' I said. 'I didn't mean to upset you.'

There was a long uncomfortable silence as Jenn glared at me. I glanced over at Daryl for support but he refused to meet my gaze. The silence was broken by Mr Murray who asked if I had time to assist him with a job after lunch.

I agreed, eager to prove how useful I could be.

I met Mr Murray outside the market and as he handed me a lantern he told me that we were going shopping. With a quickening sense of excitement I followed him along a narrow corridor and down a flight of steps carved roughly into the grey rock. He ushered me inside a large cavernous opening and I found myself in a low cave crammed with wooden shelves.

'This is where we keep our supplies,' Mr Murray explained. 'We're supposed to sign for everything we take, but the stores team are having lunch. They've just hired a new apprentice and they won't be back until they've forced her to drink at least three pints of cider.'

Mr Murray pulled a crumpled piece of paper from his back pocket and scrutinised it carefully. 'We'll take stuff from the back of the store so no-one notices it's missing,' he said as he began to check the shelves, pulling out tents, sleeping bags and a small cooking stove.

Laden with provisions Mr Murray led the way to the garage where we found Peter working on the truck, the air was pungent with a greasy, oily smell. 'Put everything in the boot,' Peter grunted, his hands busy inside the bowels of the engine.

I was struggling under the weight of my bundle and I gratefully dropped it into the boot of the truck. I stopped to catch my breath, but it seemed there was no respite. 'Come on, no time for dawdling,' Mr Murray called. 'We need to get food.'

'Make sure you only take what we need. We can hunt once we set up camp,' Peter instructed, his voice muffled under the bonnet.

My earlier conversation with Jenn had been weighing heavily on my mind. Mr Murray was my friend and I couldn't bear the thought that he might be upset with me. As we travelled back towards the stores I took the opportunity to apologise for upsetting his sister. He waved my apology away. 'I worked with the Alpha for a long time. I know that they take care of Delta. They make sure they have enough food to eat and a warm place to sleep. But however well they're treated they're still slaves, stolen from their families and forced to work in the Neighbourhood. You must be able to understand that?'

I'd always thought that the Delta were more fortunate than the Echo left to survive on the Outside. I'd heard stories about Delta who were beaten or forced to live in squalor, but it was rare. Most of them were well cared for and had a comfortable life. As we approached the stores I realised that I was viewing their situation from a position of privilege; a privilege I no longer held. How would I feel if I was taken away from Daryl and forced to work inside the Boundary? I silently berated myself. I'd lived with the Union for months and I still behaved like an Alpha. No wonder people refused to trust me.

'I understand,' I said quietly. 'Being an Alpha isn't just about money and privilege. It's about being in control of your own fate.' I realised that Delta had no such luxury; their fate was dependant on the goodwill and charity of the compassionate Alpha.

Mr Murray flashed me a smile that reached all the way to his eyes, crinkling the corners into tiny folds. 'You're a good person, MaryAnn,' he said. 'I know it's hard for people to accept you sometimes, but it will get easier. I promise.'

'But Jenn thinks I'm just like the Alpha in the Neighbourhood.'

Mr Murray shrugged, 'It's hard for Jenn. We were teenagers during the virus and it was pretty tough. She knows what the Light can do and she's terrified. Just give her some time.'

'I just want to help,' I said. 'I suppose no-one's going to believe that are they? An Alpha wanting to help the Union.'

Mr Murray's expression was grave as he considered me; no trace of a smile remained. 'The Director held you captive and tortured you and you didn't give up your family or your friends. I'd trust you with my life.'

His tone was deadly serious. I was an Alpha, the daughter of the Legislator and yet he still trusted me.

Back in the store we collected a couple of empty sacks and filled them with food. Mr Murray selected bags of oats and added packs of dried pasta, jars of bottled tomatoes, soup mix and dried meats.

After we'd returned to the garage and deposited the food in the back of the truck Mr Murray told me that I was free to go. I turned to say goodbye to Peter but he'd disappeared under the truck. I heard the sound of metal on metal as he hammered ferociously at the bottom of the truck. I hesitated uncertainly before giving the truck one last glance and leaving the garage.

CHAPTER 8

Influence & Manipulation

CHARLOTTE:

Life in the LightHouse had settled into a familiar but tedious routine of exhausting work and broken sleep. Most nights I felt like I'd just fallen into bed and closed my eyes when the siren blared to announce another assembly. This evening was no different.

'This is just stupid,' I heard Bekka mutter. 'They have to let us sleep sometime.'

I hauled myself out of bed and wearily followed the other girls out of the dorm to the Assembly Hall.

As the Warden took to the podium I stifled a yawn. Each evening assembly followed a similar format. We'd pledge our allegiance to the Light, then the Warden would follow this with a long lecture about the compassion and benevolence of the Alpha. This evening's lecture focussed on the importance of hygiene. It was a lecture I'd heard a number of times before. The Neighbourhood had strict laws about cleanliness. The Warden said it was to prevent the Sandman Virus from returning. It was the reason we were forced to wear the gloves. I hated them; they made my hands feel hot and uncomfortable. Sometimes I had to resist the urge to tear them off just to feel the air on my skin.

After the lecture we were shown a film about the work we would be given in the Neighbourhood. The first time the Warden had played a film I'd been mesmerised. I'd gasped out loud at the image of an Alpha house. Patterned paper lined the walls, bright curtains hung at the windows and a thick luxurious carpet covered the floors. I thought of my home with its rendered walls, threadbare carpets and painted floorboards. No wonder the Light despised us so much. We must seem like animals to them.

Most intriguingly the Neighbourhood had something called the Portal and PortPads that were used as a communication device. I'd recognised the PortPads as the hand held devices that the Trustees used. What I wouldn't give to get my hands on one of them and find out how they worked.

I loved machines and never grew tired of hearing Dad's stories about relics from before the virus; juice makers, sandwich toasters, washing machines. They were all so fascinating. Sometimes when Dad went to the market he would bring back broken machines for me. I loved taking them apart to see how they worked.

For my last birthday Dad had given me a broken blender. I'd spent months poring over a maintenance manual, taking the blender apart and carefully putting it back together again. When I was sure I'd repaired it I'd asked Dad to let me connect it to the generator. It had taken a lot of convincing but eventually he'd agreed to let me use some of our precious electricity. Matty had given a drum roll as I flicked the on-switch and we'd cheered as the blades whirred into life. Mum brought milk up from the cellar and Matty collected strawberries from the garden and we made milkshakes, just like the ones they sold in the milk bar. It had been a great day.

After I'd repaired the blender Dad started to let me work on the farm equipment with him. I think that's when we began to grow really close. I didn't have many friends; it was just me, Mum, Dad, Matty and the farm. That's all I ever needed.

Before I'd tested Immune Dad and I had been busy working on a secret project. We only had one truck on the farm and Mum was always grumbling that we needed another vehicle so she could deliver sewing. There were lots of abandoned cars around the Community, but most of them had rusted beyond repair. Finally Dad had found a car that he thought he could fix and convert to biofuel. We'd towed it back to the farm and hidden it in a barn on the edge of the property. Dad and I had been working on it whenever we had a spare moment. We were hoping to have it finished by Christmas.

I was ashamed to admit that when I'd first seen the PortPads and the other equipment in the Neighbourhood I'd felt a twinge of excitement. I imagined all the new things I could experience and for a short time I'd actually thought that living in the Neighbourhood might be fun. It wasn't until the Warden had shown an interview with Delta that I'd realised how wrong my first impression had been. The Delta talked enthusiastically about life in the Neighbourhood, but this enthusiasm was at odds with her flattened vacant expression. I didn't know what was wrong with the Delta but it scared me.

Today the video focussed on family loyalty. Not my real family, the one I'd left behind on the farm, but my new family. My future was the Light. It was the Light who would house me, feed me and educate me. It was the Light who deserved my loyalty.

When I'd first arrived at the LightHouse I'd missed my real family so much that I'd cried myself to sleep every night. I'd worried about how Mum and Dad would cope on the farm without me. There would be no-one for Matty to play with. Every morning I had to count the animals to make sure wild dogs hadn't taken any of them. Matty would trail along behind me telling stories he'd made up about wizards and dragons. I wondered who would have the time to listen to his stories now that I was gone.

I wasn't sure how I would have survived the last few weeks without the support of my friends. Mally and I had rediscovered our old friendship. He was shy and usually hovered on the fringes of a conversation, but he was a great listener and he was from home.

Flo had become like an older sister. Her shimmering skin and black rimmed eyes had washed away in the shower, leaving her as pale and exhausted as the rest of us, but she always had a welcoming smile. Somehow just being close to her made me feel safe.

Eric was still a mystery to me. I spent a lot of time in his company because he'd become Flo's shadow, but I wasn't sure whether we could be described as friends. Flo had taken him under her wing and they spent most evenings together in the common room chatting on the sofa. Eric had adapted more easily to the LightHouse regime than the rest of us. The hard work and lack of sleep didn't seem to bother him. While the rest of us were hollow eyed and exhausted, he'd actually put on a little weight. His problem was that he struggled with authority. The Warden ran the LightHouse with an iron fist but the strict rules just seemed to make Eric more rebellious. He always seemed to be in trouble.

'Charlotte, what are you doing?' Flo hissed. 'Get up.'

Startled, I jumped to my feet. Assembly was over and everyone was preparing to leave. I glanced around nervously hoping that a Trustee hadn't seen me daydreaming. This time I was lucky.

The following morning when Mally appeared at breakfast he was alone. 'Where's Eric?' I whispered. Mally glanced over at Flo. She'd scooped up a spoonful of porridge, but paused as she caught my question. 'Is he in trouble again?' she asked.

Mally nodded. 'He's in Detention.'

'What did he do this time?' Flo sighed.

'We were in the changing rooms and one of the Trustees yelled at him for taking too long to get undressed. He walked over to the shower, turned it on and stood underneath it fully clothed. He refused to get out.'

Flo exhaled miserably. 'I'm so sick of this,' she muttered through gritted teeth. 'Why can't he just do as he's told?'

Flo was in a horrible mood all day. We'd been given separate cleaning and work tasks so I only saw her at lunch, but I could barely get her to respond to my questions as she stabbed moodily at the food on her plate. It was unusual for her to be so quiet. She normally had so much to say.

Eric reappeared at teatime and plonked himself down at our table with a breezy 'evening all'. Flo pointedly ignored him.

Eric studied Flo for a moment and then asked her what was wrong. When he spoke I was surprised to hear real concern in his voice.

'Like you don't know,' she snapped. Her tone was unexpected. I'd never heard her speak so viciously before.

Eric opened his mouth to respond but Flo silenced him with a wave of her hand. 'I'm just sick of you getting into trouble all the time.'

'That's not your concern,' Eric replied.

'Of course it's my concern. I worry about you.'

'I never asked you to worry about me,' Eric responded.

'One day you're going to push the Trustees too far and then they're really going to hurt you.'

'You think the Trustees can hurt me?' he said with a touch of bravado.

'I told you what my dad was like. Living in here is a picnic compared with being at home. I get three meals a day and if I do anything wrong the Trustees just slap me around and put me in Detention. If that's the best they can do I'm disappointed. I should give them my dad's address. He could teach them a trick or two.'

I winced at his comment. Most of the adults in our Community had a funny drunken story to tell about Mr Castle, but the way Eric spoke about his dad made him sound like a monster. It reminded me of something that had happened a couple of years ago. Dad had returned home from the market in a foul temper. It was unusual because he was normally so calm. My mum was the bad tempered one.

Dad was in the living room, but he was shouting so loudly that I could hear him up in my bedroom. He'd mentioned Mr Castle's name and then I'd heard him say, 'People like him shouldn't be allowed to have kids.' At the time I'd thought it had something to do with Mr Castle being drunk and embarrassing his children, but now I wasn't so sure.

'Just promise me that you'll stop winding up the Trustees.' I could hear the pleading tone in Flo's voice.

Eric shook his head stubbornly. 'I'm not letting them throw their weight around, thinking they can do whatever they want to me.'

As the siren blared to signal the end of the meal Flo jumped to her feet. 'Then I can't be friends with you anymore,' she said in a choked voice as she turned and rushed away.

Eric clambered to his feet intending to follow. I put a hand out to stop him. 'I'll go and speak to her,' I said. To my surprise he didn't argue. 'Just make sure she's alright,' he urged as I left the dining hall.

I headed to the common room, expecting to find Flo inside but when I peered around the door she was nowhere to be seen. On impulse I decided to check the dorm. My heart beat wildly in my chest as I hurried along the corridor, keeping a wary eye out for the Trustees. If I was caught I would be sent to Detention.

I arrived at the dorm and when I crept cautiously inside I found Flo by the window. I flopped down beside her.

'Sorry for causing such a scene,' she said. 'You must think I'm an idiot.'

'Of course not,' I replied. 'Eric's the idiot, getting himself locked up in Detention all the time.'

She sniffed and wiped her nose on her shirt. 'I'm just scared that one day he'll push the Trustees too far and they'll really hurt him.'

'He was the same back home,' I explained. 'He was always fighting.'

'It's because of his dad,' Flo replied. 'He's a drunk. When he drinks he hits Eric and his sisters.'

I flinched in horror, 'I didn't know that,' I replied.

'Eric used to antagonise him so that he'd leave his sisters alone,' Flo continued. 'Now he thinks he has to fight everyone.'

'Did Eric tell you that…about his dad?'

'He told me some of it. The rest I figured out on my own. In the circus we pick up lots of kids that are running away from home. Most of them are just like Eric.' She sniffed again. 'I wish my mam and dad were here, they'd know what to do….' She was interrupted by the creak of the door and we both watched anxiously as it slowly swung open. I let out an audible sigh of relief as Eric and Mally shuffled nervously into the room. Eric looked completely miserable while Mally appeared terrified. His eyes flitted anxiously around the room as if he expected a Trustee to jump out from behind one of the beds.

'This is the girls' dorm,' Flo hissed. 'You can't come in here.'

'He made me come with him,' Mally mumbled.

Eric scowled. 'I wanted to talk to you.'

'Well I don't want to talk to you,' Flo snapped.

'Don't be like that,' Eric said. 'You're my best friend.' His tone was so earnest that I couldn't help but feel a little sorry for him.

'Maybe you should let him speak,' I coaxed.

'If you're here to promise me that you're going to stop causing trouble then I'll listen to what you have to say.'

Eric scuffed at the floor with the toe of his shoe. He didn't respond.

Flo shrugged. 'Then we have nothing more to say,' she snapped. 'Just go away and leave me alone.'

'You don't understand,' Eric replied, 'sometimes the Trustees make me so angry. It's like a fog in my brain and I don't know what I'm doing.'

'That's absolute rubbish and you know it is. You antagonise them on purpose.'

'Flo, I'm trying to be honest with you. I don't want to make a promise that I can't keep.'

'Then we can't be friends. I won't sit by and watch them beat you and drag you away to Detention anymore.'

'But you're my best friend,' Eric pleaded.

'Best friends are supposed to look out for each other,' Flo replied.

Eric leant back against the wall and rubbed a hand across his face. 'You're not making this easy for me.'

'I think it's very easy. Play nice with the Trustees and I'll be your friend, antagonise them and you're on your own.'

He sighed. 'Alright, you've made your point. If it upsets you so much then I'll try not to antagonise them, but I can't make any promises.' He waited expectantly for a response.

'Is that the best you can do?' she growled.

Mally and I exchanged a glance. It seemed there would be no peaceful resolution to the quarrel.

'Perhaps you should listen to him,' I urged. 'If we work together maybe we can help him stay out of trouble.'

Eric stared at me like I'd suddenly grown horns. 'You'd do that?' he asked. 'You'd help me?'

'Of course,' I replied. 'Mally will too.'

Mally responded with a nod. 'I don't particularly enjoy watching the Trustees haul you away to Detention. If I can help you stay out of trouble then I will.'

Eric peered down at Flo. 'It looks like Charlie…' he threw me a glance, 'Sorry, Charlotte and Mally are prepared to help. What about you?' He offered Flo a hand. It was a conciliatory gesture.

She considered the hand for a moment. At first I thought she was going to refuse, then she grabbed hold of it, lacing her fingers through his. He pulled her to her feet.

'You'd better not be messing with me,' she said. They exchanged a brief hug as the siren sounded for bed.

The following afternoon Flo and I were allocated work duty collecting fallen branches. It was a warm day and the sun beat down unchecked. I pushed damp hair out of my eyes, wishing I'd brought a hair band with me.

'Here, let me.' Flo appeared at my side and pulled a couple of bands from her wrist. She deftly plaited my hair into two thick braids.

'Much better,' she said as she turned me around until we were face to face. She tucked a loose strand behind my ear. 'You have such lovely thick hair.'

'I wish it was pink, like yours.'

'Are you kidding me? I hate my hair,' she complained, grabbing a tuft of pink fringe. 'Look at it. The colour's growing out.'

I glanced down at Flo, the top of her head reached just above my chin. The roots that peeked through the pink hair showed blonde. I thought it was a nice colour.

'I'm going to be blonde and boring for the rest of my life,' she moaned.

'Was your mum angry when you dyed your hair?' I asked. I tried to imagine the look of horror on my mum's face if I came home with pink hair.

'My mam dyed it for me,' Flo replied. 'She has blue hair. Most of the travellers dye their hair. We add glitter to it just before a performance to make it really sparkle.'

Flo's family sounded so glamorous. Before she tested Immune she'd lived in a circus and travelled in a caravan, putting on shows in the different Communities. I was a little overawed. The only other time I'd been away from home was when I was 10 years old and my Uncle Ethan had taken Matty and me on a holiday to the seaside. We'd had an amazing time camping on the beach and building sandcastles, but after three nights I was glad to get back to the farm and my normal life.

'Is it weird for you living in a house?' I asked.

'It's horrible,' Flo said. 'We had the cosiest caravan and our horse Mr Mumbles was so cute. I hate waking up in the same place every day and seeing the same people.' She paused uncertainly. 'I didn't mean you,' she added quickly. 'I like you. You're fun to be around.'

'I understand,' I said. 'I'd give anything to be back home on the farm.' I felt a lump in my throat and I swallowed hard.

She touched my shoulder, 'You missing home too?'

I nodded, too choked up to reply.

'Shall I show you something cool?' she said. She checked to make sure we were alone before surprising me by performing a perfect back flip.

'Wow,' I breathed. 'How did you do that?'

'I always wanted to be an acrobat,' she puffed. 'I was going to get my apprenticeship in a couple of months when I turned 18… but….' she faltered.

'You tested Immune,' I replied.

'Four months away from being 18 and I test Immune. Can you believe my bad luck? We all thought I was in the clear. My mam and dad were devastated.'

'You still have to get tested even though you travel with the circus?' I asked.

'The circus has to register with the Watch every year so we can pay our taxes. That's when the under 18s get tested. *No-one can escape the almighty authority of the Light,*' her lip curled into a sneer.

I glanced around nervously, 'Shush,' I hissed. 'What if a Trustee hears you?'

Flo scanned the woods. 'Sorry, I shouldn't have said that out loud,' she gave a humourless laugh. 'After all the things I said to Eric last night, and here I am running my mouth off.' She sighed. 'I just thought that my life would be different. I had it all planned out. I was going to apprentice as an acrobat for a few years and when I graduated get a job in the circus full time.' She paused. 'Can I tell you a secret?'

I nodded, thrilled that she trusted me enough to confide in me.

'I met a boy last year.'

'Is he in the circus?'

'No I met him at a party. He's really nice. I think I might have been able to persuade him to join the circus when I finished my apprenticeship.' She shrugged, 'I suppose it doesn't matter now does it? I'll never see him again.' She took a couple of deep breaths and I watched helplessly as a series of emotions played across her face. She stooped to pick up a large branch. 'We should get back to work,' she said in a choked voice. 'Come on, I'll need some help with this one.'

I grabbed the end of the branch and with difficulty we carried it to the clearing where Eric was chopping the wood into logs. He wielded an axe and expertly cleaved through the trunk of a fallen tree. He let the axe fall as we approached. 'Just what I need, more wood!' He flashed a smile to show that he was joking.

We deposited the fallen branch on the woodpile.

Eric frowned and pulled at his gloves. 'Don't these damn things drive you two crazy. They make my hands feel so hot.'

'Mine feel fine,' Flo replied as she unclipped her water bottle from her belt. 'The Warden said they're breathable just like skin.'

'That's because you're used to smothering that circus gunk all over your skin,' Eric replied.

I unscrewed the cap of my water bottle and took a long drink. The water was tepid and did little to quench my thirst. I screwed up my face in disgust.

Eric caught the look and laughed. He held up his bottle. 'I pretend it's a nice cool ice cream float,' he said. 'Makes it go down a treat.'

Flo laughed. 'Maybe I'll pretend mine's a nice glass of iced tea,' she said.

'Hmmm, home-made elderflower lemonade,' I added as I took another mouthful. 'My mum makes the best elderflower lemonade in the world.'

'Yum, I might have some of your mum's elderflower lemonade too,' Flo exclaimed and then froze as a Trustee emerged from the woods. I hurriedly clipped my water bottle back on my belt and prepared to return to work.

With his eyes firmly fixed on the Trustee Eric leisurely raised his bottle to his lips and took an exaggerated gulp. Panic flickered across Flo's face and I gave Eric a small shake of my head. To my surprise he responded by placing his water bottle on the floor and picking up the axe. 'See,' he flashed a wide grin as he heaved the axe above his head, 'sometimes I can play nice.'

Chapter 9

Family Ties Part 2

MaryAnn:

It was the eve of the May Day celebration and the clamour outside the boat suggested that the festivities had started early. May Day was one of the biggest events in the Union social calendar and although we were busy making last minute preparations to travel to the North I couldn't help but get caught up in the excitement.

As I pushed my way through the crowd of revellers on my way to the market to meet Daryl for breakfast I heard someone call out my name. I turned to find Cheryl behind me. 'MaryAnn, I'm so glad I bumped into you. I want to show you what I bought for the party,' she rummaged in a brown paper bag and pulled out a teal blue dress. 'Do you like it?'

'It's beautiful,' I replied as I caressed the soft material of the dress marvelling at how smooth the silk felt against my skin. Its thin spaghetti straps were decorated with a thread of sparkling diamanté that danced brightly in the candlelit cave.

'I thought you'd like it,' Cheryl gave a satisfied smile. 'Most people around here don't appreciate beautiful clothes, but I knew you would.'

'You made this?' I asked.

Cheryl laughed brightly. 'You've got to be kidding me. I can't sew. My mum tried to teach me but it turns out these hands are only good for baking bread. We've had a really good year in the bakery so I paid someone to make it for me. Bit of a luxury I know, but it's nice to have a treat every now and then isn't it.' She winked conspiratorially.

I thought back to when I lived in the Neighbourhood. I'd bought new clothes almost every week and it hadn't seemed such a luxury then. I glanced down at my flannel shirt, jeans and heavy boots and felt a little envious. Wearing a new dress to the party would be heavenly but I only had the food tokens that Uncle Patrick had given me. My limited wardrobe had been scavenged by Daryl and Peter from hand-me-down clothes donated by other members of the Union. At first the thought of wearing second-hand clothes had disgusted me, but I'd had no other choice. In the Union, clothes were reused and handed down between family members and friends until they were almost threadbare. New clothes were considered an extravagance.

Cheryl was on her way to a shift at the bakery so she accompanied me to the market. It was nice to have someone new to talk to. Usually when Daryl and Peter were busy I spent my time alone as I'd struggled to make any real friends among the Unionists.

I left Cheryl at the entrance to the bakery and went in search of Daryl. I found him sharing a table with Peter and Mr Murray. As I slipped into a seat beside Peter I heard Mr Murray say, 'We need to leave the party as discreetly as possible. We don't want to draw any attention to ourselves.'

I jumped as Peter let out a loud snort. 'Asking MaryAnn to be discreet is like forcing a herd of cows into ballet shoes and asking them to pirouette across a stage.'

I glared at him for a moment and then let my face relax into a smile. This was the first time he'd addressed me directly since the incident on the boat. If he felt comfortable enough to make a joke then maybe it was a sign that we were friends again. I tried to keep the conversation light. 'Well Petey if I'm such a liability maybe you can help me,' I fluttered my eyelashes suggestively.

Mr Murray barked out a laugh. 'Petey, maybe you can carry MaryAnn in your big strong arms.'

I gave Peter's upper arm a tight squeeze. 'Ooh, it feels like you've been working out.' He shrugged me away, 'Gerroff.'

Mr Murray leant across the table and gave Peter's arm a tight squeeze too. He winked at me. 'You're right, he has been working out.'

Peter batted him away. 'Okay folks. Peter's my name. Let's use it, shall we? And keep your hands off me!'

Mr Murray grinned, but whatever he was going to say next was interrupted by the appearance of Mr Murray's nephew, Matty, as he tore across the market place. 'Uncle Ethan. You have to come. You have to come.'

Mr Murray was out of his seat in an instant. 'What's wrong?' he cried.

'Nothing's wrong,' Matty giggled. It was the first time I'd seen him smile since he'd arrived at the caves.

'You have to come and see,' he squealed. 'It's the circus. People are eating fire! Come on.' His voice rose excitedly as he grabbed Mr Murray's hand and dragged him impatiently towards the entrance. As we scrambled to our feet Peter gave Daryl a discreet thumbs up.

The circus had gathered in the large entrance cave. The excitement and vibrancy they brought with them seemed to fill the cave to bursting. The performers were dressed in bright clothes that shimmered with colour as they danced and somersaulted across the floor. Each new trick was greeted with a yell of excitement and a round of rapturous applause from the gathered crowd.

'See Uncle Ethan, I told you. It's the circus.' Matty bounced on his toes like an excited puppy.

I caught sight of Uncle Patrick. He hovered on the edge of the crowd talking intently to a blue-haired woman. Her black ringed eyes and shimmering skin marked her out as a member of the circus.

'Isn't that Flo's mum over there with Patrick?' Peter asked. Daryl was on his tiptoes examining the performers. He nodded. 'Yeah it is. I'd recognise that blue hair anywhere.'

I could tell that there was something wrong. The blue-haired woman appeared agitated as she gestured furiously at Uncle Patrick. She grabbed his arm, seeming to plead with him. Uncle Patrick tried to pull away but she refused to let go. A short stocky man with a ribbon of red dreadlocks appeared beside her and gently removed her hand. Uncle Patrick pulled down the sleeve of his shirt, then turned and walked away, his face a mask of fury.

Daryl pushed his way through the crowd towards her and we all followed close behind. When the woman caught sight of Daryl she pulled him into a tight embrace.

'Nessa, what's wrong?' Daryl asked as she released him from her grasp.

'It's Flo,' the woman gasped, 'she tested Immune.'

'Immune,' he whispered hoarsely as the colour drained from his face. It was almost too painful to watch. When I reached for his hand he grasped it so tightly that I winced in pain.

'The Watch came for her. We couldn't stop them,' the woman was close to tears.

Daryl continued to stare at her in wordless horror.

'They took her to the LightHouse?' Peter asked.

The woman nodded, 'About a week ago.'

'We thought Patrick would help,' the dreadlocked man said, 'but he's not interested in getting involved.' There was a tightness to his jaw that implied a barely contained anger. He turned to the woman. 'You're a Steward, Nessa. He has to listen to you?'

Nessa shrugged. 'I can call a Union meeting, but Brandon's the only Steward we can rely on to stand against Patrick. The others will do whatever he says, especially his lapdog Leah.'

'I can't believe he won't help us,' the man spat angrily.

Peter shared a glance with Mr Murray, who took hold of Matty's hand, 'I'll take the boy back to his mum. Come and find me when you've had a chance to talk,' he said.

'What's going on?' Nessa asked as she watched Mr Murray disappear into the crowd.

'Let's go to the boat, where we can talk,' Peter said.

Nessa studied him carefully before nodding her head.

'Come on Daryl,' Peter said. 'You can lead the way.'

As we clambered on board the boat Peter sank down onto the deck. 'I'll keep watch,' he said. Daryl, you go inside and have a chat with Nessa and Rory.'

Daryl checked to make sure that the boat was empty before indicating that we should take a seat at the table in the galley.

'Who's she?' the man eyed me suspiciously as I slid into the seat next to Daryl.

'She's my sister, MaryAnn,' Daryl replied by way of introduction. 'MaryAnn, this is Nessa and Rory. They're my friend Flo's parents.'

'Are you going to tell us what this is all about?' Rory asked.

'Murray has a niece who tested Immune and has been taken to the LightHouse,' Daryl said. 'We're going to try and get her back.'

Nessa looked startled, 'Patrick said he wouldn't help us.'

Daryl cleared his throat. 'Patrick hasn't sanctioned the operation.'

'You haven't told Patrick?' Nessa raised her eyebrows. The surprise was evident in her voice.

Daryl looked a little uncomfortable as he shook his head.

'He's not going to be very happy with you when he finds out,' Rory responded.

'That's why we have to keep it a secret,' Daryl said. 'We promised Murray we'd help him look for Charlotte.'

'…and you'll find Flo too?' Nessa interjected. 'She was very fond of you.'

Daryl flushed red. 'We're going to leave during the party tomorrow and head north. Charlotte's dad thinks he might have found the location of the LightHouse. We're going to take a look.'

'We're coming with you,' Nessa replied.

Daryl shook his head. 'You can't Nessa. It's not safe.'

'Safe! You think I care about being safe. I can't stay here and do nothing, not when Flo needs me.' There was a slightly hysterical edge to her voice.

'Nessa, you have to stay here. We're planning to leave during your performance tomorrow evening. You have to be our cover.'

Nessa didn't look convinced.

'I'll do everything I can to get Flo back. I promise.'

Nessa and Rory shared a long look before Nessa slowly bobbed her head in agreement. 'Just bring her back to us,' she pleaded.

CHAPTER 10

May Day Madness

MaryAnn:

I was woken the next morning by the sound of singing outside the canal boat. Daryl's bed was empty, the sheets strewn carelessly aside. Peter was still asleep. I'd heard him stumble into his bunk in the early hours of the morning. He'd been up most of the night working on the truck.

As I climbed out of bed and gathered my clothes he sat up and yawned. 'Do you want to meet me here after you've had a shower and we can go get some breakfast?' he asked. I smiled in response. 'Give me five minutes.'

Peter laughed and fell back onto his pillow. 'Five minutes! More like an hour,' he replied. 'I'll be waiting when you get back.'

I clambered down onto the dock feeling optimistic that Peter and I might finally be friends again. I sniffed the air. The rich aroma of baking seemed to permeate every corner of the cave. I suspected that there would be a lot of entries in the baking competition today. Peter had been very upset the previous evening when Uncle Patrick had asked Mr Murray to help judge this year's competition. His theatrical display of disappointment had even raised a smile on Daryl's morose face.

I snaked a path through the revellers to the washrooms where

I enjoyed a long, luxurious shower. After I'd towelled myself dry I pulled on a pair of clean brown trousers and a faded pink cotton shirt. I'd chosen my least threadbare outfit to wear to the party. I thought enviously of Cheryl's new dress and the luxury of owning something that hadn't been pre-worn. My only new accessory was the leather pouch Uncle Patrick had presented to me a few weeks after I'd moved into the caves. It clipped to my belt and it was for storing my valuables. In the Union everyone kept their most treasured possessions close, never knowing when they might need to flee at a moment's notice.

I arrived back at the dock to find Peter perched on the steps of the canal boat casually throwing a ball to Flash. The dog was freshly bathed, clipped and wearing a smart new bow tie.

'You look nice,' Peter said.

I shrugged. 'It's just clean clothes.'

'I thought you might like this,' he held out a package wrapped in an old Union pamphlet. He seemed a little awkward.

Surprised, I took the parcel from him, 'What is it?' I asked.

'Why don't you open it and find out?'

I ripped open the packaging with a sense of excitement. It had been a long time since I'd received a gift. 'It's beautiful,' I gasped as I pulled out a wool cardigan.

'I thought you might want something nice to wear to the party. Look, it even has a hood to keep you warm,' he said.

I fingered the soft blue wool. 'You have surprisingly good taste. Did someone help you choose it?'

'Too right! Despite my remarkable sense of personal style I don't have a clue about girl stuff. Cheryl helped choose the wool and Mr Murray knitted it for me,' he said.

'Mr Murray made this?'

'He likes to knit,' Peter said. 'It helps him relax. He made a tie for Flash too.'

'Well he looks very handsome,' I said as I gave Flash an affectionate pat on the head.

I offered Peter my arm. 'Now that I'm appropriately attired maybe you can escort me to breakfast.'

At the mention of breakfast Flash barked loudly.

'Looks like someone's hungry,' Peter said as he slipped his arm companionably into mine.

After a noisy breakfast in the market Peter and I went in search of Daryl. We found him alone in the entrance cave, perched sullenly beside a smouldering fire.

'Is he alright?' I whispered as we approached.

'He's pretty cut up about Flo, we should try and cheer him up.'

It transpired that Peter's approach to cheering up Daryl involved taking him to the cider tent, forcing him to drink a mug of spiced cider and then coaxing him outside to watch the May Day dancing. 'You shouldn't get him drunk,' I whispered to Peter. 'We have to leave later.'

'I know what I'm doing,' he whispered back. 'He just needs enough alcohol to bring him out of his bad mood. I promise I won't get him drunk.'

With mugs of cider in hand we gathered around a brightly decorated pole that Peter told me was the Maypole. A group of children circled it, each holding a coloured ribbon.

'Why are the ribbons red, white and blue?' I asked. 'Those are Neighbourhood colours.'

Peter shook his head. 'They're Union colours,' he replied.

'How strange that the Neighbourhood and the Union both have the same colours,' I mused.

'I suppose so.' Peter nudged Daryl. 'Hey look, they're about to start.'

A white-haired man emerged out of the cave entrance. His white beard was clipped short and he carried a ukulele under his arm.

It was John, the bandleader. His group was the mainstay of any Union party. John wasn't just an expert ukulele player, he crafted the instruments too. Peter had taken me to his studio so I could watch as he shaped and sanded the wood. I loved the quiet of his workshop. After the hustle and bustle of the caves it was nice to find a little oasis of calm.

John was always very welcoming and actually seemed to enjoy my company. He'd very kindly offered to teach me how to play the ukulele, but after a few lessons we'd mutually agreed that I was hopeless so I'd settled for watching him work instead. He liked to chat while he worked and he would entertain me with stories of the time he spent touring the world in a folk band.

People rarely spoke about life before the virus, even those who were adults when the disease broke out. We'd been shown broadcasts at school about how people used to live, but it was definitely not considered acceptable dinner conversation. Sometimes it felt like people needed all their energy to survive the present and there was nothing left to remember the past. John's company made a refreshing change.

John pulled out his ukulele and waited patiently for the rest of the band to tune their instruments. For a brief moment the children balanced on their tiptoes and as the band struck the first bars of the tune, the dancing began. As the children snaked a path around the pole, the girls' patterned skirts flared and the boys' shirts billowed in the soft breeze. The onlookers began to clap in time to the music and I found myself caught up in the excitement.

I stole a glance at Daryl but it seemed that even the dancing wasn't enough to coax him out of his black mood. Before the first dance had ended he turned and walked away. I flashed Peter a look of concern. 'I'll keep an eye on him,' he whispered.

The dancing came to an end and Peter and Daryl still hadn't returned so I went in search of Mr Murray. I was hoping he might have some cake left over from the baking competition.

I jumped onto an overcrowded rowboat, which lurched unsteadily along the underground river. As we docked at the entrance cave I spotted Leah, she'd commandeered one of the fires and was surrounded by a group of friends. Her face curled into a sneer as she caught my eye. She turned and whispered something to her friends and they all burst out laughing. Embarrassed, I quickly scurried away. I heard someone call my name and turned to find Mr Murray beckoning me over to the fire. 'MaryAnn, come and join Jenn and me.'

'Everything alright?' he asked as I took a seat beside Jenn.

'Fine,' I replied as I glanced warily at Leah. She was still laughing loudly with her friends.

Mr Murray followed my gaze and frowned. 'I saved this for you,' he said as he handed me an iced bun. He glanced around. 'Are the boys with you? They don't usually miss an opportunity for free food.'

'They're outside,' I paused uncertainly. 'Daryl's a bit upset about Flo.'

Mr Murray nodded thoughtfully. 'I thought he might be. They got on really well the last time the circus visited. Made a nice couple. It must be difficult, hearing that she's been taken to the LightHouse.'

'It's difficult for all of us having the people we love taken away and locked up in that place,' Jenn interjected harshly.

Mr Murray pulled a flask from his pocket. 'Here, have some of this,' he said as he handed the flask to his sister. She took a mouthful and swallowed loudly. She handed the flask back to him. 'You want some?' Mr Murray offered. I took the flask and wiped the top with my sleeve. I took a cautious sip and savoured the tartness of the apple cider. I offered the open flask to Mr Murray but he shook his head. 'I never drink before an operation. I need to keep my wits about me.'

'Have you been on many operations?' I asked. Even though I'd spent a lot of time with Mr Murray I realised that I didn't know very much about him. He rarely talked about himself.

'You could say that. I've been with the Union since I was a boy.'

I found it hard to imagine Mr Murray as anything other than the solidly built man sitting before me. I definitely couldn't picture him as a boy.

'Why did you join?' I asked.

Mr Murray glanced at Jenn. She gave an almost imperceptible shrug.

'You remember how I told you that my mum and dad managed a hotel in Manchester. It's the house the Director lives in.'

I nodded. That was how he'd known where to find me when the Director held me captive in the tunnels.

'The hotel was attacked by a gang of thieves in the early days of the virus. They thought we had food. Truth was we hadn't had any guests in a long time and were just as hungry as everyone else. Mum told Jenn and me to go through the tunnels and fetch the police while she went to look for our dad. By the time the police arrived, the hotel had been ransacked and both our parents were dead.'

'That's horrible,' I murmured.

'We weren't the only kids orphaned by the virus,' Mr Murray said. 'Jenn and I were sent to live with our Uncle John on his farm. With all the unrest and rioting that followed the outbreak of the virus he wouldn't let us leave the farm,' he shrugged, 'but we were kids and bored so one day we snuck out to a party.'

'You mean *you* snuck out to a party!' Jenn interrupted.

Mr Murray smiled at the comment, 'Okay Miss Goody Two Shoes. I snuck out to the party and you followed me.'

'To make sure you didn't get into any trouble.'

'Of course,' Mr Murray winked at me. 'Anyway we got into a bit of bother and that's when we met Ericka. She was the leader of the Union. She helped us out of a jam and afterwards she offered me a place with the group and I accepted.'

'So Ericka was the leader of the Union before Uncle Patrick?' I asked.

'No. Patrick joined a few years later. Ericka realised the threat the

Light posed right away, but most people wouldn't listen. Even when the Boundaries were being erected people thought the Light were building sanctuaries for the sick. When they closed the Boundaries, Ericka was the only one left fighting for us on the Outside.'

'What about your uncle, didn't he try and stop you from joining the Union?'

I felt Jenn stiffen beside me.

'He died,' Mr Murray said.

'I'm sorry,' I began.

Mr Murray waved away my concern. 'It doesn't matter. It's all in the past. It was a long time ago.' From the haunted look in Jenn's eyes I wasn't so sure that she felt the same way. I had the suspicion that there was more to the story, but there was no time to question either of them further. The loudspeaker sputtered into life and announced that the archery competition would begin in 30 minutes.

'Come on,' Mr Murray said. 'We don't want to miss the start of the archery competition, it's usually very popular.'

When we arrived at the archery field there was already a large group of people gathered around the contestants. I bounced on my tiptoes, trying to see over the crowd.

Mr Murray tapped me on the shoulder. 'Do you want a better view?' he asked. Before I had chance to respond he scooped me into the air and I found myself sitting high above the heads of the crowd as I straddled his shoulders.

'Is this safe?' I squealed.

'I used to do it with Jenn all the time, but apparently she's too old now,' Mr Murray nudged his sister playfully.

'I'm a grown woman,' Jenn replied tartly, 'I can't go around riding on people's shoulders.'

'Of course not,' Mr Murray replied.

From my vantage position on Mr Murray's shoulders I watched as Brandon strode through the crowd and took his place along side the other contestants.

'I didn't know that Brandon was an archer,' I called down to Mr Murray.

'He's one of the best we've got. He's won the main prize for the last five years. Although I hear that he might actually have some competition this year,' Mr Murray said. 'One of the younger lads has been bragging about beating him.'

I spotted Uncle Patrick in the crowd and he waved.

'What about Uncle Patrick, is he taking part in the archery contest too?'

Mr Murray laughed. 'Archery isn't really his thing. Patrick likes to blow things up.'

'Blow things up?'

'Before the virus he was studying chemical engineering at university. He's a bomb maker.'

Painful memories of my parents' death resurfaced and I gave an involuntary shudder. I pushed the memory aside and turned my attention back to Brandon, trying to focus on the competition.

Brandon was a very skilled archer. His only real competition came from a tall blonde-headed boy whom I recognised as Will. His friends Jake and Max urged him on from the sidelines.

Despite the challenge from Will, Brandon was declared the winner and everyone cheered loudly as Uncle Patrick presented him with a medal.

'What's next?' I asked Mr Murray as the crowd began to disperse.

'Peter's running the assault course. We should go and cheer him on,' he said as he deposited me back on the ground.

The contestants were already lined up at the starting block when we arrived at the assault course. Peter raised a hand in greeting as we jostled for a good place in the crowd. I sighed inwardly. I wasn't sure why Peter felt the need to run the race shirtless. The other contestants had all managed to keep their clothes on.

'He's so cute,' I heard a voice exclaim behind me.

'Did I tell you that he went out with my sister Kelly last year?' came the reply.

'No, you never told me that!'

'He gave her a bunch of flowers.'

'Oh my god. That's so romantic. I wish a boy would bring me flowers.'

'I know, me too.'

'Have you seen his tattoo? It's beautiful.'

'Kelly said it's a phoenix rising out of the ashes.'

'That's so deep.'

My eyes widened in surprise, the girls were talking about Peter. I glanced over at Mr Murray and he rolled his eyes dramatically. I let out an involuntary giggle as the whistle blew to signal the start of the race.

Reluctantly I had to confess that Peter's performance on the assault course was pretty impressive. With a grace that belied his size he scrambled up a high wall and then deftly hopped across a log pile. Next he shinned up a rope, the muscles in his arms bulging with the effort. Finally, red faced and panting, he made his way across the finishing line with a large sack slung heavily across his shoulder.

The crowd roared appreciatively when he was declared the winner and within seconds he was swamped by well wishers.

'Come on,' Mr Murray said, 'we should congratulate the conquering hero.'

As we approached I realised that the majority of Peter's well wishers were female. 'Congratulations,' Mr Murray boomed as he slapped Peter firmly across the back.

Peter winked at me, 'Pretty impressive eh?'

My god, he could be so arrogant sometimes! 'I suppose so. If you like that type of thing,' I shrugged.

Peter grimaced. 'If you like that type of thing!!!! I just…I just…I climbed a wall. I carried a sack of sand for nearly half a mile…I beat the course record…'

'We thought you were very impressive,' Mr Murray replied in a conciliatory tone. 'Didn't we MaryAnn?'

I could feel the eyes of the other girls, watching me, waiting for a response. 'You were great,' I muttered.

'That's what I like about you,' Peter grumbled. 'Your enthusiasm is infectious.'

'The circus performance will commence in 30 minutes.' I followed the crowd of excited revellers out of the cave, searching for the rest of the group. We'd arranged to meet at the performance and use it as cover to sneak away undetected. 'MaryAnn!' I turned to find Uncle Patrick and Brandon by the cave entrance. 'Are you enjoying our little party?' Uncle Patrick asked.

'It's great,' I replied as my hand flew up to my face. I stroked my scar self consciously.

Brandon had never mentioned my scar, didn't even stare at it like other people, but I always felt the need to cover it up whenever I was in his company. 'Congratulations on winning the archery competition Brandon,' I said.

Brandon flashed a smile that showed white teeth against tanned skin, 'Thanks MaryAnn. It was pretty close this year. I'm going to have to watch out for some of those young kids coming up through the ranks. I thought Will might actually beat me.'

'There's always next year,' Uncle Patrick joked.

'Yeah the boy's definitely improved since last year. I think I'm going to have to put in a bit more practice on the archery field,' Brandon replied.

'Patrick! Brandon!' Peter exclaimed cheerfully as he appeared at my side. 'You having a good time?' I was relieved to see that he'd put his shirt back on.

Brandon held up a mug of cider. 'We are indeed Peter.' He peered into his mug. 'In fact it looks like I'm almost empty,' he nudged Patrick, 'and I think it's your round.'

Peter turned to me, 'MaryAnn I've been looking for you everywhere. The performance is about to start and I know how much you wanted to see it.'

'That's very gentlemanly of you Peter,' Brandon smirked. 'Escorting MaryAnn to the performance.'

Peter frowned. 'MaryAnn's been looking forward to it all day…'

I was a little surprised by Peter's tone. Of course I wanted to see the circus but he was being a little persistent.

'Come on, we should go now if we want to get a good spot.' It was the way he emphasised the words *go now* that brought me to my senses. With Uncle Patrick and Brandon around it would be impossible to sneak away.

'I can't wait,' I replied brightly as I flashed Peter a wide smile. 'I'll see you later Uncle Patrick, Brandon.' I linked my arm through Peter's, in what I hoped was a casual, friendly gesture. 'Come on, let's go.'

I suppressed the pang of guilt that surfaced as we took our leave. Tomorrow morning when the party was over Uncle Patrick would wake to find us gone. I hoped that he would be able to forgive my disloyalty.

The circus had set up in a large clearing, creating a makeshift stage at its core. A large crowd of people had gathered for the performance, sprawled out on multi-coloured blankets as a group of jugglers tossed balls high into the air. Peter and I took a seat on the grass beside Daryl.

'Did you take Flash to the truck?' Peter asked.

Daryl nodded. 'He was fast asleep on the back seat when I left.' He peered into the sky. 'It'll be getting dark. We should probably leave soon.'

'Where ya going?' I jumped in alarm as a short chubby figure stepped out from the trees. I groaned inwardly. It was Jake. I glanced behind him and as I expected his two companions Will and Max hovered close by. The three boys were rarely seen apart.

'It's none of your business,' Peter replied as he swatted them away like flies.

Undeterred by Peter's brusqueness Jake continued, 'Are you going on an operation?'

All three boys were so desperate to be involved in an operation that they pestered Peter and Daryl constantly.

'It's May Day,' Peter responded, 'we're at a party. There are no operations today. Now go away.'

Jake scowled and glanced at each of us in turn. 'You're up to something,' he said. 'I can feel it right here,' he indicated his midsection.

'Well your gut must be wrong, because nothing's happening today,' Peter replied sharply. 'So why don't you and your little friends go and find somewhere else to play and leave the grownups to talk.'

Jake opened his mouth to argue, but Peter sprang to his feet. 'Just go,' he ordered. The three boys hesitated. Peter took a threatening step towards them. 'Get lost.'

'We'll find out what you're up to,' Jake threw back over his shoulder as the boys hastily retreated.

'Good luck with that,' Peter said as he retook his seat.

As the light began to fade the jugglers were replaced by fire-eaters and I watched fascinated as they danced in the deepening twilight, swallowing blazing batons of vibrant orange flame. I was mesmerised and would have watched all night if Mr Murray hadn't arrived. 'You ready?' he whispered. As we clambered to our feet I caught a flash of blue hair. Nessa had lowered her baton and as she caught our gaze I saw an unspoken plea in her eyes. Daryl gave a small nod of acknowledgement as we turned and stole away into the night.

CHAPTER 11

Up North

MaryAnn

Daryl called 'shotgun' and jumped into the front passenger seat of the truck. Peter had volunteered to drive so I climbed into the back with Mr Murray. Flash was curled up on the seat. He grumbled sleepily as I gently pushed him out of the way.

The truck roared into life and as we pulled away from the caves I felt my stomach knot anxiously. Leaving the Neighbourhood and venturing Outside had been a terrifying experience, but now we were heading into the complete unknown. I caught Peter's eye in the rear view mirror and he winked. I returned the wink with a nervous smile.

We drove through the night, keen to cover as much distance as we could. At first we bumped along rough country tracks until finally we hit a tarmac road. 'We need to keep an eye out for the Watch,' Daryl called from the front of the truck. 'They usually stick to the North Road, but sometimes they set up roadblocks on other roads too, and they'll confiscate vehicles they take a liking to.'

The tarmac road had worn away in places and was pitted with potholes. In the blaze of the headlights I could make out the shapes of vehicles left haphazardly by the side of the road. Mr Murray explained that they'd been abandoned after the virus and left to rot.

I slept fitfully during the journey and woke in the early hours of the morning with a cramp in my neck. I stretched my arms above my head to work out the kink and heard Mr Murray's stomach growl loudly. 'There's a roadhouse not far from here,' Daryl said. 'We should stop for breakfast.'

A short time later Peter pulled off the road and came to a standstill outside a whitewashed building. As I climbed out of the truck the door to the building opened and I caught a vivid flash of yellow as a small girl raced across the yard towards the truck.

'Poppy!' Peter and Daryl chorused in delight as the girl threw herself at them. After she'd received a hug she pulled away and turned to Mr Murray. She gave a shy smile before jumping into his arms. Mr Murray turned her upside and held her over a dirty puddle of water, 'Poppy, you're getting too big for me to carry. I might just have to drop you in the water,' he threatened. She giggled loudly at this. 'Put me down, put me down,' she begged.

Safely back on her feet she peered shyly at me through hooded eyes. She was about eight years old with dirty blonde hair caught up in an untidy braid. I smiled and she hurriedly stepped back, finding a safe hiding place behind Mr Murray's leg. A man and woman exited the whitewashed building. They had to be the girl's parents, they shared the same hair colour and deep blue eyes.

'Nice to see you again Diane,' Daryl said as he greeted the woman with a hug.

'Daryl, Peter, Murray,' the man thrust a hand out to each of them in turn.

'Adam, this is my sister MaryAnn,' Daryl said as he pushed me forward. The man had a strong grip as he pumped my arm up and down.

'Come on inside,' Diane beckoned. 'There's a fair breeze outside today and you'll catch your death.'

We followed Diane and Adam across the yard to the whitewashed building. I stepped through the entrance to find myself inside a small café. Its high ceiling was intersected by a thick wooden beam and the walls were decorated with bright paintings that gave the place a cheery homely feel. The café was empty so we sat at a small table close to the window with a good view of the road.

Diane handed each of us a menu.

'I'm starving,' Peter said. 'I'm having a full English.'

'Good idea, me too,' Daryl said.

'Ooh,' I exclaimed, 'what's that?'

'Sausage, bacon, black pudding, eggs, tomatoes, mushrooms, toast…the works.'

'Oh, do you have anything without meat?' I asked.

'I can do the full English without the meat. So tomatoes, mushrooms, eggs and toast. How does that sound?'

It sounded great. I was starving. 'I'll give you a couple of extra eggs,' Diane said as she collected my menu. 'Feed you up a bit.'

Breakfast arrived and we all tucked in enthusiastically. 'Best breakfast in the North,' Daryl exclaimed with his mouth full. 'This'll set me up for the day.'

By the time we'd finished eating and Diane and Adam had cleared away our plates it was already light outside.

Back in the truck and travelling in daylight I could clearly see the dreadful state of the road. The journey was slow and torturous as Peter carefully navigated the potholes and skeletons of old cars that littered the tarmac.

'How can people drive on this?' I complained. 'You'd think someone would repair the road.'

'Who would do that?' Peter queried from the driver's seat. 'The Light don't control this road, they use the North Road so they're not going to maintain it.'

'What about the Communities? Aren't they responsible for

repairing the roads?'

'It's not that simple,' Peter replied. 'The Outside is made up of lots of small Communities. There isn't one person in charge.'

'So there's no-one in control of the Outside?'

'Not really,' Peter said. 'After the Light built the Boundaries food became scarce and it was too dangerous to stay in the cities. People moved out to the countryside so that they could grow food. They took over farms and built up small Communities. The Communities are self-sufficient; they grow their own food and make their own energy. That's how we live now. It's about growing enough food to eat, not about rebuilding what we used to have...so the roads just fall apart.'

I considered Peter's comment. It seemed strange that no-one controlled the Outside. Our lives inside the Boundary had been so completely dominated by the Light. We'd been told that it was to keep us safe and I'd never considered that we could live differently; that there was the opportunity for a freer, less controlled existence. The idea intrigued me, but at the same time the thought of all that freedom terrified me.

Having spent my life confined inside the Boundary of the Manchester Neighbourhood, I'd been taught by the Light that the Outside was a wild and feral place. What the Light had failed to mention was how vast it was. The only signs of habitation we encountered on our journey were small deserted villages with tumbledown stone cottages. In the Neighbourhood space had been a luxury. The Hub located at the very centre of the Neighbourhood was the commercial district and tightly packed with shops and businesses. Surrounding the Hub the accommodation districts - North, South, East and West - comprised row upon row of residential apartments and houses. Each district had its own park for recreation purposes, but every year these green spaces seemed to reduce in size as permission was given for new development. The only wild spaces in the Neighbourhood had been the borderlands that separated the city from the Boundary fence. We'd often visited them on a weekend for family picnics and they'd seemed like wide-open spaces for us to play in, but compared to the Outside they were tiny. Even in the caves, with so many people living close together, the accommodation felt cramped. In comparison the Outside was a vast landscape of empty space. It almost made me feel giddy as I watched the open fields roll by.

To add to the feeling of emptiness we encountered very few travellers and those we met were on foot or bicycle. 'There don't seem to be many other cars,' I observed. 'Is it because the roads are in such bad condition?'

'Partly,' Mr Murray replied, 'but there's also a problem with the fuel. Before the virus, cars used to run on petrol or diesel, but it's hard to get hold of now so we've had to convert vehicles to biofuel. It takes know-how to do the conversion and time to grow the fuel. Plus it can be a little bit volatile sometimes.'

'Volatile!' I queried nervously as I realised the truck we were travelling in had been converted to biofuel.

'You know, *"boom"*,' Mr Murray made an explosive motion with his arms. I swallowed hard. 'It's best not to think about it,' Daryl called from the front seat.

In an effort to distract myself from thoughts of the truck exploding I pointed to a field of green shrubs. I'd seen a number of similar fields along the side of the road. 'What are those?' I asked.

'It's a soya bean field,' Mr Murray explained. 'We grow it for the Light.'

'What do the Light need soya beans for?' I asked.

'They use it as food,' Mr Murray explained. 'There wasn't enough room in the Neighbourhoods to take any animals so they use it as a substitute for meat, cheese, eggs, milk.'

'You mean that the food I ate in the Neighbourhood was made

from soya beans?' I asked.

'Yeah, a lot of it,' Mr Murray replied.

'So the Communities grow the soya beans and sell them to the Light?' I questioned.

'That's not how it works,' Mr Murray explained. 'The Light can't grow enough food to feed everyone in the Neighbourhood so about 10 years ago they introduced a land tax. Each Community has to set aside a certain amount of land to grow soya beans to pay the tax.'

'It's not a tax,' Peter said from the front of the truck, 'it's theft. The food doesn't belong to the Light. It belongs to the people who grow it.'

'Why don't the Communities just refuse to grow the beans?' I questioned.

'There was a Community over in Pocklington,' Peter replied. 'They had a couple of bad harvests and there wasn't enough food to feed the Community so they decided not to waste resources growing soya beans. When the Watch arrived to collect the land tax and the Community leader told them they couldn't pay, they shot her, then they set fire to the Community. It burnt to the ground.'

I gasped in horror. 'Why didn't the people fight back?'

'Because they're farmers not soldiers,' Peter replied. 'They're not trained to fight.'

'I didn't realise the Light had so much influence on the Outside.'

'Whatever power they have it's been taken not given,' Peter said. 'The Light can do what they want because they're the ones with the weapons. The Communities have no other choice but to do as they say.'

'But if all the Communities banded together and fought them?' I protested. 'They'd have a chance, wouldn't they?'

'That's what the Union are trying to do, but it's difficult. The Communities are all so spread out that it's hard to co-ordinate them into any form of resistance,' Peter explained.

'If the people in the Neighbourhood knew what was going on Outside they'd be horrified.'

'You think that people in the Neighbourhood don't already know?' Peter replied. 'They turn a blind eye because it makes their life easier.'

I wasn't sure how to respond to Peter's comment. It was hard to believe that people in the Neighbourhood knew about the things the Light were doing on the Outside and did nothing to stop it. Then I remembered my father. In his role as the Legislator he'd tortured and killed countless people. There was more going on beneath the veneer of the Neighbourhood than I'd ever realised.

We took a short break for lunch just as the sun reached its zenith. It was warm outside and we parked in the shade of a large tree. The light breeze that rippled through its leafy branches was a welcome relief after the stifling interior of the truck. Even with the windows down it was still incredibly stuffy.

'I think we're making pretty good time,' Daryl said as he took a bite of his sandwich. 'If we carry on like this we'll be at the rendezvous in no time.'

'Can you believe that before the virus we could drive to the far north in less than a day?' Mr Murray said.

'And now?' I asked. 'How long will it take?'

'Hopefully about three days,' Daryl replied. 'As long as we only stop to eat, sleep and pee.'

We drove for a few more hours until I could feel tension begin to build in the truck. Peter was seated on the back seat beside me, he'd spent the earlier part of the journey pointing out the different types of flowers and shrubs that grew by the side of the road; now he was silent, peering anxiously out of the window. 'We should get off the road soon,' he muttered quietly to Mr Murray, who had taken over the driving.

'What's the matter?' I whispered.

'This is a tricky spot,' Peter replied. 'There's a city not far from here. No-one lives there anymore, apart from bandits and thieves. Not the type of people we really want to meet on the road.'

I swallowed nervously. 'What do we do?'

'We take the coast road,' Mr Murray replied grimly. 'It's slower, but much safer.'

As the city came into view I could make out a series of dilapidated tower blocks in the distance. They were blackened, burned out skeletons, open to the elements. It looked like a run down, derelict version of the Neighbourhood. The city gave off such a feeling of desolation and desperation that I had to avert my eyes.

'Murray, we're coming up to the turning,' Peter muttered in a tight voice. The truck slowed and as we turned off the road I heard an ear-splitting crack and a fracture split the windscreen into two pieces. 'Someone's firing at us,' Mr Murray yelled.

'Crap!' Daryl yelled. 'Murray we need to get out of here NOW.'

'That's what I'm trying to do,' Mr Murray muttered.

Daryl rummaged in the glove box and I caught a glint of metal as he pulled out a gun. We only had one gun, it belonged to Mr Murray and it was ancient. The Union had an armoury, but guns were in short supply and only issued for official operations. The armoury was so closely guarded that we couldn't risk taking any weapons with us.

Peter muttered a curse as he dragged me down onto the floor. 'I can't see where they're firing from,' he called out.

'I can see someone on the roof of the metal shed,' Daryl's voice cracked with tension. 'Damn, I can't get a clear shot from here.' He twisted around in his seat. 'They've set up a roadblock up ahead,' he yelled. The panic was evident in his voice.

'I'm going to drive through it,' Mr Murray shouted. The floor began to vibrate as the speed of the truck increased. 'Faster,' Daryl urged. 'You need to go faster.'

I could feel the vibration intensify as I cowered on the floor. There was hot breath on my neck. Flash perched on the edge of the seat and I was surprised to see the glimmer of white teeth as he issued a low growl.

'Go! Go! Go!' Daryl bellowed.

'I'm going, I'm going,' Mr Murray yelled. There was the screech of tyres followed by the scream of splintering wood. We careered down the road, the tyres squealing in protest until Peter clambered up onto the back seat. He squinted out of the rear window. 'I think they're gone,' he said.

'You sure?' Daryl called back.

'Yeah,' Peter replied. 'No-one's following us. They probably don't have a vehicle.'

'They definitely had guns,' Daryl responded.

'You didn't even get off a shot,' Peter grumbled.

'The angle was wrong, I didn't want to waste any bullets,' Daryl protested.

As the truck slowed down Peter grabbed my arm, pulling me back onto the seat.

'Phew,' Daryl whistled. He clasped a hand across his chest. 'My heart feels like it's going to explode.'

'You okay?' Peter asked as he brushed dirt off my arm. I couldn't trust myself to speak.

'We're safe now,' Daryl said.

'Safe,' I muttered. 'People were shooting at us. You didn't tell me that people would be shooting at us.'

'They weren't very good,' Peter replied. 'Otherwise they'd have shot out the tyres.'

'Is that supposed to make me feel better?'

'Yeah,' Peter frowned. 'Things could have been a whole lot worse.'

'He's right,' Daryl said. 'We were lucky. They weren't very well trained.'

'The truck still took a battering,' Mr Murray grumbled. 'Look at the windscreen.'

'I'll take a look at it when we stop this evening,' Peter said.

I peered out of the rear window and watched as the city receded into the distance. I was relieved when we turned a corner and it slid out of view.

As the light began to fade Daryl unfolded the map. 'Peter and I know a good place to camp close to here,' he said. 'Murray, you need to take the next turning.'

We turned off the main road and bumped along a dirt track until we came to a standstill in a large clearing. I clambered out of the truck, and was greeted by a breeze that brought with it a salty tang. I sniffed the air curiously.

'You can smell the salt from the sea,' Peter said.

'The sea!' my voice rose with excitement.

'You ever been to the coast before?' Peter asked. He must have detected the excitement in my voice.

'No, I've only seen it in pictures.'

Peter let out a shrill whistle and Flash appeared beside him. 'You're in for a treat. Come on,' he said.

I followed Peter along a narrow sandy track. At the end of the track he pushed his way through a clump of thick wiry bushes. As I stumbled out after him I let out a gasp of surprise. Stretching out before me was a golden beach. Flash tore across the sand, barking wildly at the waves that lapped gently onto the shore.

'Here boy,' Peter threw a stick down the beach and Flash careered after it, his ears flapping in the breeze. As Peter chased after Flash I pulled off my boots and felt the gritty sand squelch between my toes. I squealed. It was a strange sensation but not unpleasant enough to make me put my boots back on. I wandered down to the water's edge and tentatively dipped my toe into the sea. It was freezing.

Wading ankle deep, I let the frigid water lap gently over my feet. A stick flew over my head and without warning I was spattered with salty droplets of water as Flash tore past me. Peter appeared beside me laughing loudly.

Flash was paddling hard in the water, his legs flailing wildly against the undertow. He picked up the stick and paddled back to Peter. I squealed as water splashed up the front of my shirt.

'He's a bit of a clumsy swimmer,' Peter patted the dog's wet head affectionately.

We took it in turns to throw sticks until Peter said that it was getting late and we should go back to the others.

We arrived back at the camp to find the tents had been erected and, from the smell that wafted from the fire, dinner was already cooking.

'Ah! Nice to see you've come back now that all the hard work has been done.' Daryl grumbled.

'I had to take Flash for a walk, he was going crazy after spending a day cooped up in the truck,' Peter replied.

'And MaryAnn had to go with you?'

'I've never been to the coast before,' I protested. 'Peter wanted to show me the beach.'

'I'm sure he did.'

'What's that supposed to mean?' Peter asked.

Daryl ignored the question and pointed to a small blue tent. 'MaryAnn, that's your tent. I'll share the red one with Murray and Peter can share the yellow one with Flash.'

'Great,' grumbled Peter, 'I get to wake up to the aroma of wet dog.'

'He's your dog, mate,' Daryl replied, as Flash softly butted Peter's hand, looking for another stick to play with.

'I get my own tent?' I queried.

'Of course,' Daryl responded. 'Unless you want to share with one of us?'

I crinkled my nose in mock disgust. 'There's no way I want to wake up to the aroma of smelly boy.'

Daryl grinned, 'That's what I thought.'

'Hey,' Peter protested, 'I don't smell like a boy. I smell like a man.'

'I've already put your things in your tent. There's a sleeping bag inside too,' Daryl said, ignoring Peter who was making a pantomime of sniffing his shirt.

When I unzipped my tent and wriggled inside I found my rucksack sitting on top of a thick sleeping bag. I rummaged inside and pulled out my hairbrush and mirror. I studied my reflection in the mirror and found a wild looking girl staring back at me. My hair was stuck up at right angles, my face smudged with dirt. I dragged the brush through my hair and wiped the dirt from my face with the corner of my sleeve. Then I heard Daryl calling me to dinner and I shuffled out of my tent to re-join the others.

Peter crouched by the fire and busied himself pulling potatoes out of the ashes. He dropped them onto plates and handed one to me. 'Careful, it's hot.'

'Have you planned the route for tomorrow?' Mr Murray asked as he spooned beans onto his potato.

Daryl nodded. 'I've planned the whole route. If we don't hit any problems we should be at the rendezvous in two days.'

'What happens when we arrive at the rendezvous?' I asked.

'We'll look for the LightHouse,' Mr Murray replied.

'Is it going to be dangerous?' I asked.

When Mr Murray didn't respond Peter answered for him, 'Plenty of people have gone to look for the LightHouse. Either they come back without finding it or they don't come back at all.'

I gave an involuntary shudder. 'What do you mean they don't come back at all?'

Peter shrugged. 'They just disappear.'

I swallowed hard, suddenly wondering what I'd gotten myself into.

'Everyone, come here. Quickly!' Peter's voice rang out across the clearing. Daryl and I dropped the dishes we were washing and raced over to him. Peter had returned to the truck to fix the windscreen and we found him in the driver's seat playing with the radio. Static screamed from the speaker. 'Have you been able to tune it in?' Mr Murray huffed as he appeared at my side.

Peter nodded excitedly. There was another blast of static and then a voice rang out across the clearing.

'*Word up! Citizens of Earth, this is the Atlantis Warrior returning after a short hiatus.*'

'It's Radio Atlantis,' Daryl cried. 'They're back!'

'What's Radio Atlantis?' I queried.

'It's a pirate radio station. They broadcast to the Communities from a boat called the Atlantis Warrior.'

'*This is your old buddy DJ Neptune and I'll be with you for the duration of the programme. I realise that many of our listeners have been worried about the good ship Atlantis and its trusty crew of DJs. Let's just say we ran into some troubled waters. The Light issued us with a cease and desist notice in the form of a cannon ball straight through the hull. Yes my dear listeners, don't try to unblock those ears. You heard correctly. The Light decided to go medieval on us. They have a cannon and they're prepared to use it. The old lady took a bit of a battering and we've been adrift at sea. I hope we didn't give you too much of a scare.*

In true Atlantis style let's celebrate our return to the airwaves with a bit of music. Boys and girls let's get ready for a Crazy, Crazy Night.'

There was the screech of static and a hissed rebuke, '*Stanley that was your cue to flick the switch.*'

DJ Neptune barked out a laugh, '*Enjoy the music folks while I go and sack the intern.*' The screech of guitars signalled the opening bars of an unfamiliar tune.

'I can't believe they're back,' Mr Murray exclaimed over the noise of the music. 'I really thought they'd been captured by the Light.'

'Me too,' Daryl replied. 'I wonder whether Patrick's listening to the broadcast.'

'Is the radio station part of the Union?' I asked.

Daryl shook his head, 'Not officially, but we use it to send messages. Patrick's been struggling to find another solution while they've been off air.'

I was puzzled, 'How do you use the radio to send messages?'

'Listen to the broadcast and you'll find out,' Peter replied.

'That was a great little song to get things a-rocking and a-rolling this evening. Now back by popular demand… and I don't mean me! It's time for "Show 'n' Tell". Up first is a message for the Community at Hebden Bridge. We've heard that there's a lightning strike coming your way. It's time to duck and cover folks.'

I peered up at the blue sky, there wasn't a storm cloud in sight. 'A lightning strike?' I queried.

'It's code,' Peter explained. 'A warning to Hebden that the Watch are on their way.'

'Anyone heading north to Newcastle, we've had reports of bandits on the road. My advice would be to stay clear of the area or take the coast road.'

'Might have been nice if we'd had that warning earlier,' Mr Murray grumbled. 'It could have saved us a cracked windscreen.'

'Finally. Congratulations to the Community at Bodmin who have just elected a new leader. After many years of service to the Community Barry Dawkins has decided to step down to pursue other opportunities.'

Peter let out a derisive snort, *'Pursue other opportunities!* The idiot was thrown out more likely.'

'Patrick's going to be pleased. Barry wouldn't allow the Union anywhere near his Community,' Mr Murray said.

'Yeah he was a bit too friendly with the Watch for my liking,' Peter agreed. 'I never did trust him.'

'Why would someone from a Community be friendly with the

Watch?' I queried.

'Sometimes people think that making friends with the Watch will earn them special favours,' Daryl explained. 'Problem is that they lose the trust of the other Communities which means they have no-one to rely on when times are hard.

'The last few years we've had a couple of bad food harvests,' Peter said. 'I expect Bodmin wanted to share resources with other Communities and they can't do that with Barry in charge.'

'The Radio Atlantic team would like to wish Barry good luck in whatever new endeavour he plans to pursue.

Unfortunately folks that's all the news we have time for today and sadly we've come to the end of our programme. After our last altercation with the Light we need to float under the radar for a while so we're keeping our programmes short and sweet. It's time for us to pull up anchor and be on our way. We'll see you tomorrow - same time, new location. The password of the day will be Gabba Gabba Hey.

Until we meet again this is the Atlantis Warrior; over and out."

As the voice faded to silence Peter switched off the radio. He stifled a yawn.

Daryl glanced at his watch. 'We should probably head to bed if we want to get an early start in the morning.'

'Good idea,' Peter replied. 'I've taped up the windscreen, but there's nothing more I can do without replacing the glass.'

'MaryAnn are you going to be alright in the tent on your own?' Daryl asked as we made our way back to the camp.

Before I had chance to reply Peter gave me a nudge. 'If you get cold in the night MaryAnn you can always…'

I grimaced. 'Hell would have to freeze over before I shared a tent with you.'

'Now look who's being presumptuous,' he smirked. 'I was just going to offer you an extra blanket.'

CHAPTER 12

The Light is Right, The Light is Might

CHARLOTTE:

The weather was unseasonably warm and the LightHouse simmered like an oven. At home when it was hot we'd slept with the windows open so that we could keep the rooms cool, but in the LightHouse the windows were nailed tightly shut. Bekka said it was because the Warden was scared that the Residents might open them and jump out. As melodramatic as it sounded, there might have been some truth to the rumour. The routine in the LightHouse was oppressive, the schedule relentless. There was no fun and nothing to look forward to. I struggled through each day and wished more than anything that I was back home with my mum and dad. Flo warned me not to think about it, she told that it would only make me feel worse, but I couldn't help it. I just wanted to go home.

There were certain work tasks that were worse than others. Collecting and breaking rocks were tasks that every Resident dreaded. Often it was given as a punishment to people who misbehaved. This meant that, despite his promises to Flo, Eric still spent a lot of time in the yard swinging a sledgehammer. Eric was like a machine. Even when he was exhausted he refused to show any sign of weakness.

Today Eric and I were both unlucky and we found ourselves surrounded by a mountain of unbroken stone. I heard the sound of a cart being dragged across the concrete as another load of rock was tipped out onto the ground behind us. I stretched awkwardly clutching at my sore back and let out a painful sigh.

'All that time you spent on the farm feeding the chickens has made you soft.' Eric pranced around the yard pretending to throw grain to imaginary birds. 'You're not cut out for hard work.'

I giggled then glanced around to make sure that the Trustees weren't within earshot. 'Eric, stop acting like an idiot and get back to work before someone sees you messing around.'

Eric gave a mock sigh. 'Work, work, work, that's all you ever think about. You sound just like Flo.' There was a wicked glint in his eye. He wiped a hand across his face. 'It's boiling,' he said as he pulled his t-shirt over his head and dropped it onto the floor.

Without his t-shirt I could make out the twisted angry scars on his back. Mally had told me about them, but this was the first time I'd actually seen them. I didn't mean to stare, but when Eric glanced over he caught me looking.

'Everything all right?' he asked.

'Yeah,' I glanced away embarrassed and picked up the sledgehammer. 'I didn't mean to...' I mumbled, the end of my sentence trailing off self-consciously.

He shrugged. 'I'm used to it. You should have seen the guys at school. After gym we'd go for a shower and they'd be up in my face making stupid comments and asking questions.'

'What did you say to them?'

'I didn't have to say anything. Not after I'd punched a few of them in the mouth.' He smirked, but I didn't think his comment was funny so I didn't return the smile. The smirk slid from his face immediately. 'Sorry,' he said, 'it was supposed to be a joke.'

'I don't think it's very funny to joke about hitting people.'

He sighed. 'No I suppose it isn't. Look if you want to ask me about them, the scars I mean, I don't mind.'

'I just wondered how you got them,' I questioned hesitantly.

He whistled between his teeth, 'Now that's a long story. It literally took me years to build up this little collection.'

I flinched in horror, not sure how to react to such a candid response.

'It was my dad,' he explained. 'You must have seen him in the Community. You know he likes a drink?'

When I nodded he continued, 'Well it turns out that he cares a whole lot more about home brew than he does his family. Eventually Mum got fed up and left. That's when his drinking got really bad. He always bought the cheapest stuff and they don't call it *"brain rot"* for nothing. He used to sit for hours ranting at us like he was deranged. He was only happy when he was drinking, and God help anyone who got in his way,' he paused and I held my breath as he continued. 'Unfortunately I used to get in his way a lot. I'm a fast runner, but sometimes when he wasn't completely wasted he would catch me and add a few more souvenirs to my back.'

I was horrified. I thought of my own dad. He would do anything to protect me. That's what dads were supposed to do...take care of you. Wasn't it?

'Oh Charlotte,' Eric said, 'I didn't mean to make you cry.'

'I'm not crying,' I lied, rubbing at my eyes. 'It's just horrible. I wish you could meet my dad, he'd make sure your dad never hit you again.'

'I know your dad,' Eric surprised me by saying. 'He's Tracker Dan isn't he?'

Tracker Dan was my dad's nickname. He kept most of the Community supplied with meat. 'You know my dad?'

Eric nodded. 'He's a good guy. Helped me and my sisters out a few times. He gave my dad a bit of a thumping once when he caught him hitting me. Used to drop a rabbit or two by our house every now and then.'

'I didn't know that!' I said. 'He never mentioned it.'

'He's not the type of guy to show off is he? He's one of the only people who was ever nice to us. Izzy and Trina love him.' His face fell. 'I just hope he's still taking them food, because they're not old enough to get by on their own.'

'I don't know what to say,' I said helplessly.

'There's nothing you can say,' he replied. 'I tested Immune and ended up in here. It's just the way it is and there's nothing we can do about it.'

He picked up his sledgehammer and returned to the pile of rocks. I joined him, but couldn't stop thinking about Eric and his sisters. However much I missed my family at least I knew that they were safe on the farm and that no-one was going to hurt them.

The siren screamed out across the courtyard and I gratefully packed away my tools. Eric and I headed wearily back to the LightHouse. We found Mally and Flo in the dining hall. 'You look exhausted,' Flo said as she wrapped an arm around my shoulders. I heard real concern in her voice. She'd appointed herself as my big sister and took the role very seriously.

'I'm fine. It's just been a really long day. All I want to do is eat my tea and go to bed. Hopefully the Warden won't call another evening assembly. I don't think I could stay awake through another one.'

CHAPTER 13

Rendezvous

MaryAnn:

My eyes flickered open. It was hot in my sleeping bag and my damp vest stuck unpleasantly to my skin. In need of air I unzipped my tent and peered outside. The rest of the camp were sleeping. The morning sky was streaked with hues of pink as the last remnants of night were swept away. Flash was sprawled in a heap outside Peter's tent. He opened a lazy eye as I wriggled out onto the grass and then padded over to lick my face.

'Come on,' I said as I got to my feet, 'let's go to the beach.' Needing no further encouragement Flash bounded ahead of me along the track. By the time we pushed our way through the thicket of bushes onto the sand the sun was already making its appearance over the horizon and the surface of the sea shimmered with a vibrant pink glow.

I waded into the sea until the water was splashing around my knees. A small wave washed over me, wetting the hem of my shorts. Flash bounded into the water and circled me, barking madly.

'That dog never did have any sense of style.' I turned to find Peter, hands on hips, water lapping gently at his calves.

'Isn't this amazing,' I spread my arms enthusiastically.

'You should go for a swim,' Peter said.

'I don't have a swimming costume.'

'Who needs a costume?' Peter laughed as he scooped up a handful of water and poured it over my head. I kicked at him, water splashing up the front of his t-shirt. He retaliated as Flash barked furiously, a vision of thrashing legs and flapping ears. Finally Peter scooped me up and threw me into the water. I resurfaced to find him standing over me laughing loudly. 'You look like a drowned rat.'

'Oi, you two. If you've finished messing around in the water you might want to come and have some breakfast.' Daryl was on the beach, hands folded across his chest, his forehead creased into a slight frown.

'Come on,' Peter said a little sheepishly as he pulled me to my feet. I gave him one final splash before running out of the sea towards my brother.

Back at the camp I headed to my tent to change into dry clothes before joining the others at the fire. Daryl handed me a bowl of porridge and we ate quickly, anxious to be on the road as soon as possible.

After we'd packed up the camp I climbed into the back of the truck with Peter. It was Daryl's turn to drive and we followed a road that hugged the coastline. I peered out of the window framing the view in my memory. It was a sight I could never tire of. For a while I allowed myself to daydream, imagining another life where I lived in a little house by the sea. I'd grow vegetables and maybe raise a few chickens and the Light…they wouldn't even exist.

As we turned off the coast road I felt a surge of tension in the truck. 'More bandits?' I queried fearfully.

Daryl shook his head. 'No, we're getting close to the Edinburgh Neighbourhood. We'll stay off the road, but we should keep an eye out for the Watch in case they have any patrols out today.'

My stomach churned anxiously. Given the choice I'd rather meet a whole pack of bandits than a single Watch patrol.

By late morning the road had dipped into a valley bordered by the biggest mountains I'd ever seen. We'd left the Edinburgh Neighbourhood behind and the tension in the truck had relaxed a little.

'Amazing, aren't they?' Peter murmured as he stretched across the truck to peer out of my window. 'They remind me of the mountains at boot camp,' he observed. 'What do you think Daryl?'

'I'm glad I'm not climbing them with a full rucksack,' Daryl replied.

'Have you been here before?' I asked.

Peter shook his head. 'No, our boot camp is in the west, but it's a similar landscape to this…lots of mountains. The Union rarely travels this far north. Most people moved south after the virus because the weather's better for growing crops. Apart from a few small villages and hamlets along the coast the area's uninhabited.'

The area did appear deserted. Our journey took us through a bleak and desolate landscape and we met no other travellers on the road.

We stopped for a brief lunch by the edge of a deep blue lake and then continued our journey until the light began to fade. We made camp in the shadow of a mountain; its rocky sides rising steeply to a craggy summit.

While Daryl and Mr Murray went in search of firewood I stayed behind to help Peter erect the tents. I thought it would be fun, but it turned out to be a much harder task than it looked. Firstly we had to link a series of poles together to make a frame. Then we had to fit the cover. By the time we'd finished the first tent Peter was already in a bad mood. I think he blamed me for hitting his foot with the hammer, which was ridiculous because I hadn't done it on purpose. As I struggled to fit the cover over the second tent his temper grew steadily worse until finally I yelled at him in exasperation and stormed off in search of Daryl and a sympathetic ear. I heard Peter call after me but I ignored him.

I found Daryl collecting firewood along the edge of a lake. He was laden down with tree branches. 'I thought you were helping Peter with the tents?' he said.

'I was, but he's in a really grumpy mood.'

'Really?' Daryl replied. 'He seemed fine when we left.'

'You know how unpredictable his mood swings can be sometimes.'

'Not really,' Daryl replied. I glared at him and he shrugged. 'Okay, well don't just stand there, you can take some of these branches. They're heavy.'

I grabbed a handful of wood and then we scouted the area looking for more fallen branches. When we'd collected as much wood as we could carry, we headed back to the camp. We arrived to find that Peter had finished erecting the tents.

'Nice job mate,' Daryl flashed a wry smile as Peter took the pile of wood from him and placed it on the ground.

'Yeah, no thanks to your sister,' Peter growled as he glared quite unnecessarily in my direction.

'Is there something wrong with your foot?' Daryl queried. 'You're limping?'

'I don't want to talk about it,' Peter replied as he bent down to build the fire.

'See!' I mouthed to Daryl, 'I don't know what's the matter with him.'

The following morning we were packed and on the road by first light. Mr Murray was keen to arrive at the rendezvous as early as possible and refused to stop for any breaks.

Daryl was in the front passenger seat and from time to time he attempted to tune in the radio. The previous evening we'd hoped to pick up Radio Atlantis but all we found was static. I'd gone to bed feeling a little deflated. It had been nice to have a connection to the outside world.

After scrutinising the map Daryl directed Mr Murray onto a wild and rugged coast road bounded by steep cliffs. 'We're getting close,' he said, 'we should find somewhere to park.'

Mr Murray pulled off the road and brought the truck to a standstill on a patch of muddy flat ground. 'We'll leave the truck here,' he said as he switched off the engine. 'I'll go to the rendezvous. The rest of you climb to the top of one of those hills. Keep an eye out for trouble.'

The salt wind whipped savagely at my hair and clothes as I clambered out of the truck. 'That hill looks like it'll give us a good vantage point,' Daryl shouted above the squall.

It took about 30 minutes to scramble to the top of the hill and despite the cold wind I was sweating by the time we reached the summit. Peter and Daryl clambered to the edge of the hill, perching on a patch of scrubby grass. Peter pulled out a pair of binoculars and peered down to the path below. As I squatted down beside him I could make out the blurred figure of Mr Murray as he paced up and down in a harried sort of way. I pulled a bottle of tepid water out of my rucksack and took a mouthful. I grimaced; it tasted terrible.

Something caught my attention – a movement to the right. Peter stiffened beside me and focussed his attention on a figure that crept stealthily through the undergrowth. I watched as the blurry figure of Mr Murray raised a hand in greeting and then the two figures embraced.

Mr Murray turned towards the hill and waved his arms above his head.

'That's the signal,' Peter said as he packed the binoculars away. 'Come on.'

We scrambled down the hill to find Mr Murray accompanied by a wild looking man, his face covered by a thick untidy beard, a deerstalker hat pulled down tightly over a mass of unruly curls. Mr Murray introduced him as Dan Swift.

'Thanks for coming to help,' Dan said as he shook each of our hands in turn. His voice was like gravel.

'Dan has set up a camp,' Mr Murray said, 'but we can't take the truck. We'll have to walk.'

We concealed the truck in a coarse thicket of trees and followed Dan as he slashed a path through dense foliage. The ground beneath my feet was uneven and I lost count of the number of times I tripped over tree roots hidden in the thick vegetation.

'Not far to go now,' Dan called as we emerged out of the undergrowth. I followed the direction of his finger as he pointed to a high mountain ridge.

'Great,' I grumbled to myself, 'now he expects us to climb a mountain.'

'Scared of heights?' Peter teased. I jumped. I hadn't realised he was standing behind me.

'No, just scared of falling off a mountain,' I replied sarcastically.

I continued clumsily up the track. My rucksack was heavy and soon I was trailing far behind the rest of the group. Daryl and Peter stopped and waited for me to catch up.

'Come on, just one more push,' Peter said.

'Just one more push,' I mouthed behind his back. Why did he have to be so cheerful?

When we arrived at the ridge I found that it was wider than it appeared from below and there was space for two or three people to walk side by side.

'What now?' Daryl asked.

Dan grasped at a string of vines clinging precariously to the rock face. 'A little trick I learnt from the Union,' he said as he pulled the vines aside to reveal a moss-covered opening.

We followed Dan through the entrance and I found myself in a high-roofed cave. A small lamp illuminated its dank interior.

'Just like home,' Daryl muttered as he pulled off his rucksack and let it drop to the floor.

'Not as comfortable as your Union cave, but it'll do,' Dan said.

'It's just like I remember it,' Mr Murray murmured almost to himself.

Peter whipped around to face him. 'You've been here before?'

Mr Murray nodded uncertainly. 'It was a long time ago. I'm not sure I would have found it again without Dan's help.'

Peter's eyes narrowed and he shared a look with Daryl. My brother opened his mouth as if to comment but Dan interrupted him, 'The cave is well camouflaged. So it'll keep us hidden from the Watch.'

'The Watch patrol this area?' Daryl questioned. 'It's a bit far north isn't it?'

Dan crouched by the fire and busied himself with the kettle. 'Does everyone want tea?' he asked.

Peter and Daryl shared another glance and I felt a flicker of annoyance. Something was going on between them, something that I wasn't party too. 'Is someone going to tell us what we're doing here?' Peter questioned.

'What do you mean?' Mr Murray and Dan exchanged a guarded look.

Peter fixed them both with a shrewd stare. 'I think there's more going on than you've told us.'

When Mr Murray didn't respond Peter folded his hands across his chest. 'Murray, you can't keep secrets, not when we're risking so much to help you. I'd like you to explain how you know about this cave,' he faced Dan, 'and why you think the LightHouse is here.'

Dan got to his feet, 'Ethan, we should tell them the truth,' he said quietly.

CHAPTER 14

Ethan Murray's Story

MARYANN:

'We've been here before,' Mr Murray confessed. 'Jenn and I caught the Sandman Virus when we were teenagers. We both recovered, but Jenn was taken by the Light. They used people like us to test their drugs on. My uncle and I went after her and we met up with Dan on the road, his brother Tommy had also been taken. Dan tracked them to a research facility close to here. It was on an island just off the coast. We were able to rescue Jenn but my uncle and Tommy were killed in the escape. We hid out in this cave until it was safe to leave.'

'So you think the research facility where they held Jenn and Tommy might be the LightHouse?' Peter asked.

'It was just a hunch at first,' Dan replied. 'I'd heard the rumours about the LightHouse being in the north and I figured it had to be in an isolated location. The research facility fits the bill. I've been watching the island from a lookout further up this mountain. There's a tracker unit stationed at a small jetty further along the coast.'

'Crap,' Peter and Daryl both hissed.

'What's a tracker unit?' I asked.

'It's an elite Watch unit, specially trained to track down fugitives,'

Mr Murray explained.

'The research facility has to be the LightHouse,' Daryl said. 'Why else would they have a tracker unit stationed here?'

'We need to go over to the island to take a look,' Peter said.

'That's where things get a bit tricky,' Dan replied. 'The sea around here is treacherous. There are rocks really close to the surface. The whole area's littered with wrecks.'

'How did you get over to the island to rescue Jenn?' Daryl queried.

'David, a local fisherman, took us. He also showed us this cave. He used to play in it when he was a kid,' Dan explained.

'Would he help us again?' Peter asked.

Mr Murray shook his head. 'He's dead. He was shot during the escape.'

'There must be someone else who can take us to the island,' Daryl protested.

Mr Murray turned to Dan, 'Have you checked the other villages along the coast? Someone must have a boat?'

'The villages are deserted,' Dan replied. 'Everyone's gone. Apart from the Watch I haven't seen anyone else the whole time I've been here.'

'That's strange,' Mr Murray said, 'has everyone gone south?'

'I don't know,' Dan answered. 'I've searched the villages and they're all empty.'

'David did have a wife and a baby,' Mr Murray said. 'Have they gone too?'

'I walked over to his cottage a couple of days ago and it looked empty. I didn't have time to take a proper look around because I was interrupted by a Watch patrol and had to get out of there pretty sharpish.'

'We should check the cottage again,' Peter replied.

The following morning we gathered for breakfast and I enquired if there were any washing facilities. It had been days since I'd had a shower and my skin and hair were caked with dirt. Peter rolled his eyes and glanced pointedly at his watch. 'We're leaving as soon as we've eaten,' he grumbled. Dan ignored Peter's comment and climbed to his feet. 'Come with me;' he said, 'have I got a treat for you.'

Curious, I grabbed my towel and followed Dan as he led the way along a winding passageway. At a fork in the tunnel we squeezed through a narrow opening to enter a low cave. I was greeted by a torrent of water that spilled down the jagged rock face. 'This is our rain water shower,' Dan said. 'I'll leave you to enjoy the facilities.'

I stripped off my filthy clothes and stepped into the stream of water. It was ice cold but I forced myself to remain under the water until I'd rinsed away the days of accumulated dirt and grime. Feeling much cleaner I dried myself and pulled my clothes on before heading back to join the others.

'Finally,' Peter grumbled as I entered the cave. 'We were hoping to leave today, not sometime next week. How long does it take to have a wash?'

Turning a dead ear to his complaints I searched for my bag. 'Where's Dan?' I queried.

'He's at the lookout. He's going to stay here and keep watch,' Daryl replied.

We left the cave and followed Mr Murray along a dirt track that snaked around the mountain and down to the cliffs below. We trekked through miles of empty countryside until we arrived at a hamlet of whitewashed cottages. We picked our way through the deserted main street, the blackened broken windows of the houses staring sightlessly as we passed by. I spotted a village shop, its awning tattered and broken. The front door was torn from its hinges and thrown carelessly into the street.

'I don't like this place,' I shuddered, as I pressed closer to Daryl.

'Me neither,' he replied, his eyes darting from house to house.

At the edge of the village Mr Murray came to a standstill. 'This is it.' He gestured towards a squat white cottage standing alone in an overgrown plot of land. 'We should take a look around.'

'Daryl and I will check the outbuildings,' Peter offered as he opened the gate to an unkempt yard.

'Be careful,' Mr Murray warned. He gestured towards the cottage. 'MaryAnn, come with me.'

We entered the dank interior of the cottage; the light outside barely penetrated the grimy windows. A layer of dust covered the furniture and I coughed as it caught the back of my throat. 'I don't think there's anyone here,' I whispered.

Mr Murray quietly surveyed the room. 'I have a feeling that's what we're meant to think.' He padded across the room tapping on the wooden floor with the heel of his boot. As he approached the centre of the room the sound underfoot became a hollow echo. Mr Murray bent down and peeled back a dirty rug. I gasped as he revealed a wooden trap door hidden underneath.

'Go get the boys,' he hissed.

I beckoned to Daryl and Peter from the door of the cottage and they followed me back inside.

Mr Murray carefully opened the trapdoor to reveal a staircase beneath. He switched on a torch, illuminating the dark interior. 'You can come out,' he shouted. 'We're not going to hurt you.'

There was no response.

'If you don't come out we'll come down and get you,' he warned.

There was a long pause. 'I have a gun,' a female voice called out.

'Bring it with you,' Mr Murray replied. 'I told you we're not going to hurt anyone.'

There was the hollow ring of footsteps on the wooden staircase and a wild grey head emerged out of the trap door. The woman clambered up the steps, impatiently slapping away the hand that Mr Murray offered. 'I can do it myself,' she said.

'Are you alone?' Mr Murray asked as the woman eyed us warily.

'Yes. It's just me.'

'Are you Sarah?' Mr Murray asked.

The woman's eyes narrowed. 'Do I know you?'

'Your husband helped me rescue my sister Jenn from the Light a long time ago.'

'I remember you,' she said.

'The Light have taken my niece. We need a boat. I was hoping you could help us again.'

The woman pursed her lips as if she'd just swallowed something bitter. 'The last time my family helped you I became a widow.'

Mr Murray flinched. 'Your husband was a brave man. I'll be in his debt forever.'

'Better a coward than a hero…brave or not my husband is still dead.'

Sarah's comment was followed by an awkward silence.

'Can you help us?' Mr Murray finally asked.

'The Watch burnt all the boats, had a massive bonfire. I couldn't help you even if I wanted to.'

'There are no boats left?' Mr Murray questioned.

Sarah shook her head. 'The boats are the least of your problems. It's the helicopter you should be worried about.'

'The Watch have a helicopter?' Daryl breathed excitedly. 'I've only seen them in films.'

Sarah turned to face him. 'A film's the best place to see a helicopter. This one will blow you out of the water.' Daryl visibly paled under her gaze.

'Are you sure they burnt ALL the boats?' Mr Murray asked.

'Every last one of them and they evicted all the people.'

'But they let you stay?' Mr Murray queried.

'Of course not. I hid from them in the cellar. This is my home. The only way I'm going to leave it is in a box.'

'There must be some other way to get to the island,' Mr Murray murmured to no-one in particular.

'Well you won't find any answers here,' Sarah responded gruffly. 'I can't help you. I have no husband and no boat.'

Mr Murray appeared totally deflated.

'If you don't mind I'd like you to leave my property before the Watch get suspicious and start poking their big fat noses where they're not wanted,' Sarah said.

'Come on,' Peter said. 'We should go.'

'Thank you for your time,' Mr Murray murmured as we headed for the door.

Back at the cave Mr Murray disappeared up to the lookout to update Dan, while Daryl and I prepared lunch. Flash was in a boisterous mood and as he prowled the cave restlessly Peter rummaged in his rucksack and pulled out a shiny red ball. He threw it in the air and I watched as Flash raced after it, catching it deftly between his teeth. He returned the ball to Peter, dropping it expectantly at his feet. As Peter stooped to pick up the ball he stiffened. Flash let out a low growl, his attention focussed on the cave entrance. I felt a firm pressure on my arm. Startled I turned to find Daryl crouched beside me, a finger pressed to his lips.

Mr Murray and Dan climbed down from the lookout. 'There's someone outside,' Dan hissed.

With a series of hand signals Mr Murray indicated that Daryl and I should go to the lookout. We climbed up through the tunnel at the back of the cave and crawled across a rough stone platform. When I peered over the edge I spotted a girl creeping stealthily along the track below. She glanced around nervously and appeared to be searching for something. I watched as Mr Murray and Dan stole out of the cave entrance unnoticed. As Dan called out a warning, the girl spun round. She froze when she saw the gun in his hand.

'Who are you?' Dan asked, his voice floating up to the ledge.

'My name's Ruth. You came to my house to speak to my mum,' the girl spoke quickly, tripping over her words.

'You're Sarah's daughter?' Mr Murray asked.

'Yes.'

'She said she lived alone,' Mr Murray said.

'She lied. She didn't want you to know that I was in the cellar.'

'Did you follow us?' Mr Murray asked.

Ruth nodded uncertainly.

'Does your mum know you're here?' Dan asked.

The girl frowned. 'She thinks she's looking out for me but we can't stay hidden forever.'

'Why did you come?' Mr Murray queried.

'My mum lied when she said that all the boats were destroyed. We have a row boat hidden in a cave.'

Mr Murray and Dan shared a glance. 'Can you navigate to the island?' Dan urged.

'I have my dad's charts. Sometimes I take the boat out to fish,' she replied.

'What about your mum?' Mr Murray asked. 'She doesn't want to help.'

Ruth shrugged, 'I'm old enough to make my own decisions.'

'It's going to be dangerous,' Dan replied.

Ruth squared her shoulders. 'The Light killed my dad. I hate them. I want to help.'

Dan considered her for a moment. 'I understand,' he said. 'Do you think you can bring the charts and meet us here tomorrow night?'

Ruth nodded. 'I'll be back tomorrow and I can bring all the charts you need.'

CHAPTER 15

Unexpected Visitors

MARYANN:

The following evening Mr Murray assigned me my first guard duty. I perched diligently on the rocky ledge of the lookout, binoculars glued to my eyes as I searched the sea for any sign of life.

I was surprised by the sound of footsteps from behind me. I turned and let out a squeal of horror as I stared into a pair of glassy eyes. The binoculars fell from my grasp, clattering noisily across the stone floor.

Peter hooted with laughter as he dangled two dead rabbits by the ears. 'Say hello to dinner,' he teased.

'Peter,' Mr Murray called from the cave below, 'stop messing around with those rabbits and bring them down here so they can be skinned and put in the pot.'

Peter smirked before turning on his heel and scrambling down to the cave below. I made a rude gesture at his retreating back and returned to my sentry duties.

As the light outside began to fade my eyes grew heavy. I blinked furiously in an effort to stay awake. I couldn't fall asleep on my first guard duty. Mr Murray would never trust me again. I was disturbed by the snap of a twig on the path below and glanced down irritably.

If Peter was tormenting me again I was going to kill him.

Someone entered the cave. It was Peter, a bloody finger held to his lips. My heart skipped a beat. Who was on the path below?

'Is Ruth out there?' I whispered.

'I don't think so. There's more than one person.' Peter scrambled over to the ledge and quietly scrutinized the dark shapes below. I heard him utter a low curse. 'You've got to be kidding me. I'll bloody kill them.' Pushing me aside he climbed back down into the cave. I quickly followed and arrived just in time to see Peter disappear out of the entrance, accompanied by Dan and Mr Murray. They returned a few moments later draggling three familiar figures with them. The figures were deposited roughly onto the floor as Mr Murray cried, 'Will, Jake, and Max! What the hell are you doing here?'

Max clambered to his feet, shaking the mud out of his short dark hair. He turned to the other two, 'I told you we wouldn't be able to sneak up on them,' he grumbled, 'but neither of you ever listen to me.'

'It's your fault for making so much noise. Stamping around like a herd of cattle,' Will complained as he pulled Jake up from the floor. 'It's a wonder the Watch didn't find us too.'

'Oi!' Peter shouted. 'Murray asked what you were doing here. Now answer the question.'

Jake peered up at him and I had to admire his confidence in the face of Peter's blazing anger. He was the smallest of the boys, but always the most defiant. 'We were tracking you,' he said.

'Tracking us?' Daryl queried. 'Did Patrick send you?'

'Off course he did,' came a growl from the entrance and I stared open mouthed as a very angry looking Uncle Patrick climbed into the cave.

Mr Murray found his voice first. 'You'd better sit down,' he said as he led the newcomers to the fire.

I studied Uncle Patrick as he took a seat. He was blistering with a barely contained rage.

'Is someone going to tell me what you're doing here?' he demanded as he fixed the assembled group with a hard stare.

Again it was Mr Murray who was the first to speak. 'I told you I was going to look for Charlotte.'

'Yes, but you forgot to mention that you were taking Peter, Daryl and MaryAnn with you,' Uncle Patrick's tone was brittle.

'We volunteered,' Peter sounded defensive. 'Murray didn't force us to come.'

Uncle Patrick faced Peter, his eyes flashing dangerously. 'You had no right to volunteer.'

'Murray's my friend and he needed my help,' Peter protested.

'I don't care about your friendship with Murray. The Union should come first. We're your family. You should understand that better than anyone.'

A muscle twitched in Peter's cheek but he didn't respond.

Uncle Patrick turned to Daryl. 'And what have you got to say for yourself?' he demanded.

'They took Flo,' Daryl replied dully.

Uncle Patrick shook his head in disgust. 'So you think chasing after some girl is a good enough reason to put your sister in danger. I thought you'd have more consideration given everything she's been through.'

The colour drained from Daryl's face.

'He didn't force me to come. I volunteered,' I said.

Uncle Patrick continued as if I hadn't spoken. 'You're the biggest disappointment of all Daryl. How could you betray me like this?'

'I didn't betray you,' Daryl whispered hoarsely. 'I told you I came for Flo.'

'I don't care. I won't accept disloyalty from anyone. Your actions will have consequences.'

'What type of consequences?' Daryl asked fearfully.

'There will be a formal hearing when we get back to the head-quarters,' Uncle Patrick explained.

'A hearing?' Daryl whispered quietly.

'I can't let you disobey an order, even if you are my family. You'll have to justify your actions to the other Stewards. I came here to bring you all back.'

'How did you know where to find us?' Dan interrupted.

'That doesn't matter,' Uncle Patrick replied brusquely, 'you disobeyed a direct order coming here.'

'I don't take orders from you,' Dan replied. 'Now answer my question. How did you know where to find us?'

Uncle Patrick's manner was offhand. 'Jenn showed me the rendezvous on the map and the location of the cave. We tracked you here.'

'Jenn would never give up that information,' Mr Murray said.

Dan's brow furrowed. 'Not unless you threatened her.'

'I didn't threaten her. I just made it clear that if she didn't help me she would have to leave the caves and take Matty with her.'

'What!' Dan and Mr Murray sprang to their feet. As Dan took a threatening step towards Uncle Patrick Peter jumped up, placing a restraining hand on his shoulder. 'Dan,' he warned.

'You gave her no choice. She had nowhere else to go,' Dan growled. 'After I fought the Watch they turned us off the farm. She couldn't go back to the Community.' The look he gave Uncle Patrick was menacing, almost brutal. If he decided to attack Uncle Patrick I feared that even Peter wouldn't be able to stop him.

Uncle Patrick shrugged. 'We have rules.'

'Those rules include threatening children, do they?' Mr Murray asked.

Uncle Patrick surveyed the group. 'You don't seem to understand that we're at war with the Light. Sometimes that means we have to make difficult decisions.' Uncle Patrick's passionate speech was interrupted by a low growl. Flash crept to the cave entrance, the fur on his neck standing on end.

'It must be Ruth,' Mr Murray said. 'She promised to come back this evening.'

'Who's Ruth?' Uncle Patrick demanded.

'Someone who can help us,' Mr Murray said. 'I'll go and fetch her.'

A few moments later Mr Murray returned with Ruth. Her eyes widened as she surveyed the band of people gathered around the fire. Living in isolation in the cellar, I suspected that it was the first time she'd seen this many people together in one place. Seeming to sense her discomfort Mr Murray gently guided her to an empty seat.

'Did you bring the charts?' he asked as soon as she was settled. His tone was soft.

'Just a minute,' Uncle Patrick protested. 'I haven't agreed to this operation. I told you I came here to take you back to the caves.'

''We're not going anywhere, but feel free to leave anytime you want to,' Dan said as he indicated the cave entrance. I cast an anxious glance towards Peter.

It was Mr Murray who filled the tense silence that followed Dan's challenge. 'Patrick, we have two girls trapped in the LightHouse. We need your help to get them out.'

Uncle Patrick frowned.

'We've been friends for years,' Mr Murray said. 'You know I can't leave here, not until we get Charlotte back.'

'You undermined my authority Murray. I can't make an exception for you just because you're my friend,' Uncle Patrick said.

'I understand there'll be consequences and I'm happy to accept my punishment but for now I really need your help.'

'We'll have a better chance of rescuing them if you're with us,' Daryl agreed.

'Patrick, we can't go home, not until we've got the girls out,' Mr Murray coaxed.

Uncle Patrick surveyed the group. 'Do you have a plan?' he asked.

'Not yet,' Mr Murray replied. 'Ruth can get us over to the Light-House, but we'll need your help to get them out.' He turned to Ruth. 'Did you bring the charts?' he asked.

Ruth rummaged in her bag and pulled out a roll of well-worn papers. She handed them to Mr Murray, who unfurled them and spread them out across the floor.

Ruth leant over the charts. 'There's a small cove on the island that we can row over to. I've plotted a course,' she informed him timidly.

'Good work,' Mr Murray smiled.

Ruth seemed relieved and when she spoke again her voice had gained a little more strength. 'I usually take the boat out during the new moon. It makes it harder for the Watch to spot the boat.'

Mr Murray paused thoughtfully. 'That gives us just over a week to plan the rescue.'

'We'll need to find a way to warn Charlotte and Flo about the rescue so that they're ready to leave,' Uncle Patrick said.

'Someone will have to go over to the LightHouse,' Peter said.

'That's impossible,' Mr Murray replied. 'It's going to be hard enough to make one trip over there, never mind two.'

'Then how are we going to warn them?' Daryl asked.

'An idea was beginning to take shape in my mind but I dismissed it. It was too dangerous. I waited expectantly but no-one seemed to be coming up with an alternative. 'I could go!' I finally stammered uncertainly.

All eyes were fixed on me.

'I've had the vaccination,' I continued. 'If the Watch capture me, I'll test Immune and they'll take me to the LightHouse.'

Peter shook his head. 'Absolutely not.'

'It's too dangerous,' Daryl agreed.

Any reservation I'd had about volunteering disappeared instantly. I was an adult and Peter and Daryl had no right to tell me what to do. 'I don't think we have any choice,' I said. 'It has to be someone who's Immune.'

'I'm Immune,' Peter replied. 'So is Daryl; he's had the vaccination.'

'You're too old.'

'I don't care. You're not going,' Peter replied. Daryl nodded in agreement.

'You can't tell me what to do.'

'Patrick, you have to talk some sense into her. Tell her it's too dangerous,' Daryl said.

I prepared to argue my case with Uncle Patrick too and was stunned when he agreed with me. 'She has a point,' he said. 'She is the only one who can get into the LightHouse.'

'What if she gets into trouble? There'll be no-one to help her,' Peter argued.

'She hasn't had any training,' Daryl said.

'That didn't stop you both from bringing her on this foolish mission.' He turned to me. 'Are you sure about this? It's going to be dangerous.'

I nodded, my confidence bolstered by the proud glint in his eye.

'You can't let her do this,' Peter continued to rage. 'She'll get hurt.'

'She's a Hunter. Fighting is in her blood.'

'What! That's crazy. It's too dangerous.'

'Better she understands the danger she's getting into rather than being captured because of an amateur mistake, don't you think?' Uncle Patrick's voice was pure poison.

All the air seemed to leave Peter's body as he visibly deflated. He cast an anxious glance in my direction. 'I didn't want to leave her at the Director's house; I wanted to take her with us.'

'That may be so, but it was your incompetence that led the Director to her,' Uncle Patrick accused. 'All you had to do was to remember to sign out of the security system.'

'Someone should be on guard duty,' he muttered as he jumped

to his feet. He gave me another anxious glance before he turned and strode away across the cave.

'How could you say those things?' I challenged Uncle Patrick as I watched Peter disappear through the entrance to the lookout. 'It wasn't his fault.'

'Yes it was,' my uncle replied. 'He made an amateur mistake.' 'Where are you going?' Uncle Patrick asked as I got to my feet and prepared to follow Peter out of the cave.

'I'm going to find Peter,' I replied. I marched angrily across the cave, pausing for a moment at the entrance to the lookout. I turned to face my uncle. 'And Peter was right; he wasn't the one that left me behind.'

I found Peter on the ledge, his back against the wall, knees pulled to his chest. 'I'm not in a very sociable mood,' he muttered as I dropped into the space beside him.

'That's fine,' I replied, 'neither am I.'

I felt an odd tension between us as I followed his gaze out into the night. The cloudless sky was so clear that I could make out the arc of the Milky Way. The stars were one of the things I'd first noticed about the Outside. In the Neighbourhood they'd barely been visible, but out here they filled the sky to bursting.

I shivered as a cold breeze whipped across the ledge sending a chill through me. Peter shrugged off his jacket and handed it to me.

As I pulled it on I heard him murmur, 'Patrick's right. It was my fault.' There was more than a hint of sadness in his words.

'It wasn't anyone's fault,' I replied.

'You have to understand I didn't mean for you to get hurt,' Peter's tone was pleading.

'It was a mistake,' I replied.

'I'm trained not to make mistakes,' his voice broke, 'when I saw you at the Delta camp. What they'd done to you…if I could have swapped places…' he trailed off helplessly.

'You didn't torture me, that was the Director.'

'But I gave you to the Director.'

'You didn't give me to anyone. It was a mistake. You have to stop blaming yourself.'

When Peter didn't respond I took his hand in mine. He tensed but didn't pull away. 'It wasn't your fault,' I repeated.

I felt his grip tighten around my hand. 'That's what everyone said about my family too,' he replied morosely. 'That it wasn't my fault they were killed, but if I hadn't tested Immune then the Watch wouldn't have had a reason to come to my house.'

'That's ridiculous. None of it was your fault. You can't blame yourself every time something bad happens.'

When he didn't respond I continued, 'Remember how you once told me that I wasn't responsible for the things my father did? Well I'm giving you the same piece of advice. You can't blame yourself for one stupid mistake.'

My comment produced a weak smile. 'It looks like I should be careful about the advice I give out in the future,' he said.

A rush of cold air sliced through the cave, blowing my hair into a tangle of curls. I shivered and pulled Peter's jacket tighter around me. I felt Peter's body give a shudder and he rubbed at his arms briskly.

'Are you cold?' I asked. 'Do you want your jacket back?'

Peter shook his head. 'I'm fine, you keep it.' I could make out the blonde hairs standing to attention on his forearms as his tattoo peeked below the sleeve of his t-shirt.

'You never did tell me about your tattoo,' I said. 'Remember at the farm, you explained the one on your back, but not the one on your arm.'

Peter exhaled slowly and I realised he was about to tell me something important. 'It was my first tattoo. I had it drawn after the Watch killed my family.' His voice had changed. Somehow it sounded raw, exposed. He turned his shoulder towards me, pulling up the sleeve of his t-shirt so I could get a better view of the design. 'See the intersecting grey with the reds, oranges and yellows…that's the sunrise over the farm. My dad and I got up early every morning to milk the cows and we watched the sunrise every day. I didn't want to forget it so I had it tattooed on my arm,' he paused for a moment and then continued. 'The eight stars are my family. The larger ones are my mum and dad and my auntie and uncle who lived on the farm with us. The smaller ones are my little sister and brother and my twin cousins. I didn't have any photographs so it was the only way I could remember them.'

His comment caused me to hesitate for a moment, before I unclipped the pouch from my belt and rummaged inside. 'I saved this for you,' I said as my hand found the thing it was looking for. It was the family photograph I'd taken from the farm a few months earlier. I pulled it out and offered it to Peter.

Peter took the photograph from my outstretched hand and quietly unfolded the picture of his family. 'I thought I told you to leave this,' he said. His voice was rough.

I peered at him anxiously, unsure whether he was angry or not. I watched as he carefully stroked the surface of the photograph with his thumb. 'It was nice of you to keep it for me.' His voice broke and he paused for a moment. 'Especially after I behaved like such an idiot. It was hard being back there.'

'You were no more idiotic than usual,' I said in an attempt to lighten the mood. It was unlike Peter to be so morose.

He smiled and gave me a gentle shove.

We remained side by side, neither feeling the need for further conversation until even Peter's jacket couldn't keep out the chill air. 'Are you ready to go back to the others?' I shivered.

He shook his head. 'No. You go back. I'm going to stay here a little while longer.'

'I can sit with you,' I offered.

He shook his head. 'I'd like to be on my own for a while if you don't mind.'

I left Peter alone on the ledge, the photograph grasped tightly in his hand, staring intently at the picture of his family.

CHAPTER 16

Two and Two Make Five

Charlotte:

The siren shrieked and I woke with a sinking heart. The sound signalled another evening assembly.

I met Mally in the corridor. 'More lectures,' he murmured. I didn't have the energy to respond.

Based on the collection of scratches on Bekka's bedframe we'd been at the LightHouse for about three weeks. Sometimes it seemed like much longer. The exhausting work, the interrupted sleep and the bland food was taking its toll on all of us. I felt like I was sleep walking through each day.

I could hardly keep my eyes open during the assembly. My brain was like cotton wool and I had to force myself to make the desired responses to the Warden's lecture. I peered around at the other Residents as they focussed intently on the podium. I noticed that we all shared the same hollow eyed look.

Eric had taken the seat next to mine and he grinned as I caught his eye. Eric was the only Resident who didn't seem to be affected by the harsh regime. Flo said it was because living with his dad had been like living in a war zone, so he'd always had to be alert and ready to flee at a moment's notice. He was used to the stress and lack of sleep. She also said he was eating better than he'd ever done at home.

My parents didn't have a lot of money and we had to forage in the woods to supplement the food we grew on the farm, but we never went hungry. My mum was an amazing cook and we always had something tasty to eat at mealtimes. Flo said that sometimes Eric would go days without having anything to eat. It seemed that in our current situation Eric was better equipped to survive than I was.

When the assembly came to an end, we reaffirmed our allegiance to the Light before trudging back to the dorm.

It felt like I'd only been asleep for a few moments when the siren sounded to signal the start of a new day.

After suffering the torture of the showers I headed to breakfast. I collected my food and slipped into the seat next to Mally. I silently shovelled porridge into my mouth, swallowing it automatically without even tasting it.

After we'd finished breakfast we filed into assembly and as the Warden prepared to read out the work detail I crossed my fingers hoping to be given an easy task. I was exhausted from breaking rocks the previous day and I needed a quiet day in the laundry or the kitchens. '*Not collecting or breaking rocks,*' I mentally pleaded. '*Please not collecting or breaking rocks.*' My fingers were pressed together so tightly that they started to cramp. I didn't dare unfold them in case it brought bad luck.

'*Charlotte Swift...rock collecting.*' My body slumped and my eyes watered. I let out an involuntary whimper. I couldn't spend the day on the beach carrying rocks. I really couldn't.

'You okay?' Eric whispered. I jumped at the sound of his voice. I'd forgotten that he was sitting next to me. I was so close to tears that I couldn't trust myself to speak.

'What's the matter?' he asked. I detected a note of concern in his voice. All I could do was shake my head in response.

'Hey, it's going to be alright,' he said and his hand briefly grazed mine. It was a small movement, designed to show support without drawing unwanted attention from the Trustees. 'I'm collecting rocks today too so we'll get through it together.' I nodded miserably, wanting to believe him, but too exhausted to really care.

I filled a bucket with water and with aching limbs I dragged it wearily across the tiled floor to the bathrooms. I scrubbed at the floor, my arms leaden and sluggish. I heard the creak of the door and a Trustee entered the room. The Trustee gave me no acknowledgement so I bowed my head and dipped my scrubbing brush into the bucket. The Trustee ran a finger across the top of a cubicle door then held it out for inspection. 'What is this?'

When I glanced up I could see that the Trustee's gloved finger was coated with dirt. I looked down at the floor, praying that the Trustee would just give me a warning and leave. 'What is this?' the Trustee repeated. Before I had time to respond I felt pain flare across my side. I inhaled sharply. I curled up into a ball to protect myself from the blows that followed. The Trustee's boots catching me across my back and shoulder.

I heard the bang of the door and I was alone. I remained curled up on the floor long after the Trustee had left. How could this be happening to me? I just wanted to go home to my family.

The Trustees ordered us to walk two abreast as they escorted us down to the beach. Eric occupied the empty space beside me. My legs were like lead and my side hurt from the beating I had taken from the Trustee. I hadn't mentioned the incident to the others as I didn't want to make a fuss. I was also scared that Eric might use it as an excuse to antagonise the Trustees.

My head was pounding by the time we arrived at the beach and I could barely concentrate as Eric whispered in my ear, 'Follow me to the end of the beach.' I staggered after him, stumbling across the sand. As soon as we were out of sight of the Trustees he came to a standstill.

My lip quivered. 'I can't do this.' I was ashamed to sound so weak, but I couldn't keep the whine from my voice.

'I know,' he said. 'You look done in. Stay here and try not to attract any attention. I'll collect our quota of rocks for today.'

'I can't let you do that,' I protested feebly. 'It's not fair.'

'Don't worry about it, everyone has a breaking point and you've just reached yours. You can repay the favour some other time.'

'You're like a robot,' I said. 'I can't imagine you ever reaching your breaking point.'

'That's not true,' he said. 'Everyone has their limits. We can't let the Trustees play their mind games with us. We have to stick together.'

'What do you mean by mind games?' I queried.

'Do you think it's a coincidence that you're collecting rocks today when you look so exhausted?' he asked.

I hadn't really thought about it. 'You obviously don't think so,' I queried.

'I think they have people working for them who can read that type of thing.' He stooped to pick up a rock. 'If they want to break us it's easier to do it if we're exhausted and can't think straight.' He hugged the rock to his chest and left me considering his comment as he staggered away across the beach.

I watched as a familiar face approached. It was Mally. I took note of the violet smudges under his eyes. His wiry frame was thin to the point of emaciation. He was exhausted too.

'You look like death, mate,' Eric said as he approached from behind, clapping a hand on Mally's shoulder. Startled, Mally jumped into the air. When he realised that it was Eric he smiled. 'Maybe you should take a look in the mirror sometime. You're not exactly a vision of beauty yourself.'

The change in dynamic between the two boys was interesting. In the Community they would never have been friends, but here in the LightHouse they'd grown close. I think the friendship had really begun when Mally had stuck up for Eric and spent time in Detention. It had earned Eric's respect. I suspected that very few people had ever defended him before.

'Have you come to help?' Eric asked Mally.

'Yeah if you don't mind? It'd be good to have some company.'

'I'd appreciate it seeing as Charlotte's having a day off.'

'Oi!' I reprimanded. 'As if I'm not feeling bad enough already.'

'I'm joking, I'm joking,' he interrupted with a grin.

'Ignore him,' Mally said. 'You didn't see him last week after he'd been breaking rocks all afternoon. Dale and I had to help him out of his clothes because he couldn't undo the buttons on his shirt. Not exactly a superhero moment.'

'Hey. It wasn't just one day. I spent four days breaking rocks while you were in the laundry fluffing up pillows and folding bed sheets. How hard can that be?'

'I got a very nasty burn from the iron,' Mally said as he held out his arm. 'Look.'

Eric sniggered, 'Ooh, that looks nasty. You should get it checked out sweetheart.'

The afternoon dragged on and by the time the Trustee called to signal the end of the work duty even Eric was looking pale. Mally was so tired he could barely stay upright as we stumbled back to the LightHouse.

At teatime I scarcely had the energy to lift the spoon to my mouth. As we were finishing our meal the Warden entered the dining hall. She normally ate her meals alone so it caused a stir among the Residents. She clapped her hands and a hush descended across the room.

'I have some good news,' she called out. 'You've all worked very hard over the last few weeks and have shown a real commitment to the Light. As a reward I wanted to inform you there will be no evening assembly. We've also cancelled leisure time to give you the opportunity to catch up on any sleep you may have missed. Thank you for your continued devotion to the Light. You are dismissed.'

I was shocked at the intense rush of gratitude, almost love that I felt for the Warden. She might be stern and unswerving, but today she was my saviour. I was almost ready to weep with relief at the thought of a full night's unbroken sleep.

Mally yawned widely, not even bothering to cover his mouth. 'I'm off to bed,' he said as he got up from the table. It seemed that everyone else had the same idea as we all filed out of the dining room and headed straight to the dorms.

CHAPTER 17

Beach of Bones

MARYANN:

'MaryAnn, I've been looking for you everywhere.'

Daryl's head appeared around the entrance to the small cave where I'd secreted myself with a book. The arrival of Will, Jake and Max made our living space feel overcrowded and I was desperate for some quiet.

Without being invited, Daryl flopped down into the empty space beside me. 'Can we talk?'

I reluctantly closed the book and set it aside.

'I want you to reconsider your plan,' Daryl said.

I sighed. I'd been expecting this conversation ever since I'd volunteered to go to the LightHouse. 'You know I can't do that.'

'It's too dangerous,' he replied.

'I thought you wanted us to rescue Flo?'

'I do…'

'Then you know that this is the only way to get her back,' I said.

He exhaled. 'This is so hard. I want to find Flo, but not if it puts you in danger.'

'I'll be fine,' I said.

He grabbed my hand for a moment, holding tight. 'If anything happened to you or Flo I don't know what I'd do.'

I gave his hand a reciprocal squeeze. 'You really like her don't you?'

He smiled. 'Yeah, she's great. You'd like her too.'

'Tell me about her.'

Daryl's face lit up. 'She's tiny. Even smaller than you,' he joked.

I gave him a dig in the ribs. 'I'm not that small.'

'She has this cool pink hair and she wants to be a circus acrobat. She practises all the time. She's really good.'

'So you like her more than the other girls you've been out with?' I asked.

He seemed puzzled. 'There haven't been any other girls.'

I blushed. 'Oh! I just…well…Peter's been out with a lot of girls. So I thought…'

Daryl smiled. 'I grew up in the Neighbourhood, remember. Just because I live on the Outside now, it doesn't mean that I'm going to go out with a different girl every night.'

'It's strange how people on the Outside have relationships without any serious commitment,' I replied. 'No-one would do that in the Neighbourhood.'

'I suppose it's because there aren't any restrictions on the number of children you can have. You don't even need to apply for a licence on the Outside.'

'I know. Its crazy I met some people in the Union who have three or four children,' I replied.

'Out in the Communities they have even bigger families. I met one with eight children.'

I was appalled and clasped a hand across my mouth. 'Eight children!'

'If you have a lot of land to farm it helps to have a big family.'

'I suppose so, but I can't imagine having seven brothers and sisters,' I replied. 'One brother is more than enough for me.'

Daryl grinned. 'What about you?' he asked. 'Did you have anyone special in the Neighbourhood?'

'Not really.' I thought of Reese. 'There was this boy I liked, he was a good match, but he turned out to be a bit of an idiot. He threw up on my shoes.'

'He doesn't sound like the type of boy I want hanging around with my sister,' Daryl threw an arm around my shoulder.

'I don't think you would have liked him very much.'

Daryl gave my shoulder a squeeze. 'I really appreciate what you're doing for Flo. I just don't want you to get hurt.'

'I'll be careful. I promise.'

'You'll be more than careful,' he replied. 'I'm going to teach you how to defend yourself.'

'I'm not planning on getting into any fights,' I protested.

'No arguments,' Daryl scrambled to his feet. 'We'll start your training in the morning.'

The following morning I'd barely had time to finish breakfast before Daryl appeared and told me to follow him into the small cave.

Once inside the cave he produced two sharpened sticks and handed one to me. 'Pretend it's a knife,' he said.

I turned the stick over in my hand. 'It looks like a stick, how can I pretend it's a knife?'

His exasperated reply set the tone for the lesson. 'Just try,' he said.

He began by teaching *"defensive techniques"*. This involved jabbing at me with the stick to feign a knife attack. He then coached me on the best way to avoid the attack.

Daryl's training was relentless and as the morning wore on I grew more exhausted. Each time I asked for a break he patiently urged me to try 'just one more time'.

'Isn't it lunchtime yet?' I whined. My stomach growled in response.

'Let's try a few more moves and then we can go and get something to eat,' Daryl coaxed.

'I don't want to do this anymore, I don't like fighting.'

'We're not fighting, I'm teaching you to defend yourself.'

'I don't care. I don't want to defend myself anymore and you can't force me.' I let my stick drop to the floor.

'I'm not forcing you to do anything. I just want to keep you safe.' He bent down to retrieve the stick I'd dropped. 'Some people take a bit longer to pick this stuff up. You just need practice.' He held the stick out to me.

I mouthed a curse as I snatched the stick from his outstretched hand.

'Just one more time,' he said. 'Try and block my attack. Then I promise we'll go and get something to eat.'

He lunged at me but I moved too slowly and his stick scraped painfully across the flesh of my arm. A thread of blood appeared along the length of the wound. Exasperated, I threw my stick at him and marched out of the cave. I'd had enough self-defence lessons for one day.

I climbed up to the lookout to find Peter on guard duty with Flash. I threw myself onto the ground beside him.

'You alright?' Peter asked with a raised eyebrow.

'No I'm not alright,' I raged. 'Daryl's driving me crazy with his self-defence lessons. Look at what he did to my arm.'

'He just wants to make sure you can take care of yourself,' Peter said as he dabbed at the wound with a corner of his shirt.

'You have to talk to him. Make him stop.'

'You know I can't do that.'

'Of course! I should have known you'd take Daryl's side.' I wrenched my arm out of his grasp.

He sighed. 'I'm not taking sides.'

'Yes you are. He's your friend so you can't see how unreasonable he's being.'

'He's just worried about you. That's all.'

'There's nothing to worry about. I'm only going to be in the LightHouse for a few days. You'll come and get me before anything bad can happen.'

'Of course we're coming to get you. But there's no harm in learning how to look after yourself. You should listen to Daryl. He has some good skills to teach you.'

When I didn't respond, he continued, 'Can't you let him do this? It'll make him feel better.'

'So you're telling me I have to let him stab me with a stupid stick just so he can feel better. What about me? I'm the one that's bleeding!'

'Just think how worried you'd be if Daryl was the one going into the LightHouse on his own,' Peter said.

I considered his comment. The thought of Daryl trapped in the LightHouse sent a chill through me. I'd be frantic with worry. 'You might have a point,' I reluctantly confessed.

Peter threw his hands up in the air in mock horror. 'Do my ears deceive me or did you just agree with me? This truly is a miraculous day.'

Despite myself I giggled. 'Just don't get used to it,' I replied.

'Why don't you go and speak to Daryl?' Peter urged.

'I will, but not right now, otherwise Daryl will be the one who needs the self-defence lessons.'

I remained at the lookout with Peter until Uncle Patrick called to tell us that Ruth had returned.

I entered the cave to find everyone assembled around the fire. Daryl caught my eye and patted the empty space beside him.

'Sorry about your arm. I didn't mean to hurt you,' he said as I sat down.

'It's fine, just don't be so rough next time.'

'So there's going to be a next time?' he asked. The corners of his mouth lifted into a tentative smile.

'Maybe,' I replied.

'Alright, let's have a bit of quiet,' Mr Murray surveyed the group and everyone fell silent. 'Now that we're all here I want to go over the plan,' he said. 'This operation is going to be dangerous so we need to make sure it's water tight,' he paused, 'no pun intended.' Mr Murray turned to me, 'MaryAnn you'll need to be ready to leave for the LightHouse in a few days.'

'Do we have a plan for getting MaryAnn inside the LightHouse?' Daryl asked.

'I've been thinking about that,' Uncle Patrick replied. 'MaryAnn you'll have to go down to the jetty and let the Watch capture you.'

'They'll question her,' Peter said.

'I know. She'll have to make them think she's lost and scared. Do you think you can do that?' Uncle Patrick asked.

I nodded. It wouldn't require much acting on my part.

'Once they test your blood and confirm you're Immune they'll take you to the LightHouse,' Uncle Patrick continued. He rummaged in his pouch. 'I had a new identity card made for you but you left before I had chance to give it to you.... Here.'

I took the card from his outstretched hand and scrutinised it. The name on the card read Beth Summers and I was officially designated as an Echo. The photograph had been taken in shadow so my scar wasn't visible.

'Beth Summers,' I murmured, rolling the name over my tongue, familiarising myself with my new identity.

'A Unionist gave us her daughter's name. Not all Echo deaths are registered so you should be fine using it,' Uncle Patrick said.

Shocked, I looked up. I hadn't expected Beth to be a real person. I wasn't sure that I felt entirely comfortable using a dead girl's name.

Once you're inside you'll have to find Charlotte and Flo and tell them about the plan. I don't know how easy it's going to be to locate them,' Mr Murray said.

'I can draw you a layout of the building,' Dan offered. 'It's been a long time since I was inside, but I think I still remember it.'

'Thanks,' I replied.

'You have to be ready to leave on the night of the new moon,' Mr Murray continued. 'As soon as it's dark you'll escape out of the front door. We'll meet you outside the gates and take you to the boat.'

'Do you know if there's a HealthScan?' Uncle Patrick asked Dan and Mr Murray. 'They might set off an alarm when they leave the building.'

'I can disable it,' Mr Murray said. 'I've had plenty of practice in the Neighbourhood.'

'There's just one other matter that we need to resolve.' Uncle Patrick's voice had lost its usual authority and he paused uncertainly. 'We have the problem with MaryAnn's scar.'

I touched my cheek self-consciously. 'What's the matter with my scar?'

'The Director has the Watch looking for you. They might recognise the scar.'

'I've tried to cover it, but nothing works,' I said.

'I was thinking that we might be able to hide it if we caused enough damage.'

'Damage,' I swallowed.

'If someone hit you hard enough to cause bruising…' Uncle Patrick couldn't meet my eyes as he spoke.

'No way!' Daryl and Peter both yelled in unison.

'We can't risk the Watch recognising her,' Uncle Patrick said. 'Unless either of you have a better idea.'

'The Watch stationed here are isolated from the Manchester Neighbourhood; they may not know about MaryAnn,' Daryl said. 'The Director's trying to keep her disappearance a secret.'

'Are you willing to take the risk?' Uncle Patrick asked.

When Daryl didn't reply my uncle continued, 'It's the only option.'

I swallowed hard.

'Who's going to do it?' Peter asked.

'Not me,' Daryl said immediately. 'Yeah me neither,' Peter added almost at once.

'She's not much older than Charlotte,' Dan said. 'I can't do it.'

'Don't look at me,' Mr Murray said.

'Jake could do it,' Will piped up. 'He has a great right hook.' Jake glanced uneasily in Peter's direction before replying, 'I'm not hitting MaryAnn.'

'Too right,' Daryl replied. 'You're not laying a hand on my sister.'

Uncle Patrick exhaled loudly. 'I'll do it.'

'How's the swelling?' Daryl asked as he removed the cold towel from my throbbing cheek. He scrutinised my face, pulling my chin towards him. I flinched.

'You can hardly see your scar,' he said as he examined the bruising.

'That's great,' I murmured as I grabbed the towel from his hand and hugged it back to my cheek. The cool water helped to soothe the throbbing.

Peter entered the cave carrying a cup of water. He squatted down in front of me. 'Take these,' he said as he handed me two white pills. 'It'll help with the pain.'

As I swallowed the pills Daryl got to his feet and strolled over to where Dan, Mr Murray and Ruth were studying maps of the island.

'Do you know what I find really strange?' Daryl said. 'How come we're the only ones to find the LightHouse?' He turned to Dan. 'I know you have ninja tracking skills but don't you think it's a bit weird?'

Ruth glanced up from the note she was scribbling. 'Other people have been here before,' she said.

'Then why haven't they told anyone about it?' Daryl replied.

Ruth chewed on her bottom lip.

'Did something happen to them?' Daryl enquired. He shared an anxious glance with Dan and Mr Murray.

'You really don't want to know,' Ruth murmured as she turned back to her notes.

'Oh I think we do!' Uncle Patrick clambered through the entrance, a dead rabbit swinging from his hand. He'd left the cave immediately after *"attending to my face"*, claiming that he needed some fresh air.

Ruth paused, pen hanging in mid-air. Her hand was shaking slightly.

'I'm waiting for an answer,' Uncle Patrick declared.

Ruth licked her lips and slowly folded up the map. 'It would be easier if I showed you,' she said as she got to her feet. She refused to say anything more, insisting that we had to see for ourselves.

After ordering Will, Jake and Max to remain on guard duty Uncle Patrick indicated that the rest of us should go with Ruth. 'You want to come?' Daryl asked.

I nodded, the painkillers had reduced the throbbing in my cheek to a dull manageable ache.

Ruth steered us along a muddy track that circled the base of the mountain. We hiked across barren moorland, finally pushing our way through a low thicket of bushes to pause at the edge of a steep cliff. Ruth swallowed. 'Down there,' she said in a strained whisper.

Puzzled, I followed the others to the brink of the cliff and peered over the edge. My breath caught raggedly in my throat and I gave a strangled gasp. The beach below was littered with hundreds of broken bodies. My stomach tightened as the pungent smell of decay filled my nostrils and I sprang back in horror.

Uncle Patrick was the first to speak. 'What happened to them?' he demanded.

'Most of the people who come here aren't like you,' Ruth stammered. 'They don't hide in caves. The Watch find them and bring them here,' she waved towards the edge of the cliff. 'My mum said that there are people from our village down there too. The ones who refused

154

to leave. That's why we hide in the cellar.'

'It's barbaric,' I whispered hoarsely.

'Now do you understand why I've been pushing you so hard,' Daryl said as he gripped my upper arm. His face was pale. 'This isn't a game.'

We walked back to the cave in silence. The sombre mood that pervaded the camp even affected Will, Jake and Max, who spent the evening whispering quietly, carefully observing the rest of the group.

After dinner I didn't resist when Daryl collected the sharpened sticks and suggested that we spend the evening practising self-defence. For the first time I truly understood how high the stakes really were.

CHAPTER 18

From the Inside

MARYANN:

The day of my *"capture"* was heralded by a flurry of birdsong from outside of the cave. I'd spent a restless night tossing and turning in my sleeping bag and with the arrival of the dawn chorus I finally gave up on sleep altogether.

Not wanting to disturb the others I crept across the cave and climbed up to the lookout to where Peter and Flash were on guard duty.

'Nervous?' Peter asked, pushing a disgruntled Flash out of the way so I could sit down beside him.

'A little,' I replied, not wanting to admit that I was terrified.

'I remember after Daryl and I graduated from boot camp, we were so desperate to go out in the field, we pestered Patrick for weeks. Eventually he gave us a job delivering messages during an operation. I was so nervous that I threw up twice.'

'Lovely,' I replied with a grimace.

Peter laughed, 'I'm just saying that it's all right if you're scared. Nerves are good. It means you understand the danger.'

'I am slightly terrified,' I admitted.

'You'll be fine. You should try and locate Flo and Charlotte as soon as you arrive,' Peter advised. 'Bring them up to speed with the plan and make sure they're ready to leave. They're both going to be scared so it's up to you to reassure them and keep them calm.'

'I have to reassure myself first,' I muttered.

'You can do this, MaryAnn. I saw you practising last night with Daryl and you might not be the most elegant fighter I've seen but you did alright.'

'Thanks, I think.'

'You'll only be in the LightHouse for a few nights. All you have to do is keep out of trouble and remember that Daryl and I will be coming for you.'

I heard the echo of soft voices drift up from the cave below. 'It sounds like the others are waking up,' Peter said. 'We should go and get some breakfast. You'll feel better once you've had something to eat.'

We found the rest of the group assembled around the fire. As I took a seat Daryl handed me a mug of tea. I took a sip. It was hot and sweet, just the way I liked it.

Flash emitted a low growl as someone stumbled through the cave entrance. It was Dan. He was walking with a pronounced limp.

'What happened?' Mr Murray asked as he jumped up from the fire and hurried over to help.

'I was collecting firewood and I tripped over a damn tree root. I think I might have twisted my ankle.'

Peter unclipped a small first aid kit from his belt. 'Let me take a look,' he said. He untied Dan's boot and pulled a face at the sight of his puffy ankle. 'It looks like a pretty bad sprain,' he said. 'You'll need to stay off your feet for a while.'

'I can't do that. We have to go and get Charlotte in a couple of days.'

'Not with that ankle you won't,' Peter said in a firm voice.

Mr Murray surveyed his ankle and pursed his lips. 'Dan, you can't walk on that. You have to let Peter strap it up.'

Dan shook his head. 'I'll be fine.' He tried to pull his ankle out of Peter's grasp.

'No, it won't be fine,' Mr Murray replied.

'But she's my daughter,' Dan protested. 'She's counting on me.'

'Are you forgetting that she's my niece too?' Mr Murray replied firmly. 'I'll bring her back, I promise.'

As the day wore on I grew increasingly anxious. Lunch was a muted affair. My throat was so tight I could barely swallow any food.

After we'd cleared away the dishes it was finally time to leave. As I made my goodbyes Peter seemed excessively jovial. He reassured me that he would see me in a couple of days and surprised me by giving my hand a firm shake. For some reason I'd expected something more; a hug or an expression of regret, anything other than the handshake I received.

Daryl had volunteered to accompany me to the jetty. 'You alright?' he asked as we hurried along the path. I nodded silently, but couldn't trust myself to speak. 'You can always back out,' he said. 'There's no shame in it. Just say the word.'

His offer was very tempting, but the success of our plan depended on my capture by the Watch. I gave Daryl a weak smile. 'I'll only be gone a few days,' I said in a voice that I hoped was reassuring.

Daryl came to a halt when we arrived at a clearing close to the jetty. 'I can't go any further. You'll have to go the rest of the way on your own,' he said.

I paused apprehensively.

'You know I'll be worried about you every second you're away,' he whispered.

'I'll be worried about me every second I'm away too,' I replied. We exchanged a tight hug and I was about to turn away when he grabbed my arm and pulled me back.

'What!'

'You need to look as if you've been wandering around lost for a couple of days,' he said as he picked up a handful of mud and smeared it down the front of my shirt.

'Urgh. It smells bad,' I complained.

Daryl ignored my protests and continued to wipe mud across my face and down my neck and arms. He stepped back to survey his handiwork. 'Perfect,' he said. He wrinkled his nose in disgust, 'And you're right, you do smell bad.'

'They'd better have showers at the LightHouse,' I hissed as Daryl pushed me out of the clearing.

'Be careful,' he whispered.

When I turned back for a final reassuring glance he'd already disappeared.

I strolled purposefully towards the jetty where a large blue and white boat was anchored. I spotted a group of Watch standing beside a wooden hut and waited until one of them pointed in my direction. I turned and stumbled away. There was a shout behind me but I continued to run until a harsh voice called out, 'Stop where you are or I'll shoot you.' The threat had the desired effect and I came to an immediate halt.

I turned to find myself face to face with three Watch. Each had a gun aimed at me. I had to fight to control the panic that threatened to overwhelm me. The last time I'd been this close to the Watch I'd been handed over to the Director.

'What's your name?' one of the Watch barked. He was tall with a shaved head and penetrating blue eyes. He took a threatening step towards me as he spoke.

I gaped at him. I didn't have to pretend to be afraid. I was terrified.

'What's your name?' he repeated.

'Beth Summers,' I mumbled nervously, giving him the name on my fake identity card.

'What are you doing here?' he asked. He tried to hold my gaze but

I feigned shyness and peered down at my feet. 'What are you doing here?' he repeated, more forcefully this time. I shuffled uncomfortably but still didn't respond.

A Watch detached himself from the group and stepped towards me. 'Can't you see she's scared?' he said as he peered at me with a kindly expression. 'Honey, why don't you tell us what you're doing here?'

I took a step backward and his expression faltered for a brief instant. 'Why don't you tell me what you're doing out here?' he repeated, his kindly expression firmly back in place.

'I can't,' I stammered.

He scrutinised me for a moment. 'Take her to the shed for questioning,' he ordered.

I made a pretence of struggling as the Watch grabbed my arms, but they just gripped tighter. They dragged me to the hut where I was shown into a small windowless room. They left the room and I was alone with the kindly Watch.

He pulled out a chair. 'Take a seat,' he said. I sat down tentatively as he strode around the table, taking a seat opposite.

'Honey, I know you're hiding something. Why don't you tell me what you're doing here?'

When I didn't respond he leant across the table and brushed his fingers across the bruise on my face. 'It looks like you've had a bit of trouble,' he said. I shrank away from his touch. Cold eyes passed over me, scrutinising my face, searching for the truth. The Watch frowned. 'If you don't tell me what you're doing here I'll have no option but to call in the other Watch. If that happens things could go very badly for you.'

When I grimaced, I saw the ghost of a smile play across his face.

'Just tell me what you're doing here,' he urged.

'I can't,' I replied, feigning indecision.

'Then you leave me with no option.'

'Don't,' I squeaked.

'Then answer my question. What are you doing here?' he demanded.

I paused like I was about to make an important decision. 'You promise you won't let them hurt me?' I asked.

'Of course. You have my word.'

'I was with my parents. They went out hunting and didn't come back. I don't know where they are.'

'What are your parents doing all the way out here?' he asked.

'We had to leave our Community,' I stammered.

'Why? Did your parents do something wrong? Are they criminals?'

'No, they're not criminals,' I protested.

'Then why did they leave your Community?'

'It was because of me,' my voice wavered. 'They had to leave because I'm Immune.'

My confession had the desired impact. The Watch leant forward, searching my face looking for any indication that I might be lying. 'You're Immune?'

I nodded miserably. There was the clatter of wood as the Watch jumped to his feet. 'Wait here,' he ordered, as the door slammed loudly behind him.

When the Watch returned a few moments later, he was carrying a small box. He opened it and pulled out a syringe. 'I need to take a sample of your blood,' he said.

I rolled up my sleeve and winced as the needle pinched my skin.

When the syringe was full the Watch pulled it out of my arm and placed it back in the box. 'I'm going to test this,' he said as he left the room.

I padded over to the door and as I pressed my ear against the wood I could make out voices on the other side. 'If the feral's telling the truth then there could be a nice bonus in this for us.' The Watch's voice was no longer kindly; it had a hard ruthless edge to it.

'How long before we know the results?' another voice said.

'About two minutes, I'm just processing the blood now.'

I returned to my seat and waited for the Watch. When he re-entered the room a few moments later I could detect a greedy glint in his eye. 'The test shows that you're telling the truth. You are Immune,' he said.

'What will happen to me now?' I asked.

'We're going to take you to the LightHouse.'

I cringed, 'No, you can't. I have to find my parents. They'll be worried about me.'

'You don't need to be concerned about your parents anymore, you've been given a great opportunity to serve the Light.' He was interrupted by a knock at the door. The blue-eyed Watch entered.

'The boat's ready to leave,' he said.

'Good, you can take her away.'

The boat docked on the island and I stepped onto the beach under the inquisitive gaze of a group on onlookers. Strangely it looked as if they were collecting rocks. I surveyed each person in turn, hoping to identify Charlotte or Flo, but I couldn't spot them among the crowd.

I followed the Watch up the cliff and along a narrow path until we arrived in the courtyard of an imposing grey building. After stepping through the HealthScan I was greeted by a skeletal woman who introduced herself as the Warden. She escorted me to a room where I was searched by an androgynous-looking servant that she referred to as a Trustee.

Next I was taken to the showers. It had been a long time since I'd enjoyed a proper shower so I luxuriated in the warm water. I wasn't expecting the chem rinse that followed and I gagged with shock as the noxious liquid sprayed over me. I'd forgotten how horrible it could be.

After the indignity of the shower I was handed new clothes; a pair of scratchy red trousers and a shirt. I was also given a pair of gloves. I pulled at them absent-mindedly as the Warden escorted me down a long corridor. They felt tight and uncomfortable.

The Warden guided me to the dining hall where she apologised for the brevity of the tour. She explained that it was quite unusual for someone to arrive at the LightHouse unannounced and she hadn't had time to make the appropriate arrangements. She called out to a plump, red-headed girl who had followed us into the dining hall, 'Bekka, this is Beth. She's a new arrival. I'm releasing her into your care. Please familiarise her with the rules. I'll hold you responsible for any indiscretions.' The red-headed girl looked a little startled and peered at me curiously. 'I'll leave you to get better acquainted,' the Warden said.

'Why do I have to babysit the newbie, it's so unfair,' Bekka moaned as the Warden left the room. I was slightly underwhelmed by her welcome.

Bekka led me over to the counter and showed me how to use my new identity card to get dinner. As we sat down to eat I noticed that she was observing me curiously.

'Is there something wrong?' I asked.

She shrugged, 'You're the first person who's arrived here on their own. Didn't they collect anyone else from your Community?'

'I wasn't taken from a Community,' I said. 'I was on the run with my parents, but the Watch captured me.' I wasn't sure whether I could trust Bekka so I stuck to my cover story.

'That's bad luck,' she said sympathetically.

I took a mouthful of food and chewed it carefully. It reminded me of the Neighbourhood.

We were joined at the table by Bekka's friends, two blonde-haired girls, Clara and Robyn, and a pair of twins, Megan and Marissa. They also expressed surprise when she explained that I'd been picked up by the Watch while trying to escape. It seems that my arrival really was quite unusual.

As I feigned interest in Bekka's conversation I peered curiously around the dining hall hoping to identify Charlotte or Flo. I caught a glimpse of pink hair at a table a few rows in front. It had to be Flo! She was chatting animatedly to a girl who bore such a strong resemblance to Mr Murray that it could only be Charlotte. I smiled at my good fortune. If Charlotte and Flo were already friends it would be so much easier to make contact with them.

A siren sounded and I watched as the two girls got up to leave the room. I could see that Charlotte favoured her uncle in stature as well as looks; she towered above the petite Flo. The girls were accompanied by two boys; one skinny and ginger, the other dark -haired and insolent looking.

Bekka got up from the table and told me that I had to follow her to the common room for leisure time.

Flo and Charlotte were already in the common room when I arrived. They were sprawled across a sofa chatting animatedly with the two boys. I was disappointed when Bekka headed to a table on the other side of the room to join the twins in a game of cards. It seemed that Bekka was taking her mentoring duties very seriously and wasn't going to let me out of her sight.

When the siren sounded I followed Bekka along a winding corridor until we arrived at our bedroom, or dorm as she referred to it. I was delighted to find that I'd been assigned to the same room as Charlotte and Flo. What a stroke of good luck.

There was a bag on my bed and I opened it to find a pair of pyjamas, a toothbrush and some soap.

As I changed into my pyjamas I quietly watched Flo, curious to learn as much as I could about the girl that Daryl cared so much about.

Flo caught me staring at her and she gave me a warm smile. 'You okay?' she asked.

I nodded shyly in response.

'It can be a little bit scary in here at first,' she said as she yawned widely, 'but you'll get used to it.' She climbed into bed. 'I'm here if you need a friend to talk to.'

A siren blared and I bolted upright. For a moment I stared around in confusion, then I heard the other girls and realised I was no longer in the caves, I was a prisoner in the LightHouse.

Bekka escorted me to the showers and then insisted that I sit with her at breakfast. Charlotte and Flo joined us at the table, accompanied by the two boys, who they introduced as Mally and Eric. I didn't get the opportunity to speak to them in private until later in the day when we shared a work task in the laundry. As we fed bed sheets into a washing machine I peered around the room to check that we couldn't be overheard.

'Can we talk?' I whispered, my voice barely audible above the clanking machine.

Charlotte and Flo both stared at me curiously, but didn't respond.

'Can anyone hear us?' I urged.

The girls exchanged a nervous glance. 'I don't think so,' Flo said.

'That's good,' I replied. 'My name isn't really Beth,' I said. 'It's MaryAnn Hunter and I'm here to rescue you.' I almost giggled. I sounded like one of the heroes from the films that Peter and Daryl liked to watch.

The girls gaped at me in shock. Charlotte's eyes were as round as saucers. 'Rescue us?' she whispered uncertainly.

'Mr Murray sent me.'

She looked puzzled. 'Your Uncle Ethan,' I corrected. 'He's here with your father.'

'My dad's here?' she squeaked loudly and peered around the laundry as if she expected him to jump out of one of the washing machines.

I made a hushing noise. 'He's not here in the LightHouse. He's on the mainland,' I explained. 'But we have a plan to rescue you.'

Charlotte's face broke into a wide grin. 'My dad and Uncle Ethan are here,' she giggled excitedly.

'What about my mam and dad, are they on the mainland too?' Flo asked.

'No, but my brother is.'

'Your brother!' there was a flicker of recognition. 'Hunter,' she whispered excitedly. 'You said your last name was Hunter. Is Daryl your brother?'

I nodded. 'Your mum and dad wanted to come with us, but they had to stay behind with the Union.'

'You're a Unionist?' Charlotte breathed.

'No, not really,' I replied. When she looked confused I added, 'Well, sort of...I suppose. My brother and uncle are.'

'The Union are going to rescue us.' Charlotte pulled Flo into a hug and then to my surprise and slight unease she grabbed me and hugged me too.

'Charlotte,' Flo warned, 'you need to calm down. The Trustees might hear you.'

'How can you expect me to be calm,' Charlotte hissed excitedly. 'My dad and Uncle Ethan are on the mainland waiting for me. They're going to get us out of here.'

'Charlotte, take a few deep breaths,' Flo urged. She turned to me, 'I assume you have a plan?'

'We need to leave in a couple of days. The rescue is organised for the first night of the new moon. Mr Murray, Charlotte's uncle, will disable the HealthScan and meet us outside. He'll have a boat waiting to take us to the mainland.'

'I can't wait to tell Eric and Mally,' Charlotte said. 'They'll be so excited.'

I shook my head. 'I'm sorry, I'm only here for you two. We can't take anyone else with us.'

Flo's face grew hard. 'I won't leave them behind. They're our friends.'

'We only have a small rowing boat,' I explained.

Flo shook her head determinedly. 'I'm not going without them.'

'We can't leave them,' Charlotte added.

'The Trustees know we're friends,' Flo said. 'If we escape they'll think they know something about it. They'll get into trouble.'

I sighed in frustration. I wasn't sure how I was going to explain the two additional escapees when we arrived at the rendezvous.

CHAPTER 19

New Hope

CHARLOTTE

It was another warm afternoon without a cloud in the sky. The chickens scratched around pecking at loose bits of corn as I collected the eggs from the henhouse and carefully placed them into my basket. I counted twenty, holding each of them in turn, enjoying the warmth as I cupped them in my hand. The eggs reminded me of the stones Dad would warm by the fire when we went out foraging in the winter. He'd wrap them in thick fleece material and slip them into my gloves to keep my hands warm.

Working in the chicken shed was usually my favourite task because it reminded me of home, but today I had another reason to be happy. The new girl, Beth, or MaryAnn, as she said her real name was, had come to rescue us. When she'd arrived at the LightHouse with her face swollen and bruised I'd been a little bit scared of her, but she said she was a Unionist like my Uncle Ethan.

'Charlotte, have you finished with the eggs?'

I jumped. It was Mally and Eric.

I held out the basket of eggs with a wide grin. 'All done.'

'You seem very happy this morning,' Mally said as he took the basket from my outstretched hand.

'Why wouldn't I be happy?' I dropped my voice to a whisper. 'We're going to be rescued. We're going home.'

When we'd met up in the common room the previous evening Flo and I had taken Mally and Eric aside and told them about the escape plan.

Mally and Eric shared a brief glance. 'What's the matter?' I asked.

Eric thrust his hands into his pockets. 'You think she's telling the truth, this girl, Beth or MaryAnn, or whatever her name is?'

I nodded enthusiastically. 'Don't you?'

He pulled a face. 'I really want to believe her, but I've never heard of anyone escaping from the LightHouse.'

Mally sighed. 'Neither have I.'

'But she's in the Union. They wouldn't have come all this way if they didn't think they could rescue us.'

'That's the other thing,' Eric said. 'If the Union really could rescue people from the LightHouse why haven't they done it before? What makes us so special?'

'It's because of my Uncle Ethan. He must have convinced them to help us.'

'I want to believe her,' Mally said.

'But you don't?' I queried.

'I'm worried that the Trustees are playing a trick on us and that this is another one of their mind games,' Eric replied.

'What do you mean mind games?' I asked.

'The Trustees are always messing with our heads,' Eric said. 'This could be just another cruel trick.'

I frowned. 'The Trustees are horrible,' I said, remembering the time I'd been attacked in the toilets, 'but I don't understand how they can mess with our heads.'

'You've seen the way that Amber and Green population behave at evening assembly; like they're robots or something. It's weird right?'

I shrugged, 'I suppose so.'

'Well something must happen to make them like that. I think that whatever it is starts in Red population. That's why the Trustees work us so hard and make us sit through evening assemblies so we don't get enough sleep and we're tired all the time. They're messing with our heads.'

'I'm still not sure I understand,' I said.

'Do you remember when the Warden came into the dining hall and said there wouldn't be an evening assembly because we needed our rest and we'd worked hard to prove our devotion to the Light?'

I nodded. 'I'd been so exhausted that day. I could still remember how happy I'd felt to get a full night's sleep.'

'I bet you felt really grateful didn't you.'

I blushed, remembering the rush of love I'd felt for the Warden.

'Don't worry. You're not weird,' Eric said. 'I felt the same way too. What about you Mally?'

Mally thought for a moment, 'I wanted to hug her. I was so happy.'

'That's what got me thinking,' Eric said. 'It was like when my dad hit my mum. He'd do something really nice afterwards; buy her a present or cook tea and she'd be so grateful that she'd forgive him. It's how people like that work. They mess with your head; beat you down until you feel worthless and then you'll do anything to please them.'

Mally shuddered. 'So you think we'll end up like Amber and Green population if we stay here?' he asked.

'Exactly,' Eric said. 'Haven't you ever wondered why Delta don't try to escape from the Neighbourhood? They're not under guard. So why don't they just sneak over the Boundary? Something must happen to make them want to stay.'

'I still don't understand what this has got to do with MaryAnn?' I questioned. The idea of being brainwashed was disturbing, but why did it make Eric suspicious of MaryAnn?

'Maybe she's working for the Light and it's all a trick, giving us hope, when there is none.'

I shook my head. 'I don't believe that. I think she's telling the truth. MaryAnn said that my dad and Uncle Ethan are on the mainland. How would she know that? You know how good a tracker my dad is. He must have followed us here.'

'I hope you're right,' Eric said, 'for all our sakes.'

'I am,' I replied with as much conviction as I could muster. 'If anyone can rescue us from the LightHouse my dad and Uncle Ethan can.'

CHAPTER 20

The Return of the Director

MaryAnn

The morning assembly buzzed with excitement as the Warden clapped her hands and ordered everyone to be quiet. I stared at her in horror as I tried to make sense of the announcement she'd just made. The Director, the monster who had imprisoned and tortured me, would be arriving at the LightHouse tomorrow.

I jumped in alarm as I felt a light pressure on my arm. 'Are you alright?' Charlotte whispered.

I nodded. The movement had a dreamlike quality, the room receding at an alarming rate.

'You look awful,' Charlotte murmured.

I clasped a hand to my mouth, fighting an overwhelming urge to throw up.

'You're really pale,' Charlotte whispered, her eyes searching my face anxiously. 'If something's wrong, you can tell me.'

I studied her for a moment. How could I confide in someone I barely knew? She touched my arm again and something in the kindness of the gesture reminded me of Mr Murray.

'I know the Director,' I murmured quietly, making sure no-one else could overhear.

Her eyes widened in surprise. 'You know the Director?'

'He was my guardian after my parents died.'

'Your guardian,' she stammered. 'You lived with the Director?'

'For a while.'

'You're from the Neighbourhood. You're not an Echo?'

I shook my head. 'I'm Alpha.'

'Alpha?' Charlotte gasped a little too loudly.

'Shush, not so loud.' I glanced around nervously in case anyone had overheard, but despite the Warden's best efforts the room still buzzed with excitement.

'I never met an Alpha before,' she whispered.

'Well technically I'm not an Alpha anymore. I live on the Outside with the Union.'

'What will happen if the Director finds you here?'

'He'll take me back to the Neighbourhood…' I couldn't finish the sentence. What would come next was too awful to contemplate.

'We can't let that happen. We have to tell the others.'

I shook my head vehemently. She clearly didn't understand the danger the Director posed.

'They'll want to help,' she coaxed.

The siren signalled the end of assembly and the Warden ordered us all to stand.

'We'll speak to them this evening in the common room,' Charlotte whispered as we filed out of the room.

I arrived at the common room to find the others waiting for me. They watched in quiet anticipation as I took a seat at the table. 'Charlotte told you about the Director?' I sighed.

'She said that he knows you?' Flo questioned.

Eric's eyes narrowed suspiciously. 'She told us that you used to live in the Neighbourhood.'

'He was my guardian after my parents died,' I replied.

'You told us you were a Unionist,' Eric accused.

'I live with my brother and uncle now and they're both Unionists.'

'So you expect us to believe that you left your comfortable life in the Neighbourhood to join the Union,' Eric sneered.

'Eric,' Charlotte reproached, 'why are you being so mean?'

Eric turned to Charlotte. 'I'm just trying to get to the bottom of this. She,' he pointed a finger accusingly at me, 'hasn't exactly been truthful with us has she? What if she's been sent to spy on us?'

'Why would I want to spy on you?' I protested.

'I don't know, maybe you're reporting back to the Warden. You could be working for the Light.'

'I am not working for the Light,' I hissed.

'I believe her,' Flo said.

Eric rounded on her. 'You know her brother. Did he tell you he was from the Neighbourhood?'

Flo nodded. 'He told me he was born there, but now he lives on the Outside.'

'So you knew that MaryAnn was from the Neighbourhood?' Eric snapped.

'Yes I guessed she must have lived there with Daryl,' she replied quietly.

'...and you didn't think to mention it?' he questioned.

'Daryl doesn't like to talk about it so I assumed MaryAnn felt the same.'

'So you didn't mention that MaryAnn was best buddies with the Director because you were worried about embarrassing her! That's just great Flo.'

I was outraged by Eric's comment. 'Don't you ever say that to me again,' I hissed through gritted teeth. 'I am not best buddies with the Director. He's a monster. The last time I saw him I was strapped to a chair and he was slicing my arms to pieces.'

My comment seemed to grab Eric's attention. 'How do we know

you're telling the truth?' he challenged.

'Take a look,' I pushed up the sleeve of my shirt to where a ribbon of thin white scars was still visible against the skin. 'Is that enough evidence for you?' I said as I thrust my arm across the table.

He leant towards me and for a brief moment I thought he was actually going to touch the scars. He withdrew his hand at the last minute and dropped it down into his lap. I watched as the anger and accusation drained from his face.

'If what you say is true.'

'It is true,' I snapped.

'What will the Director do if he finds you here in the LightHouse?' Eric challenged.

'He'll take me back to the Neighbourhood.' I swallowed hard.

'We won't be able to escape,' Mally said.

'Of course you will. It won't stop the Union coming for you.'

'Are you sure?' Eric questioned. 'If they see the Director they might abandon the rescue.'

Charlotte stared at him in horror. 'They wouldn't do that would they?'

'Your uncle won't leave you here,' I said. 'Daryl wouldn't abandon you either,' I reassured Flo.

'It doesn't matter,' Flo replied, 'we're not leaving without you. You risked your life to rescue us.' Charlotte nodded in agreement.

'You can't protect me from the Director,' I said. 'Once he finds me, there's nothing you can do. He'll take me back to the Neighbourhood.'

'Then we just have to make sure he doesn't find you,' there was a determined set to Flo's face. 'No arguments,' she said as I opened my mouth to protest, 'we're going to do this.'

Eric studied me for a moment; there was a wicked glint in his eye. He smirked. 'I never did like the look of that slimy Director, with his shiny hair and white teeth. Consider me part of your protection detail.'

I spent a restless night, my nerves on edge, too scared to sleep in case I woke the others with a nightmare.

The morning passed in a blur. I joined the others for a subdued lunch and once we'd eaten and the food had been cleared away a Trustee arrived to escort us to the assembly hall. I approached the room with a feeling of trepidation. The others gathered around me, offering their protection, but I'd never felt so exposed in my whole life.

Green and Amber population were already seated at the front of the hall when we arrived. The Trustee ordered Red population to fill up the back rows and we quietly filed into our seats. I could feel the anticipation build as the Warden took her place at the podium. She clapped her hands. 'Residents. I've been informed that the Director has arrived and will be here in a few moments. As a special treat he has brought his daughter with him.'

My heart sank. The Director *and* Maud! The news couldn't be worse.

I heard a commotion in the corridor. The moment I'd been dreading had finally arrived. I took a deep breath and waited with nervous anticipation as the doors to the assembly hall swung open. The Watch entered first and lined the hall. Next the Director appeared. He strode confidently into the room, closely followed by Maud. I could sense her discomfort as she followed her father to the stage, her head bowed, hands clawing nervously at a yellow cardigan.

As the Director and Maud climbed up to the podium I nestled deeper into my seat wanting to make myself invisible.

The Director greeted the Warden with a small bow. 'Good health and wellbeing,' he said.

The Warden returned the bow. 'In the Light we trust.' She turned to face the audience. 'Residents, I would like to present to you our esteemed patron, the Director of the Manchester Neighbourhood, and his daughter Maud.'

The Director surveyed the crowd with a warm smile. 'Residents,' he began. 'It is an honour to be invited here today to meet you and to see first-hand some of the great work being undertaken by the Warden and her team of hard working Trustees.' He flashed the Warden a warm smile and she flushed crimson, running a nervous hand across her immaculately groomed hair.

'It's a pleasure to meet the future of our Neighbourhood,' he paused and spread his hands wide indicating the audience. 'Many of you have a long road ahead of you but we fully expect you to flourish under the expert tuition of the Warden and her Trustees. I urge you to make the most of your time at the LightHouse. Listen to the Warden and let her team guide you until we are ready to welcome you into our glorious Neighbourhood.'

His speech was greeted with rapturous applause from the Warden and her Trustees. Amber and Green population joined in wholeheartedly. Red population clapped politely but I noticed a number of amused glances. As the applause died down I was taken by surprise when the Warden asked if anyone had a question for the Director. Four hands, two Green and two Amber, shot into the air. The action was so effortlessly choreographed that it almost seemed rehearsed.

The Director turned to the first volunteer, a girl from Amber population. She jumped eagerly to her feet and asked what we could expect when we arrived at the Neighbourhood.

The Director smiled warmly in response. 'That's a very good question. Once you've successfully completed your residency at the LightHouse you will be taken to the Neighbourhood, where we will help you integrate into your new environment. We expect everyone to contribute to the success of our Select Neighbourhoods Project so the Light will provide you with an appropriate job and a place to live.'

The girl gave a nod of thanks before retaking her seat.

The Warden pointed to a blonde-haired boy from Green population. 'You next.'

'What type of work will we be doing in the Neighbourhood?' The boy was so nervous his question came out as a squeak.

The Director flashed him an indulgent smile. 'You're really testing me with your questions today,' he stroked his chin, considering his response before he continued. 'Towards the end of your stay at the LightHouse you will undergo a series of aptitude tests. The tests will be used to better understand the type of work you are suited to. Some of you will be given jobs with an Alpha family as a maid or a butler. Others will assist some of our Bravo population, working as health care assistants or administrators. Some of you might even be given interesting jobs in our food processing plant. Whatever your skills, we will ensure that there is a stimulating and exciting position waiting for you in the Neighbourhood.'

The next volunteer stood up so quickly that she almost knocked over her chair. This provoked a few stifled giggles from the Red population.

'What's it like living in the Neighbourhood?' the girl stammered.

'That's a very good question,' the Director responded warmly, 'and very brave of you to ask me something that I'm sure every other person in the room is thinking. You'll find that the Neighbourhood is a wonderful place to live. You will have a warm place to stay with electricity and running water and as much food as you can eat.'

The final volunteer got to his feet and asked another insipid question that allowed the Director to extol the virtues of the Neighbourhood. I tuned out the response and instead studied the Director as he held court over his audience. He was relaxed and completely at ease. In stark contrast Maud appeared terrified as she remained timidly in the background, hands clasped tightly across her stomach, her head bowed to the floor.

With the questions over the Director thanked the assembly for taking the time to listen to the *"ramblings of an old man"*. His attempt at humility caused the Warden to reassure him with an effusive gesture of her hand that his words of wisdom had resonated with every Resident in the LightHouse.

The Director informed us that he had enjoyed his visit so much that he personally wanted to thank each and every one of us for our devotion to the Light. I watched with trepidation as he surveyed the crowd, taking the time to nod and smile at each Resident. He really was going to thank each of us in turn. He moved through the first row and I shrank deeper into my seat, fighting an overwhelming urge to flee.

'Oh no!' I heard Charlotte mutter as she grasped awkwardly for my hand. Instinctively I pushed it away. I didn't want her to be guilty by association.

Unexpectedly a red arm shot into the air. The Director pulled his gaze away from the audience and turned towards Eric. His brow furrowed as he gave the Warden a puzzled glance.

'Resident, the questions are over,' the Warden snapped.

'That's not fair, Amber and Green population had a chance to ask a question. What about Red population?' Eric protested.

A shockwave echoed through the audience.

'I said that there will be no more questions,' the Warden's words were clipped.

'Our esteemed Director claims that the Light is waiting to welcome all of us to the Neighbourhood. Surely Red population should have the opportunity to ask a question as well?'

There was no mistaking the sneer in Eric's voice. For a moment I was confused by his behaviour. Then, horrified, I realised what was happening, he was sacrificing himself for me.

The Warden's face contorted with unconstrained fury as she signalled to the Trustees.

'Doesn't anyone want to hear my question?' Eric demanded as

he jumped to his feet and pushed his way down the row of seats towards the advancing Trustees. I watched in horror as he disappeared beneath a scrum of brown cloth.

The room was in a state of chaos. The Trustees hauled Eric to his feet, dragging him towards the door, he struggled, breaking free from their grasp. With a single bound he leapt onto a chair. 'Power to the Union,' he yelled above the fracas, punching a solitary fist into the air. His actions provoked outraged gasps from the Residents. A Watch roared loudly and pulled him down from the chair. I saw a flash of wood and Eric yelled, clasping a hand to his forehead as blood leaked through his fingers.

I couldn't be a spectator in this horror. I wouldn't let Eric sacrifice himself for me. It was too much to ask.

Unexpectedly Charlotte put a restraining hand on my chest, pushing me back into my seat. 'He did this for you. Don't let his sacrifice be for nothing,' she murmured. The hand she used to restrain me was shaking uncontrollably.

Assisted by the Watch the Trustees grabbed Eric's arms and legs and hauled him from the room. As the doors closed I heard him yell, 'Look after my sisters,' before he disappeared from view.

With Eric gone the clamour in the room died down immediately, to be replaced by an uneasy silence. I struggled to breathe, battling a peculiar mix of guilt and gratitude. In sacrificing himself Eric had given us the chance to escape, but at what cost to his own wellbeing?

A cold shiver of dread coursed through me and with a shudder I stole a glance towards the podium. My heart skipped a beat as I caught myself staring into a pair of familiar blue eyes. I watched as a range of emotions played across the Director's face before his eyes narrowed into serpent-like slits. Maud followed her father's gaze out into the audience. At first her face registered shock but this quickly hardened into a look of unfettered hatred. 'Oh no,' I heard Charlotte murmur. 'Oh no.'

Blood pounded in my ears and I gripped the arms of my chair, willing myself not to faint. I inhaled sharply, the noise cutting through the stillness of the room. I was aware that every face was turned towards me, a sea of bewilderment.

The Warden gave the Director a puzzled glance before turning to the crowd. 'You will go back to your dorms immediately and remain there until further notice.'

A Trustee escorted us back to the dorm. We followed in silence, too scared to speak.

Once inside the room Flo collapsed onto her bed. 'Did you see the look on the Warden's face? She's going to kill him,' she sobbed.

'I'm so sorry,' I exclaimed. 'This is all my fault.' Eric's sacrifice had been for nothing. The Director was coming for me.

Tears streamed down Flo's face as she shook her head, 'It's not your fault,' she sobbed, 'we all agreed to protect you.'

Flo was wrong. It was my fault. I was supposed to rescue them, not put them in danger. I lowered myself onto the trunk at the end of Flo's bed. 'The Director is going to come for me,' I said. 'You have to let him take me.'

'Why is the Director coming for you?' Bekka extracted herself from the other girls and strode towards Flo's bed.

'We can't let him take you,' Charlotte replied, ignoring Bekka's question.

I stared at Charlotte determinedly, I couldn't let her see how frightened I was. 'You don't have a choice,' I said. 'You and Flo have to keep out of this. I won't let him hurt you too.'

'Oi, will you stop ignoring me and tell me what's going on?' Bekka demanded. 'How does Beth know the Director?'

Before I was able to respond I heard the heavy thud of footsteps in the corridor outside. With my heart in my mouth I watched as the door opened and I came face to face with the Director.

The charming, genial man from the assembly had transformed into something sinister, the air around him seemed to crackle with untold menace. I could feel the other girls in the room instinctively shrink away from him.

As the Director strode towards me I caught sight of Maud framed in the doorway. She made no attempt to enter the room but instead observed me impassively through cold eyes.

Sweat prickled at the back of my neck, threading its way down the length of my spine. This was a scene from one of the many nightmares I'd had since I'd escaped from the Neighbourhood.

'My darling,' the Director murmured softly, 'we've been so worried about you.' He surprised me by grabbing my shoulders and holding me at arm's length. I cringed at his touch.

'What have they done to you?' he asked sadly as his eyes searched every inch of my face.

'She's in shock,' the Director informed the Watch. 'We need to get her home straight away.' He placed a hand under my chin and peered into my eyes. 'You'd like that wouldn't you MaryAnn? To go home to the Neighbourhood where Maud and I can take care of you? Your room is waiting for you. It's just as you left it.' My knees nearly collapsed under me as I remembered the metal chair.

'MaryAnn!' I heard Bekka squeak. 'That's not her name. She's called Beth.'

The Director turned to Bekka. 'Are you her friend?' he asked.

After a moment's hesitation she nodded uncertainly.

'I'm MaryAnn's guardian, she's like a daughter to me.' He stroked a finger across my cheek. I closed my eyes and swallowed. 'Thank you for taking such good care of her.'

'You're her guardian?' Bekka whispered faintly. She gave me an uncertain look.

'We thought we'd lost her. Maud and I had given up hope of ever seeing her again. We were so worried.' He placed a protective arm around my shoulder. 'Come on,' he said softly, 'it's time to go home.' I gave Charlotte and Flo a final desperate glance as I was escorted from the room.

CHAPTER 21

Escape Plan

CHARLOTTE:

I watched with horror as the Director led MaryAnn from the dorm.

'What was THAT all about?' Bekka hissed as the door closed behind them.

I knelt down beside Flo's bed. 'What are we going to do?' I whispered. I was close to tears. We'd lost Eric and now MaryAnn was gone too.

'I don't know,' Flo murmured, her voice hoarse from crying.

'Did you see how scared she was?' I said. 'We can't let the Director take her back to the Neighbourhood.'

Bekka took an impatient step towards the bed. 'Will someone tell me what's going on?' she demanded.

'Not now Bekka.' Flo waved her away impatiently.

'Yes now,' she replied in a firm voice. 'Tell me what's going on.'

Clara extracted herself from the huddle of girls. 'Bekka, this has nothing to do with you. We should keep out of it.'

'The Director just came into our dorm and took Beth or MaryAnn... or whatever she's called and you don't think that's strange?'

'He said he's her guardian. He can do what he wants,' Clara protested. 'It's got nothing to do with us.'

'Nothing to do with us!' Bekka's nose wrinkled with disgust. 'What was she doing here in the LightHouse in the first place, why wasn't she in the Neighbourhood? None of this makes any sense.'

'Bekka stay out of this, otherwise you'll just ruin it for everyone.'

'What exactly am I going to ruin?' Bekka challenged Clara.

'You heard the Director. He thinks we're special. We've been chosen to live in the Neighbourhood.'

Bekka barked out a humourless laugh. 'Don't tell me you're starting to believe all of that crap. We aren't special, we're slaves.'

Clara took a step back, hands raised as if fending off an attack. 'You're crazy. Whatever's going on I don't want to be part of it.'

'You all agree with Clara?' Bekka addressed the other girls. They each responded with a silent nod.

'Then it looks like I'm with you,' Bekka said as she took a seat at the foot of Flo's bed.

Clara hesitated for a moment and then guided the other girls to a bed in the farthest corner of the room.

'You have to tell me what's going on,' Bekka demanded, her eyes fixed firmly on Flo and me.

I glanced at Flo, raising an enquiring eyebrow.

'We have to trust her,' Flo replied.

'Of course you have to trust me,' Bekka exclaimed as she peered across the room, 'I've just lost all of my friends.'

In quiet whispers Flo and I told Bekka everything. Her face lit up when we explained about the rescue.

'You're telling me that we could get out of here,' she whispered joyfully. 'That I could go home?'

'The problem is we're supposed to leave tonight but the Director has MaryAnn and Eric,' Flo explained.

'Then we have to rescue them,' Bekka said. 'I bet the Director took them to Detention.'

'What if they've already taken MaryAnn to the Neighbourhood?'

Flo replied.

Bekka shook her head, 'I was cleaning the kitchens this morning and the cook was busy preparing a special dinner for the Director. I bet he won't leave until he's eaten.'

'If we're going to try and rescue them we can't do anything until tonight,' Flo said. 'Not until after everyone's gone to sleep.'

We were released from the dorm at teatime and a Trustee arrived to escort us to the dining hall. We found Mally already seated at one of the tables. 'The Director took MaryAnn,' I whispered as I slipped into the seat beside him.

Mally's face fell. 'Oh no! What are we going to do now?'

'You have to be ready after lights out,' I said. 'We're going to look for her. We're going to rescue Eric too.'

'How are we going to do that?' Mally queried.

'Bekka thinks they might have been taken to Detention,' I said.

'Bekka! What has she got to do with this?'

'It's a long story,' I replied, 'but we can trust her. She's coming with us.'

'What about the other girls in your dorm?' he asked.

I shook my head. 'We can't trust them.'

I climbed into bed fully clothed and waited anxiously for the other girls to fall asleep. The room quieted and quickly filled with the sound of rhythmic breathing. Flo slipped out of bed and Bekka and I immediately followed.

We padded across the room, taking care not to wake the others. Once in the corridor we headed to the boys' dorm, Bekka rapped lightly on the door and Mally exited immediately.

'Let's go to Detention,' Flo whispered.

We stole along the corridor, making our way stealthily towards Detention. When we arrived at an intersection I felt Mally stiffen beside me. 'I think there's someone coming,' his eyes widened with fear.

'Crap, crap, crap,' Bekka muttered frantically.

I scanned the corridor. There was nowhere to hide. 'What are we going to do?' I whispered.

Flo took a deep breath. 'We're going to have to take them out,' she hissed savagely. 'We don't have any choice,' she said when I stared at her in horror. 'Unless you want the Trustees to capture us?'

'Okay, we can do this,' Bekka said. I detected an edge of excitement in her voice.

'When they arrive at the intersection we're going to have to jump them,' Flo said. 'Once they're on the floor we have to make sure they don't get back up again.'

I inhaled deeply, preparing myself for the fight. I'd learnt some self-defence from Mum and Dad, but I wasn't sure I had the skills to take on the Trustees.

'Ready,' Flo breathed as the tap of footsteps on the stone floor drew closer. My breath caught raggedly in my chest.

'Let's go,' Flo hissed as the footsteps reached the intersection. She leapt cat like from her position in the corridor and as we followed her lead I caught a flash of grey. I sucked in a cry of surprise. We weren't fighting the Trustees, we were fighting the Watch and we were about to die.

I kicked the Watch hard in the shin and heard him utter a low cry. For a brief moment the sound gave me hope. We'd taken the Watch by surprise. Maybe we had a chance after all.

My optimism was extinguished moments later as I was grabbed from behind and I felt a pair of strong arms crush the air from my lungs. Gasping for breath I struggled against my attacker but he wouldn't let go. As the edges of my vision began to blur I saw a large bear of a man grab hold of both Mally and Bekka. The man glanced in my direction and I found myself staring into a pair of familiar brown eyes.

'Uncle Ethan,' I rasped in a strangled voice. My uncle's eyes widened with surprise. 'Charlotte!'

'It's Charlotte. It's my niece. Let her go,' he cried. I felt the arm around me tense and then relax. I dropped to my knees.

My uncle still had a tight grip of Mally and Bekka, who were red faced and choking.

'Uncle Ethan, can you let my friends go?' He glanced down in surprise and immediately loosened his grip. Mally and Bekka joined me on the floor sucking in air.

Without warning I was hoisted off the ground and enveloped in a familiar bear hug. 'I've never been so happy to see anyone in my whole life,' Uncle Ethan breathed as he squashed the remaining air out of my lungs. He dropped me back onto the ground. 'I hope Peter didn't hurt you?'

'I'm fine,' I replied.

'That was a pretty impressive kick you gave your uncle,' Peter smiled. 'He'll have a nice bruise to show your dad when we get back to the mainland.' Peter offered Flo a hand and pulled her up from the floor. 'Glad to see you Flo, hope I didn't hurt you.'

'What's a couple of bruised ribs between friends?' she grimaced.

'Do you two know each other?' I asked.

'He's Daryl's friend,' she replied. She scanned the corridor, 'Is Daryl with you?' she asked.

Peter shook his head. 'No, he's waiting for us outside.'

Bekka gave Peter and Uncle Ethan an appraising glance. 'Why are you both dressed like the Watch?' she asked.

'We saw the Director arrive at the jetty earlier today. We were afraid that he'd recognise MaryAnn so we decided to change our plan and come in and get you. We got these courtesy of the Watch guarding the front of the LightHouse.'

'The Director did recognise MaryAnn,' Flo said. 'He took her away.'

Peter uttered a curse.

'Do you know where he took her?' Mr Murray asked.

'We think she might be in Detention. We were on our way to find her,' Flo said.

'Can you take us there?' Peter asked.

'It's this way,' Flo replied. 'Follow me.'

As we approached the stairs to Detention, Mally hesitated. 'They usually have a Trustee guarding the cells,' he whispered.

'Right, we'll take care of that,' Peter said. 'Stay here.'

Uncle Ethan and Peter crept down the stairs and through the door at the bottom. I heard muffled voices coming from inside, followed by a loud thud and a strangled yell. A few moments later Peter appeared at the door and beckoned us inside. 'It's all clear,' he said.

I entered Detention and was immediately engulfed in a wall of noise. I spotted a Trustee slumped in a chair.

'Someone turn off that racket,' Uncle Ethan ordered.

Mally edged his way around the unconscious Trustee and flicked a switch on the wall. Instantly the room was bathed in blissful silence.

'That's better, I couldn't hear myself think,' Peter grumbled.

'Peter, is that you?' MaryAnn leapt up from a bed in one of the cells.

'The one and only,' Peter said as he reached for her hand through the metal bars, 'are you alright?' She grasped his hand, gripping it tightly.

'Did they hurt you?' he asked.

She shook her head. 'Not yet.'

'Let me get you out of there.' Peter withdrew his hand and bent down beside the lock. He unclipped a pouch at his belt and pulled out a long thin key. He inserted it into the lock.

'Is there a problem?' Uncle Ethan asked as Peter played with the lock.

'Damn thing won't open,' Peter muttered.

'Please hurry,' MaryAnn pleaded. She gripped the bars so tightly that her knuckles showed white against the metal.

'I'm going as quickly as I can,' Peter huffed.

'Well go quicker,' she urged.

Peter paused and opened his mouth as if to reply then shook his head. He returned his attention to the lock, working on it for a few moments longer until there was a pronounced click.

Peter jumped to his feet and pushed the door open. MaryAnn almost fell out of the cell, wrapping her arms around his waist. 'Thank you,' she sobbed. 'I thought he was going to take me back to the Neighbourhood.'

Peter looked a little taken aback, but after a moment's hesitation he patted her on the back. 'It's alright,' he said.

Uncle Ethan observed MaryAnn anxiously, his eyes darting nervously towards the door, 'Peter!'

'MaryAnn,' Peter coaxed, 'we have to go.'

When she didn't respond he pushed her away from him, holding her at arm's length. 'MaryAnn? I know you're scared but we have to get out of here.' MaryAnn responded with a sniff and wiped her nose and eyes on the hem of her shirt. 'I'm fine,' she replied in a faltering voice.

'Good,' Peter replied firmly. Then his voice softened. 'We'll be out of here soon. I promise. Then you'll be safe.'

'Just don't let the Director take me back to the Neighbourhood,' she whispered.

Peter shook his head. 'It's not going to happen,' he said.

Flo was at the far end of the room examining each cell in turn. 'Where's Eric?' she demanded.

'Who's Eric?' Uncle Ethan queried.

'He's our friend. The Trustees took him too. We have to find him,' Flo urged.

'We don't have time,' Peter said. 'We have to go.'

'I'm not leaving without him.' There was a determined set to her face.

Peter sighed. 'Flo, I'm sorry about your friend but we have to get out of here before someone discovers that the Watch at the entrance are missing.'

Flo crossed her hands combatively across her chest. 'I said I'm not leaving without him.'

'Me, neither,' Mally agreed.

'He's not here,' MaryAnn said. 'He was in the cell next to mine for a while but they took him away.'

'Was he alright?' Flo asked.

MaryAnn hesitated uncertainly. 'He was unconscious the whole time.'

Flo bounced on her toes anxiously. 'Do you know where they took him?'

'I heard someone mention the labs,' MaryAnn said.

'The labs?' Flo queried. 'What's that?'

MaryAnn shook her head. 'I don't know.'

'We have to find him,' Flo said. 'We can't leave him behind.'

'There's nothing we can do for him,' Peter said firmly. 'We have to get MaryAnn out of here before the Director comes back.'

'I'm not leaving him behind,' Flo responded savagely, 'he's my friend.' She turned to MaryAnn accusingly. 'You have to help him. He sacrificed himself for you.'

MaryAnn flinched.

'Flo,' Peter snapped. 'This isn't MaryAnn's decision. It's mine.'

Flo scowled and took a step towards him. Mally jumped in between them. 'I'll find him,' he said.

'What?' I cried.

'We can't wait for you,' Peter warned.

'I know,' Mally replied.

'I'll stay too,' I said. I couldn't bear the thought of leaving Mally behind.

'Oh no you will not.' Uncle Ethan grabbed my wrist. 'I promised your dad that I'd get you out of here.'

'We have a boat, it's moored in a cove on the north west side of the island,' Peter said as he pulled something out of his pocket. 'You know how to use a compass?'

'Yes,' Mally replied.

'When you find your friend you need to go to the kitchens. There's a service lift that will take you down to the basement. Go through the boiler room and out into the courtyard. We'll leave a ladder for you,' Peter said. 'Whatever you do, don't use the front entrance. We had to disable the guards. If they've been discovered then the Watch will be waiting for you.'

Peter handed Mally the compass. 'Once you're out of the grounds head north west through the woods and down to the coast.'

'Thank you,' Mally said.

'We can't wait,' Peter repeated. 'If you don't make it back in time, we'll have to leave without you.'

Mally gave a nod of understanding and then turned to me. 'I'll find Eric and then we can all go home together.'

'You promise?'

'I promise,' he replied.

Over the Wall

MARYANN:

Mr Murray peered into the dining hall. 'Come on,' he said. 'It's empty. We can get to the kitchens from here.

We threaded our way through the rows of tables towards the door that led into the kitchens. Once inside Mr Murray indicated a small opening in the wall. I recognised it immediately, it was a dumb waiter. We'd had one installed in my house in the Neighbourhood. 'This will take us down to the basement,' he said. 'We'll have to take it in turns.'

Mr Murray was the first to climb inside. His bulk took up most of the interior and Flo was the only one small enough to squeeze in beside him. She looked very uncomfortable as he pulled down the shutter. Next it was Bekka and Charlotte's turn to make the cramped journey down to the basement.

When the lift returned Peter clambered inside and I squashed in beside him. As he grabbed for the door he crushed me against the metal sides of the lift and I gasped. 'You okay?' he asked.

'Your elbow's sticking in my back,' I grumbled as I struggled to find a more comfortable position.

'Maybe if you weren't jabbing your bony knees into my ribs then

I could move my elbow,' he muttered as he yanked the door closed and I found myself enveloped in a thick cloying blackness.

As the lift descended to the basement I could hear Peter breathing heavily beside me.

'Will you stop that,' I complained.

'What?'

'You're panting in my ear. You sound like Flash.'

'I don't like small spaces,' he murmured.

The lift came to a halt and I blinked as Peter hauled up the shutter and the interior was suddenly flooded with light. Mr Murray was waiting outside and offered me a helping hand as I unfolded myself out of the cramped space. Peter scrambled after me. He looked a little pale.

'The boiler room's this way,' Mr Murray directed.

We exited the building through the boiler room and entered a courtyard bounded by a high wall.

'What now?' Flo asked.

'Daryl said you were a good climber?' Mr Murray queried.

'I'm alright,' Flo said.

'Can you climb to the top of the wall and catch a rope ladder?'

'It looks easy enough.'

I peered quizzically at the wall. The sides were almost sheer.

'You'll need these to cut the razor wire at the top,' Mr Murray advised as he handed her a pair of wire cutters.

Flo slipped the wire cutters into her pocket and strode purposely to the wall. I watched in admiration as, with a series of cat like movements, she scaled its steep flank. Once she'd reached the top she hacked at the razor wire and nimbly straddled the wall.

A whistle floated up on the evening air and as she caught the sound Flo leant over the wall. When she straightened up I saw that she was holding a rope ladder. She tugged sharply and pulled it over the top of the wall, feeding it down to Peter and Mr Murray who secured it to the ground with two pegs.

Mr Murray tested the ladder and then beckoned to me. 'You first,' he said.

'This should be fun,' Peter muttered.

I threw him a poisonous look before I took hold of the ladder and climbed awkwardly onto the bottom rung. By the time I'd made it clumsily to the top of the wall and down the other side my arms were burning with the effort. Daryl and Flo were waiting for me on the ground.

'Glad you're alright,' Daryl exclaimed as he pulled me off the ladder into a tight hug. 'I was so worried about you when we saw the Director at the jetty.'

'I'm fine,' I replied, giving him a squeeze. 'Thanks for coming to get me.'

Daryl released me from the hug and stepped forward to help Charlotte off the ladder, she was quickly followed by Bekka.

Next Mr Murray's head appeared over the wall and with a series of swift movements that belied his bulk he clambered down the ladder and landed lightly on the ground beside Daryl. 'Peter's making sure the ladder's secure for the boys,' he said.

'What boys?' Daryl queried.

'Charlotte's friend Mally has gone to look for someone. They're going to follow us to the boat.'

Daryl nodded. 'There's going to be more people than we expected in the boat. Murray, you should go and tell Patrick. Make sure he's ready to leave straight away.'

Mr Murray nodded in response. 'Come on,' he said.

'I'm staying here with Daryl,' Flo protested.

'I'll be right behind you,' Daryl replied.

'I don't care. I'm not going anywhere without you,' she replied.

Daryl sighed. 'Alright, I'll take everyone back to the boat. Murray, you stay here and wait for Peter.'

Mr Murray shuffled uncomfortably. 'I promised Dan that I wouldn't let Charlotte out of my sight.'

'Well someone needs to wait for Peter. We can't leave him on his own,' Daryl replied impatiently.

'I'll wait for him,' I volunteered.

Daryl began to protest but I silenced him. 'Someone needs to make sure that Uncle Patrick has the boat ready. Peter and I will be right behind you.'

Daryl hesitated. 'Go on,' I urged.

Flo grabbed his hand. 'She's right. We need to get to the boat. She'll be safe with Peter.'

'Okay, but be careful,' Daryl instructed. 'I'll see you soon,' he said as he left with the others and disappeared into the night. Alone in the darkness it was eerily quiet and I gave a small sigh of relief when a familiar blonde head appeared over the top of the wall.

'Have the others gone back to the boat?' Peter asked as leapt lightly to the ground.

I nodded in response. 'I volunteered to stay behind and make sure you were okay,' I replied.

'Very reassuring,' Peter grinned. He handed me a torch. 'Come on, let's get out of here. This place gives me the creeps.'

As we skirted the perimeter of the LightHouse Peter pulled out a compass. He studied it for a moment and then tapped it with his finger. I heard him issue a muttered curse.

'Is something wrong?' I asked.

'I gave my good compass to Mally,' he said as he shook it violently and checked it again. 'Okay, that seems to have done the trick. It's this way,' he pointed.

We arrived at the edge of a wood and Peter studied the compass again. 'The cove isn't too far from here.'

As we picked our way along a leafy path Peter stopped suddenly and without warning crouched down behind a rock. He made a grab for my hand, but it was too late! The light from my torch picked out a flash of grey as someone stepped out from the treeline. The Watch raised his gun. 'Stop where you are,' he barked.

Peter was concealed behind the rock but I was completely exposed. I raised my hands above my head.

'Turn around,' the Watch barked.

As I cautiously turned to face the Watch I caught a glimpse of Peter as he crept out from behind the rock, pulling a gun from the belt of his uniform.

Peter faced the Watch and raised his gun. He fired, once, twice, three times. All I heard was a series of empty clicks. Throwing the gun aside with a grunt of frustration he pulled out a knife and lunged at the Watch. He knocked the gun out of the Watch's hand and it skidded away across the dirt, coming to rest in a pile of damp leaves.

'Get the gun,' Peter yelled in a strangled voice as he continued to grapple with the Watch.

I ran and picked up the gun, but once it was in my hand I wasn't sure what to do with it.

'Shoot him,' Peter yelled. He gave a cry of pain as the Watch punched him in the stomach.

I stared at the gun and the world slipped sideways. I couldn't shoot someone.

'Shoot him,' Peter bellowed.

I could feel my hands shaking uncontrollably.

'For crying out loud, just shoot him.'

I held up the gun. 'Hands up.' My voice was weak and the Watch ignored me. 'Hands up,' I repeated. This time my tone was harder, more determined. The Watch responded by putting his hands in the air.

'Get up,' I said, summoning all the authority I could muster.

The Watch slowly clambered to his feet and Peter staggered after him. 'I told you to shoot him, not act out a scene from a bad gangster film,' Peter said. He threw me a look of disdain before holding out a hand. 'Give the gun to me,' he said. 'I'll do it.'

Before I had chance to hand it to him I heard the crunch of dry leaves and a second Watch appeared from out of the trees. 'I suggest you drop the gun,' he snapped. 'Unless you want me to shoot your boyfriend.'

As I crouched down to place the gun on the ground I caught a blur of brown fur as Flash bounded excitedly out of the treeline. He gave a *'yip'* of delight when he spotted Peter.

Peter responded with an almost undetectable hand gesture. Flash froze, his body rigid, his attention focussed wholly on Peter. Distracted, the Watch turned quizzically towards the source of the noise. Seizing the opportunity Peter cried out a single word, 'STRIKE.'

What followed next was completely unexpected, as sweet lovable Flash transformed into a snarling mass of fury. He flew at the Watch, who let out a scream of terror, dropping his gun as he was wrestled savagely to the ground.

As Peter stooped to retrieve the fallen gun I saw him sway slightly and I noticed that he appeared a little unsteady on his feet.

'Are you alright?' I asked.

'I'm fine,' he snapped as he swung round to train his gun on the other Watch, who was making a furtive attempt to crawl away into the woods. 'Oh no you don't, go and join your friend over there.'

With a cautious eye on Peter the Watch scrambled over to where Flash restrained his companion, a large paw placed firmly on his chest. I could hear him snarling ferociously.

Peter made a gesture to Flash who released the Watch and allowed him to join his colleague.

'MaryAnn, search them for a radio,' Peter demanded. I hesitated uncertainly. 'Do it now,' he snapped.

I shot forward and tentatively searched each Watch in turn. I found a radio in the pocket of one of the uniforms and Peter ordered me to throw it onto the ground. Using the heel of his boot he crushed it into a pile of broken plastic.

When Peter ordered the Watch to kneel, his voice was so cool and devoid of emotion that I glanced over at him in alarm. I stared in horror as he cocked one of the guns and aimed it at the Watch.

'What are you doing?' I hissed.

'We can't leave any evidence,' he replied. His tone was glacial. It took a moment for me to understand the intent behind his words.

'You're going to kill them?' I muttered in quiet disbelief.

Peter scowled. 'We can't leave them here.'

'They're unarmed, you could just tie them up.'

Peter's expression was hard. 'MaryAnn, if they escape and raise the alarm before we get back to the mainland, then we're all dead.'

His response sickened me. How could he even consider killing the Watch in cold blood?

'This is my decision,' he said. 'So there's no reason for you to feel guilty.'

'But it's murder,' I stammered.

He let out a derisive snort. 'And you don't think they'd kill us?'

I couldn't let him shoot someone in cold blood and there was only one way I could think of stopping him. I took a deep breath and stepped out in front of the gun.

'What are you doing?' Peter demanded. 'Get out of the way.'

I shook my head.

'Move out of the way NOW.' His voice held such a ruthless edge that I feared he might actually shoot me.

'I can't,' I squeaked, nerves making my voice high pitched and strangled.

Peter's eyes narrowed as he considered me carefully. With Flash by his side, alert and focussed I realised I was seeing them both clearly for the first time. Peter and Flash were a fighting unit. They'd both been trained to kill.

Peter continued to glare at me as the seconds ticked away. Finally he shook his head. 'If anyone gets hurt because we let this scum live, then it's all on you. You understand?'

When I didn't respond he gestured at me impatiently, 'Get out of the way. I'm not going to shoot them.'

As I stepped aside Peter approached the Watch. 'Take off your handcuffs and belts and throw them onto the ground,' he ordered. The Watch hurriedly complied.

'MaryAnn. Tie them up,' Peter barked.

I stooped to pick up the handcuffs and fitted them clumsily over each Watch's wrists. When I was sure that they were secure I collected the belts and gave Peter a quizzical look. I wasn't sure what he wanted me to do with them.

'Use them to bind their ankles,' he ordered.

When I'd finished Peter checked the bindings to make sure they were tight enough. Next Peter told me to use their ties as a gag.

After I'd finished Peter pushed me aside and dealt each of the Watch a glancing blow across the head with the butt of his gun. They slumped to the ground, unconscious.

'What did you do that for?' I cried in horror. 'They were tied up.'

'You see the blue star on the collar of their jackets? That means they're Trackers. Those restraints won't hold them for long and Trackers don't like to lose their prey. You've just caused us a whole lot of trouble.'

CHAPTER 23

Enemy Contact

Mary Ann:

We arrived at the cove to find the others waiting impatiently. 'What happened?' Uncle Patrick cried out as we scrambled down the cliff. 'We were just about to come and look for you.'

'We ran into a bit of trouble,' Peter replied. 'We really need to get out of here now.'

'Murray, get the oars,' Uncle Patrick called as he untied the boat. I climbed on board and slumped quietly into an empty seat. Flash flopped down into the space at my feet.

'We can't go,' Flo exclaimed. 'We have to wait for Eric and Mally.'

'There's no time,' Peter replied. 'The Watch know we escaped. We have to leave.'

Flo sprang to her feet and I felt the boat rock alarmingly. 'I'm not leaving without Eric.'

'Flo, sit down.' Daryl grabbed at her arm, forcing her back into her seat.

'There's no time. We're leaving now.' Uncle Patrick's voice was firm as he helped Peter push the boat from the shore. Once the boat was afloat they both jumped on board and Peter dropped into the seat beside me. Uncle Patrick took a seat next to Mr Murray and picked up an oar.

'We have to go back,' Flo yelled.

'We can't leave Mally!' Charlotte's voice joined the protest.

'You both need to be quiet,' Peter snapped. 'If you keep making all that noise you'll alert the Watch.'

As we left the shelter of the cove the boat was buffeted by strong waves and I could feel my stomach churn anxiously. I wasn't sure whether it was nerves or seasickness.

'We're heading to the pass between the rocks,' Ruth whispered as she flicked on her torch and examined the map. The tension in the boat was almost palpable as Ruth issued terse directions to Uncle Patrick and Mr Murray.

The anxious silence was broken by the sound of a distant humming.

'What's that?' Daryl hissed as he peered around the boat.

'I can see something over there,' Flo pointed out to sea. I followed the line of her finger to where I could make out a light flickering brightly in the sky. It was moving quickly towards us.

'Damn it,' Uncle Patrick cursed as the helicopter passed overhead and the boat was buffeted by a gust of wind. Water splashed up the sides, soaking my arms and legs.

I heard a distinctive click and Uncle Patrick dropped his oar. 'Into the water,' he yelled. I could hear the panic in his voice. 'NOW!' he roared as he clambered to his feet.

Rigid with fear, I stared at him in horror. I couldn't move. A pair of strong hands grasped my shoulders, tossing me overboard. I hit the water with a thud and icy shards of salt water pierced my lungs. My arms flailed helplessly as I tried to swim towards the surface. There was a tug at the back of my shirt and I was propelled upwards. I burst through the surface of the water gasping for air.

The helicopter hovered overhead, churning the sea into a reeling mass of waves. A charred burnt smell filled my nostrils. The boat was on fire!

'Swim,' a voice yelled. It was Peter. I heard a low-pitched scream, and then Peter's voice in my ear yelling at me to duck.

Before I had a chance to respond he grabbed my arm and pulled me under the surface. I choked on a mouthful of salt water and struggled against his tight grip. Just when I thought my lungs would explode Peter released me and I burst through the surface of the water, gasping for breath.

'What did you do that for?' I spluttered as I coughed up salt water.

'The helicopter was shooting at us. Come on, we need to swim to the beach.'

'Where are the others?' I asked.

'I don't know,' Peter yelled.

'Daryl!' I called out. 'Uncle Patrick!' There was no response.

'MaryAnn!' Peter shook my arm. His teeth were chattering. 'We have to get out of the water.'

'What about Daryl and Uncle Patrick?'

'They'll head to the shore too. Come on. Stay close.'

The water was bitterly cold and the icy chill quickly seeped into my bones until my arms and legs felt numb. The helicopter roared overhead, its searchlight illuminating the water. When I heard the scream of bullets again I instinctively ducked under the water. I resurfaced to find Peter paddling beside me. The helicopter was gone and I could make out its faint lights as it flew towards the mainland.

'Come on,' Peter yelled. 'We need to get out of the water before the helicopter comes back.'

My legs where leaden by the time we staggered onto the pebble beach and I collapsed into an exhausted heap.

'We have to keep moving,' Peter panted. He was bent double, his hands clasped over his knees.

I tried to scramble to my feet, but my legs wouldn't respond and I stumbled. I grasped at Peter's arm for support and heard him yelp in response.

'What's the matter?' I asked as he pulled away.

'Nothing. I'm fine. Come on, we need to keep moving.'

Shivering, I followed Peter to the edge of the beach. He paused as he surveyed the dark landscape. 'I think the cave is this way,' he said as he directed us along a sandy path. 'We should hurry.'

We stumbled through the darkness until we arrived at the mountain track that led to the cave. My legs were so weak that I barely had the energy to stagger up its steep sides. Peter seemed equally exhausted as I watched him weave an unsteady path to the cave.

I was hoping that we'd find the others waiting for us inside, but when we entered, the cave was empty. 'Where is everyone?' I muttered.

I was startled by a deep moan and turned to find Peter slumped against the wall. 'What's wrong?' I asked as I hurried over and helped him to the ground. He responded with a painful grunt.

When I glanced down at my hand I was horrified to find that it was slick with blood.

'You're hurt,' I whispered.

'It's just a scratch.' Peter was deathly pale, his breathing uneven.

'A scratch?' I pulled up his shirt and he responded with a sharp hiss of pain. I recoiled at the sight of the ragged wound underneath.

'What happened?'

'It was the Watch,' he explained. 'With my own knife,' he grunted in disgust.

'Why didn't you tell me?'

He shook his head. 'No time.'

'What do we do?' I asked.

With a groan he unclipped the first aid kit from his belt. 'You're going to have to sew me up.'

My stomach squirmed nervously and I let go of his shirt, 'I don't know any first aid.'

Peter ignored me. 'Here, just take the first aid kit,' he coaxed.

'Peter, are you listening to me? I don't know how to sew up a knife wound.'

'Then you'll have to learn,' he replied quietly.

'Shouldn't we wait for the others?' They'll know what to do.'

'Take a look around MaryAnn, there's only the two of us here and I can't do it.'

I paused uncertainly.

'MaryAnn please, just take the first aid kit.' As I watched him drag a weary hand across his face I realised he was right, there was no-one else to help.

I accepted the first aid kit and pulled it open. 'There should be some antiseptic inside,' Peter whispered in a voice that was hoarse with pain. 'You can use it to clean the wound.'

I had to use all my self-control not to throw up when I lifted his shirt and saw the blood bubble wetly from the jagged wound. I soaked a cloth with the antiseptic and dabbed tentatively at the blood. Peter tensed and let out a low grunt. I paused, 'Are you alright?'

'Stings a bit,' he hissed through tightly gritted teeth.

'Do you want me to stop?'

'No, just keep going. I'll be fine.'

After I'd cleaned away the blood he surveyed my handiwork and gave a weary nod. 'You can sew it up now,' he mumbled.

My hand was shaking as I attempted to thread the needle.

He patted my arm. 'There's nothing to it,' he said. 'You'll be fine.'

I bent over the tear in his side. The edges of the wound were ragged and raw and I could hardly bear to touch them.

'You'll need to pull the two pieces of skin together,' Peter instructed, his voice a faint whisper.

The broken skin felt slimy to the touch and bile rose in my throat as I took hold of it. Peter inhaled sharply as I pushed the needle through the flesh. The first stitch was the hardest but once it was done I was able to focus on the task until the skin was knitted together and the wound was closed. With each stitch Peter muttered a low curse.

I cut the end of the thread and surveyed my handiwork. Peter would have an ugly scar, but at least he wasn't going to bleed to death.

'You did good,' Peter said as he patted my arm. 'You can go and throw up now,' he murmured as he fainted.

Peter was shivering slightly as he slipped into an uneasy sleep. I covered him with a blanket and settled down beside him, but it was impossible to sleep as I waited anxiously for the others to return. When dawn arrived I got up and headed to the bathroom, where I washed and changed into dry clothes. Peter was still asleep when I returned to the cave so I clambered up to the lookout and trained my binoculars on the empty landscape. I could see no sign of the others.

Peter woke at midday and pulled himself into a sitting position.

'How are you feeling?' I asked as he let out a loud groan.

'Thirsty,' he rasped through cracked lips.

I handed him a cup of water and he drained it in a few noisy gulps.

He glanced around the cave. 'Are the others back?'

'No. Not yet.'

He paused thoughtfully. 'We'll wait until it gets dark, then we should leave.'

'Shouldn't we wait for them?'

'It's too dangerous. The Watch will be looking for us. They have Trackers. It's only a matter of time before they find this place,' Peter explained.

'Where will we go?' I asked.

'Daryl and I agreed on a rendezvous in case we were split up. It's on the coast close to where we camped on the first night. We'll head there.'

He yawned. 'I need to sleep. Wake me up when it gets dark,' he said as he slumped back down on the floor. He closed his eyes and was asleep within seconds.

A lonely afternoon stretched before me and with nothing else to occupy my thoughts I found myself consumed by worry. Something terrible must have happened to the others. Why hadn't Daryl and Uncle Patrick come back to the caves? In an effort to drive off impending insanity I grabbed two rucksacks and busied myself packing the things we would need for our journey to the rendezvous.

As the sun dipped below the horizon I shook Peter awake. He looked tired and pale but he assured me that he was feeling better. With some difficulty I helped him change out of the Watch uniform. The uniform was tattered and torn and useless as a disguise. Once he was back in his normal clothes I handed him a bowl of soup and some painkillers. While he sipped on the soup I showed him the rucksacks I'd packed earlier. He gave his seal of approval. 'It looks like you've got everything we need,' he said.

After he'd finished his meal it was time to leave.

We left the cave and followed the mountain track back to where we'd hidden the trucks. I noticed that Peter's pace was slower than usual but at least he was steady on his feet.

As we approached the clearing where we'd camouflaged the trucks I felt Peter place a restraining arm on my shoulder. 'What's wrong?' I mouthed.

Peter glanced around nervously and then let go of my arm, 'I don't know. Just stay here,' he whispered as he melted into the shadows.

He returned a few moments later. 'They've found our truck,' he whispered. 'There's a patrol guarding it.'

'What about Dan's truck? I asked.

'It's gone,' Peter confirmed.

Despite the seriousness of our situation I felt a momentary sense of relief. 'Do you think the others have taken it?' I whispered. It was the first indication we'd had that they might still be alive.

'Maybe,' Peter replied.

'What do we do now?' I asked. 'How do we get to the rendezvous without a truck?'

'We walk,' Peter replied.

CHAPTER 24

The Long Way Back

MARYANN:

Peter explained that it would take about three weeks to walk to the rendezvous. As I was trying to digest this piece of information he delivered even more bad news. We would have to ration our food to one meal a day.

We hiked through the night, stumbling along the mountain track in the pitch black. Peter refused to use a torch in case it alerted the helicopter to our location. At times we could still hear its faint buzz in the distance.

The sun was high in the sky by the time we reached a small wooden hut clinging desperately to the side of the mountain. Peter came to a halt outside and pushed tentatively at the battered wooden door. It opened with a creak.

'We can rest here until it gets dark,' he said as he sank down onto the dirty floor.

'We're going to sleep here?' I wrinkled my nose as I peered into its dank interior.

'Sorry, the penthouse suite was taken,' Peter replied.

Ignoring his sarcasm I shrugged off my rucksack and rummaged inside. I pulled out a bag of dried fruit and poured a large handful.

I could feel Peter's eyes on me. 'Steady on,' he said. 'We need to ration the food. We won't be able to hunt regularly.'

I chewed the fruit slowly, trying to make each mouthful last as long as possible, but even when it was gone I was still hungry. I unlaced my boots and pulled them off with a groan. I attempted to rub some life back into my aching feet.

I heard Peter give a hiss of pain. 'Do you want me to help with that?' I asked as he unwound the bandage from around his waist.

'I'm fine,' he replied through clenched teeth. 'You should get some sleep. I'll take the first watch.'

It had been a long time since I'd slept properly and I was exhausted. I was grateful for Peter's offer to take first watch. I was about to pull out my sleeping bag when he bent forward to pull a clean bandage from the first aid kit and his face was illuminated by a shaft of light from the door. I noted how pale he looked and suspected that his wound was causing more pain than he was willing to admit.

'It's fine. I'm not very tired. I'll take the first watch,' I replied, desperately trying to stifle a yawn.

Peter's raised an eyebrow in response. 'Really?'

'I can sleep later,' I replied.

Peter observed me for a moment then shrugged and spread his sleeping bag out on the ground. 'Wake me in four hours,' he said as he climbed inside.

I crept over to the open door, resting uncomfortably against its timber frame, and peered down the mountainside. I had to fight a rising sense of vertigo. We were so high up I could barely make out the valley floor below.

I kept my silent vigil for the remainder of the afternoon. After four long hours I shook Peter awake. I didn't have the energy to roll out my sleeping bag so I climbed into the one that Peter vacated. It was still warm and I fell asleep almost immediately.

I woke to the sound of someone calling my name. I yawned and blinked. My eyes felt scratchy and raw. Peter was crouched beside me. 'We have to go,' he whispered softly.

I climbed sleepily out of the sleeping bag and pulled on my boots. It was already getting dark outside. I got to my feet and Peter handed me my rucksack. 'Come on,' he said, 'let's go.'

As we exited the hut my stomach gave a hungry growl and it made me think longingly about the bag of dried fruit stowed away inside my rucksack. Despite my gnawing hunger I was going to have to survive on one meal a day.

Peter and I traversed a narrow mountain pass bordered by a deep ravine. In the failing light I had to tread carefully so that I didn't accidentally plummet down its steep side. As the night grew darker I stumbled more frequently and soon my knees were skinned and raw, the flesh stripped away by sharp stones.

Peter's strength seemed to have returned and he set a brisk pace. He had to pause frequently to wait for me to catch up. Although he didn't say anything I could tell that he was irritated by my clumsiness. Even in the dark we were horribly exposed and he was eager that we get off the mountain as quickly as possible.

Daylight announced itself with a dirty grey sunrise. Peter said we should walk for a few more hours, and then rest. We left the mountain path and entered a lush green valley. The morning was sunny and warm and I pulled off my jumper. By the time we stopped to rest I was hot and sticky and felt disgusting. This time there was no hut to provide shelter, instead we had to take cover in a thicket of scrubby bushes. Peter offered to take the first watch and gratefully I agreed.

I was completely exhausted, but the moment I closed my eyes I was consumed by a feeling of despair. I could handle the near constant hunger and endless hiking, but the unknown fate of my family was almost too much to bear. Hopelessness overwhelmed me and I bolted upright in my sleeping bag, my breath coming in rapid gasps.

'I thought you were going to get some sleep,' Peter said.

'I'm not as tired as I thought,' I said, trying to keep the tremor from my voice.

Peter studied me for a moment. 'You really should get some sleep.'

'I know,' I muttered as I struggled to get my breathing under control.

'I'm just saying that you need to be properly rested for tomorrow. We have a lot of travelling ahead of us and we have to pick up the pace a bit.'

I bristled at his comment. I'd walked all day without any food and my feet were blistered but I hadn't complained once. 'I'm doing my best,' I snapped.

'I know you're doing your best, but we're really exposed out here and we need to get to the rendezvous as quickly as possible.'

'I said I'm doing the best I can. I don't know what more you want from me.' I swallowed hard, hoping Peter hadn't heard the catch in my voice.

Peter sighed. 'I didn't mean to upset you.'

'I'm not upset,' I snapped. 'I'm just worried about Daryl and Uncle Patrick, that's all.'

'Daryl and Patrick can take care of themselves.'

I was taken aback by his comment. 'Daryl's your best friend. You sound like you don't even care about him.'

Peter eased out a slow breath. 'Of course I care about him, but the most important thing at the moment is our own survival. We can't think about anyone else.'

'How can you be so callous?'

My comment was met with a strained silence. Peter held my gaze for a few moments and then scrambled to his feet. 'Try and get some sleep and I'll wake you in a couple of hours,' he said as he moved to the edge of the thicket.

Nestled in his sleeping bag, his face relaxed in slumber, Peter had the appearance of someone without a care in the world. He was able to sleep peacefully despite the unknown fate of our friends and family.

I woke him after four hours and we ate a silent meal of dried fruit and nuts. As he ate he cleaned one of the guns he'd taken from the Watch. It was waterlogged, but he was hoping that he could get it working again. He carefully pulled the gun apart, examining each piece in turn before laying them out on the grass.

'Would you have really killed the Watch?' I asked. It was hard for me to accept that Peter could be a cold-blooded killer. When he didn't respond to my question I continued, 'You'd taken their guns, so they weren't a threat.'

Peter gave a derisive snort. 'Of course they were a threat, and yes, I would have killed them.' I was shocked by the ferocity of his tone.

'Don't look at me like I'm a monster,' he replied. The Union trained me to be a soldier. What do you think we did? Throw sticks, shout some bad words at the Watch and then run away?'

'So if you had the chance to do it again,' I questioned. 'You'd kill them?'

He fixed me with a hard stare. 'Yes, to protect the people I care about.'

'It doesn't make sense, you didn't agree with the Union planting a bomb in the Neighbourhood, but you'd kill someone in cold blood.'

'You can't compare the two things. Planting a bomb is wrong. You can't control the blast and you put innocent people in danger. If someone threatens you with a gun and they want to kill you or someone you care about, then you have a right to stop them.'

'You could stop them without having to kill them,' I protested.

'I'm not asking you to understand,' he said, 'but you have to stop questioning every decision I make. I need you to trust me.'

'I do trust you,' I replied indignantly.

'It doesn't seem like it.'

'I've trusted you enough to follow you this far haven't I?'

He looked surprised. 'I just don't think you realise how much danger we're in.'

'Of course I understand how much danger we're in. I was in the LightHouse, remember? The Director locked me in a cell.' I indicated his side, 'I sewed you up.'

'I'm worried that if something were to happen to me you wouldn't be able to find your way off these mountains.'

I dismissed his comment with a wave of my hand. 'I'm sorry that I'm such a burden, that you're stuck with me rather than Daryl or Mr Murray.'

'I didn't say you were a burden,' he protested.

'You don't have to. I can see it in your eyes every time you look at me. You're forgetting that Daryl, Mr Murray, they were just like me once, before they trained as soldiers. I don't want to be a burden, I want to get to the rendezvous so that I can see my brother again. So why don't you let me help you?'

'You don't have any skills.'

'Then teach me.'

'It's not that easy, Daryl and I spent months training at boot camp.'

'I don't want to be a soldier, I just want to survive. I don't need months of training.'

Peter studied me for a moment. 'We can't lose any time,' he said hesitantly.

'We won't,' I promised.

'Alright, if you really want to learn then I'll teach you what I can.'

CHAPTER 25

Survival Skills 101

MARYANN:

Peter was as good as his word and he spent the rest of the day teaching me how to navigate using his compass. It was much harder than I'd expected and Peter wasn't the most patient of teachers.

We made camp in a small cave, but before he would let me rest Peter taught me how to light a fire. I'd watched the others make a fire plenty of times, but I'd never been responsible for building one myself. Peter demonstrated how to start the fire with flammable bits of wood and foliage he called tinder, then how to gradually add bigger branches until the flames burnt brightly. While he built the fire he explained about the different types of wood and how they each burnt differently. He spoke so earnestly that I tried my hardest to take everything in.

Next Peter informed me that he was going to show me how to set a snare. At first I protested. I wasn't ready to kill an animal, but our supplies were low and he explained that we needed food. I followed him out of the cave and watched as he set the trap. I feigned interest, knowing that I would never be able to do something so cruel.

After we'd had some rest Peter took me back to check the snare. My stomach churned at the sight of the animal trapped by its leg.

At first I thought it was a rabbit, but Peter pointed to its large ears and explained that it was a hare. Fortunately it was already dead, so we didn't have to kill it.

'Are you ready for what's coming next?' he asked as he released the hare and held it up by its ears. I stared at him numbly. I wasn't ready for this at all.

Peter began by removing the head. 'This is a good animal to prepare because it's small and easy to butcher,' he said as he laid the hare on its back and pierced the skin. I felt the ground sway alarmingly beneath my feet.

'If you need to throw up, then go and do it now,' Peter said firmly, 'but when you're done you come right back here so we can finish this.'

I took a couple of deep breaths to steady myself. 'I'm fine,' I mumbled.

Peter demonstrated how to slit open the hare's stomach and pull out its organs. He held them comfortably in his hand but I could hardly bear to look at them. 'This is the really important bit,' he said. 'You have to remove the internal organs very carefully so you don't puncture the stomach. Look, it's right here,' he pointed at something indistinguishable within the handful of guts. 'If you puncture this you'll poison the meat and it'll make you sick.'

He paused. 'MaryAnn, are you listening to me?'

'Don't puncture the stomach,' I repeated, 'or I'll be poisoned.'

He grinned, seemingly satisfied with my answer.

'Here you go,' he said as he held up a pink slimy lump of meat, 'dinner's almost ready.'

Despite feeling ravenous, I found that I could choke down only a few mouthfuls of the meat. It wasn't the first time I'd had to eat an animal. Living on the Outside it was sometimes difficult to maintain a vegetarian diet, but I hated the unnatural feel of it in my mouth.

'Maybe tomorrow you could teach me how to pick berries,' I suggested helpfully.

There was a spring in my step, my mood vastly improved. We'd arrived at a tarmac road. It was the first sign of civilisation we'd encountered since setting off on our journey to the rendezvous. After days of stumbling across moorland and skinning my knees on sharp stones it felt good to have firm ground beneath my feet.

Unexpectedly Peter grabbed hold of my hand and I followed his worried gaze. In the murky half-light between night and day I watched as a horse and cart made its way around the bend in the road.

'Is it the Watch?' I whispered fearfully.

'No, they wouldn't use a horse and cart. It must be a local.'

'Maybe we can ask for a ride?' I suggested as I thought longingly of the easy miles we could cover in the back of the cart. My aching feet would certainly welcome the rest. Peter hesitated, chewing thoughtfully on his bottom lip. 'We'll get to the rendezvous quicker,' I coaxed.

'Okay,' he said as he stepped into the road and hailed the driver.

If the driver of the cart was surprised to encounter two strangers on the lonely road, he didn't show it. He came to a halt and sucked noisily on his pipe while Peter asked for a ride. When he'd finished the man indicated that we should climb into the back of the cart.

The smell in the back of the cart was dreadful and I wrinkled up my nose in disgust. It was pretty revolting. Peter grinned as I searched for a clean space to sit. 'Not exactly the limousine lifestyle you were used to in the Neighbourhood, is it?' he teased.

The sun was high in the sky and I judged it to be almost midday as we came to a standstill in the yard of a whitewashed farmhouse. The man turned to the back of the cart. 'Ye'll both be wanting something to eat, I expect,' he said, before clambering down and disappearing into the building.

I cast a wary glance at Peter. 'Should we follow him?' I asked.

Peter jumped lightly to the ground. 'Come on,' he replied.

'What if it's a trap?' I whispered. 'What if he's calling the Watch?'

'We're both starving and we can't turn down a free meal,' he said as he helped me down from the truck. 'Just keep your wits about you.'

When we cautiously entered the kitchen the delicious aroma that wafted from the stove made me feel slightly giddy. It had been a long time since I'd eaten a proper meal. As we took a seat at the kitchen table the man poured out two bowls of food and slopped them down in front of us. 'Ye'll eat these and then ye'll be on your way,' he said. 'I don't want no trouble.'

'We don't want to cause any trouble,' Peter replied as he ravenously shovelled food into his mouth.

'To my mind anyone you pick up in the middle of nowhere has got to be in some type of trouble. You just don't bring it here. You understand?' The man cut two slices of thick bread and handed one to me. His hands were coated with a layer of dirt and the grime was imprinted on the bread. I was so hungry I ate it anyway.

The man switched on the radio and we were greeted by a familiar voice. '*Howdy folks. Yup it's time for your daily dose of* DJ *Neptune. Today I can promise a programme filled with endless mirth and sparkling wit.*'

This announcement was greeted with a high-pitched cackle. '*Sparkling wit! Nice one granddad.*'

'*Ignore my intern,*' DJ Neptune continued. '*He wouldn't understand sparkling wit if it jumped up and bit him on the end of his rather large nose.*'

I caught the sound of a muffled curse. '*That's a lie. I don't have a big nose.*'

'*Stanley, I would never lie to our valued listeners. Your schnozzle is indeed large; it's so big I have to duck under the desk every time you turn your head. Pinocchio called the station earlier today and said he wants his hooter back…Yep you get the picture folks, Stanley has a big conk.*'

The DJ cleared his throat, '*Okay dear listeners that's more than enough talk about noses. You've tuned in to be engaged and enthralled so let's get on with the show… oh! And if there are any lumberjacks willing to assist Stanley with his problem proboscis then please call the station.'* The DJ barked out a laugh. The muttered curse in the background was unmistakable.

'In our next item, aptly titled "rumour and conjecture", we've received an unconfirmed report of a raid on the magpies' nest. We don't have any other information at the moment, but let's hope it's true. There are chicks in the nest that need our protection.'

There was a scream of static as the radio lost the signal. I caught the old man's eye, he was staring curiously at Peter and me. We'd both stopped eating, spoons hanging in mid air, our attention focussed on the radio programme. As the man picked up the radio and slapped it hard the familiar voice returned.

'Whatever's happening in the far north I should warn you that we've also received reports that the roads are infested with cockroaches. For your own safety we'd advise you to keep away. We're hoping that pest control will arrive soon…something big is happening folks. Stay tuned and we'll update you as soon as we receive further information.'

'Now it's time for our favourite part of the programme. It's Shoooooooow and Tell. First up is a message we've been running every day for the last few weeks. If we have any pest control friends out there who are lost and alone remember you'll always have friends at the wall.'

I felt Peter stiffen beside me. When I stole a glance at him, his face was expressionless but the message had clearly meant something to him.

'What's wrong?' I hissed. Peter glanced over at the man, who was busy washing dishes. 'Later,' he whispered.

We continued our meal in silence, our attention focussed solely on the radio. When the show ended the man cleared away our empty bowls.

'Thanks for the food,' Peter said as we stood up to leave. 'I'm sorry we can't pay you anything.'

'I didn't reckon you could,' the man replied. 'You don't look like someone with money to pay for food.'

'We're really grateful for the hospitality,' Peter added.

'The wife always told me to do right by strangers. Never know when you might be the one needing help.'

'She sounds like a clever woman, your wife,' Peter replied.

The man nodded. 'Yeah, she was. Died a long time ago, so it's just me now. Not that I can't look after myself,' he added defensively. 'I have a gun.'

'That's good,' Peter held the man's gaze. 'Never know when you might run into trouble.'

'Well I expect you'll be wanting to be on your way,' the man urged.

Firmly holding his gaze Peter shook the man's hand. 'Thanks for the food.'

I gave the man a quick nod of thanks and followed Peter out into the hall.

As we reached the front door the man called after us. 'If you're wanting to meet your friends at the wall you should stay off the roads. The Watch have patrols everywhere. You're best going overland.'

The comment caused Peter to stop in his tracks. 'Thanks for the tip,' he replied cautiously.

'I'm no friend of the Watch,' the man said. 'I lost a son to them. The wife too, when she got in the way.' He glanced at a portrait hanging on the wall. It showed a dark-haired boy perched on the knee of a thin angular woman. The woman looked tired and worn, but the corners of her mouth were lifted into a warm smile.

'I'm sorry,' Peter said.

'Long time ago. Another life.' The man indicated the door, 'You should go,' he turned back towards the kitchen. 'I hope you find your friends,' he said as he disappeared through the door.

'We have to get to the wall,' Peter said as we exited the farmyard.

'Was the message on the radio meant for us?'

'Yes, we have a safe house near Hadrian's Wall, I think someone's waiting for us there.'

'Maybe it's Daryl and Uncle Patrick?'

'I don't think so. We arranged to meet them at the rendezvous I showed you on the map.'

'Who can it be?' I questioned.

'I don't know, but it has to be someone from the Union,' he replied. 'We should check it out. It's closer to here than the rendezvous and they might have a truck.' His face broke into an optimistic grin. 'Maybe our luck's about to change.'

It seemed that Peter's optimism was misplaced. We'd been walking for only a few hours when thick black clouds began to gather overhead and a gloom settled over the moorland. Without warning the temperature plummeted and a blustery wind whipped at our clothes.

'There's a storm coming,' Peter said as he surveyed the threatening sky. I could hear the anxiety in his voice.

The flat featureless landscape offered little shelter from the deluge of rain that followed and soon we were soaked to the skin. We pushed on through the storm hopelessly looking for refuge. Finally Peter indicated a small clump of bushes. We clambered into the scrubby undergrowth but it offered very little protection. I pulled my sleeping bag around me and nestled beside Peter as the wind moaned eerily, the sky a maelstrom of black.

As the last remnants of light drained from the sky the rain continued to fall. It was too cold to sleep and even huddled beside Peter I could find little residual warmth. Finally Peter grabbed his rucksack. 'Come on,' he said. 'We're going to freeze if we stay here. We need to keep moving.' I nodded dully, my teeth chattering uncontrollably as I followed him out of the undergrowth.

The rain continued throughout the following day, but we marched on, picking our way across the uneven terrain, shoulders squared against the relentless downpour.

Finally, while we were traversing a shallow ravine, the rain stopped and a weak sun broke through the clouds. At the top of the ravine Peter came to a halt beside a narrow ditch bordered by thick fragrant weeds. The ditch had been sheltered from the rain by a wedge of rock and was relatively dry.

Peter flopped onto the ground. 'We should rest here,' he sighed.

My whole body was weak with fatigue and I gratefully collapsed beside him. As I rested my head on my rucksack my eyes began to close. 'Someone should keep watch,' I mumbled as I tried to force myself to stay awake.

'We both need to rest,' Peter said in a voice thick with fatigue. 'We haven't slept properly in days.'

'What if someone finds us?'

He gave an incoherent response as my eyes flickered once, twice and then remained closed. Peter threw an arm across me, pinning my shoulder to the ground. Then nothing; just welcome sleep.

CHAPTER 26

What I've Done

MaryAnn:

'Get up,' a grainy voice pierced the murky depths of sleep. My eyes flew open. My heart quickened as a blurry grey image came into focus. At first I thought it was another nightmare, but then I saw the gun the Watch held in his hand and an icy cold dread gripped at my insides.

Peter stirred, his breath tickling my neck. He groaned softly and rolled onto his back. 'Go back to sleep,' he murmured.

'Wake up!' I hissed. Peter's eyes flew open and I felt his body stiffen.

'Hello again!' the Watch said.

I scanned the man's face and recognised him immediately. Peter had been right. The Watch from the island had followed us.

I glanced behind him expecting to see a patrol but he appeared to be alone.

'Out of the ditch, both of you,' the Watch ordered.

I followed Peter out of the ditch. As I huddled beside him I tried to catch his eye, desperate for reassurance, but he ignored me. His eyes, wolf-like, observed the Watch's every move. Somehow this helped control my panic. Despite our desperate situation and the gun the Watch had trained on us, Peter wasn't ready to give up.

The Watch barked something into a radio. There was a whistle of static and he tapped the cover sharply. Taking advantage of the distraction Peter delivered a high kick, dealing the Watch a glancing blow. The gun flew from his hand and skittered over the side of the ravine.

With a sickening crunch Peter threw himself at the Watch, grappling him to the ground. Blood spattered across the grass as the Watch struck Peter across the face. Peter retaliated with a succession of punches. He didn't stop until the Watch was still.

Peter staggered to his feet, blood pouring from his nose. As I ran towards him I caught sight of the Watch clambering up behind him. He stooped to pick up a rock. Peter's attention was focussed solely on me. I stared at him in horror, my mouth opening and closing wordlessly.

The Watch struck Peter a glancing blow across the side of his head. His face registered surprise as he swayed unsteadily and his knees buckled. He grasped wildly for a handhold and stumbled against the Watch. The weight of Peter's body thrust the Watch backwards and with arms flailing he plummeted over the edge of the ravine.

I darted over to where Peter lay sprawled across the grass. He sat up and gave a low moan. 'We have to kill him.' A thick stream of blood flowed from his head wound. He groaned and grasped for my arm. 'Help me up.'

As Peter got to his feet he staggered and his eyes lost focus. I tried to catch him as he slowly pitched backwards, but he was too heavy and he hit the ground with a sickening thud.

I crouched beside him and quietly called his name. His eyes were closed, his face the colour of putty. 'Peter!' I frantically grabbed for his wrist and let out a sigh of relief as I felt the faint flicker of a pulse. He was alive. He'd just fainted.

My attention was drawn to the glint of metal. I pulled the knife from his slack grasp. It felt unwelcome in my hand and I resisted the temptation to throw it away. 'I can do this,' I whispered to myself. It was my turn to keep us safe.

I scrambled to the edge of the ravine and peered tentatively over the side. The Watch was sprawled at an awkward angle on the rocks a short distance below.

'I can do this,' I muttered as I stole a quick glance at Peter. He was still unconscious. 'I can do this,' I repeated. I used the words almost like a mantra.

Grasping the knife purposely in my hand I scrambled down to the rocky ledge below. As I straddled the Watch's unconscious body I tried to quell the sense of horror at what I was about to do.

The Watch's face was slack and I prayed that he would remain unconscious until the task was done. I gripped the knife tightly with both hands, raising it high above my head. As I prepared to thrust downwards and despatch the Watch into a painless sleep he issued a low groan. The Watch's eyes flickered open and I saw them widen with fear as he caught sight of the knife in my hand. He tried to struggle but his arms where imprisoned by my thighs. He gasped loudly, the panic building on his face.

I looked away as the knife travelled down in one fluid movement. There was resistance as the blade tore through the coarse material of his uniform. Then it plunged into his flesh like a hot knife through butter. 'I'm so sorry,' I muttered hoarsely.

My face was wet, the tang of iron on my tongue. The Watch's mouth formed a circle, a cry of surprise. A gurgling noise rose from deep within his throat, bursting out in a long continuous moan. A whispered word, 'Helen', and then his body fell slack. I felt as if I was pitching forward and when I hit the ground I would shatter into a million pieces. I remained immobile, staring at the man I'd killed, lost in the empty void where his eyes used to be.

There was pressure on my arm, a voice calling my name, but so distant it was barely audible. I was propelled upwards. My hands oddly empty. The knife was gone.

I flinched at the sting of cold water. As I blinked, Peter came into focus. He squatted before me, his face a horror of dried blood. He'd taken off his shirt and was using it to rub at my hands. When I looked down I was shocked to discover that they were painted red.

'I killed him,' I whispered in a choked voice.

'Yes,' Peter replied quietly.

'He's dead because of me.' My voice sounded hollow.

'He's dead because he tried to kill us,' Peter replied coldly as he wiped at the sticky mess of blood that coated my arms and hands.

'He called out for *Helen*.'

'MaryAnn, don't,' he warned.

'Oh Peter, what if Helen is his daughter? What if I killed her father?' The hysteria threatened to consume me.

Peter's face was grim. 'Stop it. You can't think about his family.'

'I can't help it,' a sob caught in my throat.

Peter took my hands in his. 'If you think about his family it will drive you crazy. You did what you had to do.'

I pulled away from him in disgust. 'I killed someone. I can't forget about it.'

'If you hadn't killed him he would have tracked us down and killed us,' Peter's voice was brusque.

I turned away, unable to hold his gaze. Peter gripped my shoulder, forcing me to face him. 'MaryAnn. Listen to me. You can't fall apart on me. Not now. We have to find the others.'

'I never killed anyone before,' I croaked.

His face softened. 'I know and I'm sorry. It should have been me. I should have killed him.' I heard his voice falter, and then the hardness returned. He gave my cheek a final wipe with his damp shirt. 'You're done,' he said as he got to his feet. He crouched at the edge of the river to wash away the dried blood from his hair and face. There was a large gash on the side of his head where he'd been hit by the rock.

When he clambered to his feet he grabbed his rucksack. 'Come on. We have to go.'

'That's all you have to say?' my voice was high pitched.

He frowned and put a finger to his lips. 'Keep your voice down. The Watch had a radio. There could be a patrol close by.'

I was desperate for him to say something more, anything to make me feel better, but his manner was rough as he pulled me to my feet. 'We have to go,' he repeated as he picked up my rucksack and thrust it into my hands.

We picked our way along an overgrown trail that bordered the river. We travelled in a tense silence that was only broken when Peter stopped to point out animal tracks or wild foods that were safe to eat. He was as determined as ever to teach me to survive, but he didn't seem to realise that his hardest lesson was behind me. How could I flinch at the thought of trapping an animal when I'd taken a human life?

The river fed into a large lake and we set up camp on its rocky shore. When Peter left in search of food I peeled off my blood-splattered clothing and waded into the frigid water. I floated on my back letting the river envelop me, feeling it wrap around me like a cloak. Entombed in its frigid embrace the water filtered out all sound, numbing my senses. I was cocooned, floating in the void, suspended in nothingness. Time had no meaning.

Finally I dragged my heavy limbs out of the lake and clambered across the pebbles to the shore. With each step the comforting numbness I'd felt in the water fell away. My emotions were rubbed raw. Guilt gouged a channel through me as a desperate regret tugged at my insides.

Peter had returned to camp and was crouched at the foot of a gnarly tree. I could sense him watching as I approached. He held out a plate of food, but I shook my head.

'You should eat something,' he coaxed.

I ignored him.

'MaryAnn.'

I turned away, needing to put some distance between us.

'You can take the first watch,' I said as I pulled out my sleeping bag and climbed inside. I lay down on the hard ground and behind my closed eyelids I imagined myself floating in the icy lake, the frigid water enveloping my body, bringing with it a comforting numbness. Detached from reality I drifted painlessly into oblivion.

It was dark when I woke.

'I missed my watch,' I said as I sat up.

Peter shrugged. 'It's fine. I wasn't very tired.' There was a tense silence, broken only by the sound of his knife as he sharpened it on a stone. When he saw the wary glance I gave it he quickly stowed it in his belt. 'Are you going to be alright?' he asked.

It was my turn to shrug. 'I'll be fine,' I said as I climbed out of my sleeping bag and got to my feet. 'Come on. It's dark, we should go.'

'When we get to the rendezvous if you want to talk about, what happened yesterday, then I'm…' he trailed off uncertainly.

I shook my head. 'You're right. I need to get over it.' I stuffed my sleeping bag into my rucksack and slung it over my shoulder. 'Are you ready?' I queried as I headed down the path.

Peter cleared his throat uncertainly.

'Peter, I don't want to talk about it anymore,' I called back over my shoulder.

'Okay,' he replied quietly, 'but just so you know, you're going the wrong way.'

CHAPTER 27

Lost Friends Found

MARYANN:

As we approached the remains of a ruined wall I could detect the smell of woodsmoke on the air. Peter put out a cautious hand. 'Careful,' he mouthed. We climbed to the crest of a hill and peered over the summit. My heart leapt with joy. The valley floor below was littered with brightly coloured caravans. 'It's the circus,' Peter exclaimed.

We scrambled down the hill and made our way towards the camp.

'Who goes there?' a voice called out of the shadows. I stopped and turned towards the sound. In the gloom I could make out two vague silhouettes.

'It's Peter Mallory and MaryAnn Hunter,' Peter replied. I heard a squeak of surprise and shielded my eyes from the sudden glare of a torch.

'Step closer,' the voice ordered.

'As I moved towards the source of the light I recognised Rory as the bearer of the torch. He was accompanied by Nessa.

Rory gave a smile of recognition. 'Peter, MaryAnn, it's good to see you.' I was surprised when he enveloped me in a tight hug. He smelt of smoke and grass and something sweet like raspberries.

'Is Flo with you?' Nessa peered anxiously behind us.

Peter shook his head. 'No, she isn't. It's just the two of us.'

Nessa's face fell.

'What happened to her?'

'I don't know,' Peter said. 'We lost the others.'

Nessa gave him an appraising look. 'You look awful.'

'It's been a rough couple of weeks,' Peter replied. I could hear the exhaustion in his voice.

'You look fit to drop,' Nessa said. 'Come join us by the fire.'

We followed Rory and Nessa through the camp to where a fire burnt brightly. I gratefully took a seat within its comforting embrace, eagerly soaking up the warmth.

While Rory handed around mugs of soup, I was conscious of Nessa's scrutiny. As soon as we were settled she turned to Peter. 'Tell us everything that happened,' she said.

I quietly sipped my soup and listened as Peter relayed our story. 'We found the LightHouse,' he explained. 'We rescued Flo and Charlotte.'

'Then why isn't she with you?' Nessa interrupted.

'We escaped by boat, but we were attacked by a helicopter,' Peter explained.

I heard Nessa make a small noise in the back of her throat.

'The Watch have a working helicopter?' Rory questioned.

Peter nodded in response. 'When it attacked the boat MaryAnn and I jumped overboard and swam for the shore.'

'What about the others?' Nessa interrupted again.

'I don't know. We didn't see them after that.'

Nessa and Rory shared a worried glance.

'One of the trucks was missing,' I tried to reassure her. 'We think it might have been taken by the others.'

'But you don't know if Flo was with them?' she questioned.

I shook my head.

'Flo's a resourceful girl,' Rory replied. 'We taught her to take care of herself.'

'Daryl and I arranged a rendezvous in case we were separated,' Peter said. 'MaryAnn and I are on our way there.'

'Daryl wouldn't let anything bad happen to our Flo,' Nessa stated confidently. 'If she's with him she'll be safe.'

'We don't even know if Daryl's still alive,' Rory exclaimed.

I let out an involuntary gasp. Peter didn't respond but I could see his jaw tighten. Rory glanced uneasily in my direction, 'I'm sure Daryl's fine,' he said. 'The Union trained him well.'

'Have you been waiting here long?' Peter asked.

'About three weeks,' Nessa replied. 'We assumed if you got into trouble you'd head to the safe house. We didn't know you'd arranged a different rendezvous.'

'Daryl and I thought it best to keep away from the safe house,' Peter explained. 'Our operation wasn't exactly sanctioned by the Union and Patrick told us that the Stewards weren't very pleased. We didn't want to cause any more trouble.'

Nessa barked out a humourless laugh. 'Patrick told you that did he?'

'There's going to be a hearing when we get back to the Union,' Peter explained.

'There's going to be a hearing alright!' Ness exclaimed, 'but I think it's Patrick who's got some explaining to do. Brandon's keen to understand why he abandoned the Union to chase after you. He's furious. Especially with the tension in the Neighbourhood.'

'What's happening in the Neighbourhood?' I asked.

'They're still having problems after Boundary Day. People have started to question how safe the Neighbourhood is,' Rory replied.

'The Director's doing his best to suppress the rumours but there's a lot of unauthorised chatter on the Portal,' Nessa continued. 'I also hear the new Legislator's a bit heavy handed, he doesn't have the experience of his predecessor.' She hesitated and glanced awkwardly in my direction.

I could feel Peter's eyes rest on me at the reference to my father. I stared at the floor, studiously avoiding his gaze until he turned his attention back to Nessa. 'Go on,' he urged.

'The Legislator's been arresting protestors. I heard there's been a number of deaths in custody. Too many to hide.'

'Do you think it's going to escalate?' Peter asked.

Ness nodded. 'People are starting to ask questions.'

'That's why Brandon's angry with Patrick,' Rory added. 'It's not a good time for him to be away from headquarters. Brandon's hoping the Director will be forced to quit and the new leader will open up negotiations with the Union,' he continued. 'The new Director will expect to speak to the Leader of the Union. Patrick's left the Union dangerously exposed.'

'So what do we do?' Peter asked.

'We'll take you to the rendezvous,' Nessa said. 'We'll find Flo and if Patrick's waiting there for you we can take him back to headquarters.'

'We should leave in the morning,' Rory said.

'You both need rest,' Nessa said as she collected our empty cups. 'You can sleep in our caravan tonight.'

'What about you and Rory?' I asked.

'We've got a lot of packing to do. We won't sleep tonight. Come on. Follow me.'

We followed Nessa through the camp until we arrived at a bright yellow caravan. 'This is ours,' she said.

The interior of the caravan was dominated by a large double bed, draped in a thick red blanket and covered with plump gold cushions. Peter must have sensed the covetous look I gave the bed as he promptly offered it to me.

'If she's having the bed you can sleep on this,' Nessa pulled a mattress and blanket from a drawer. 'I'll wake you in the morning when it's time to leave,' she said as she headed for the door.

I sank luxuriously onto the bed. It was soft and springy and very comfortable. 'Are you sure you don't want to sleep on the bed?' I asked Peter. I eyed his thin mattress dubiously. 'That doesn't look very comfortable.'

'It'll be fine,' he replied.

I untied my boots and dropped them onto the floor.

'You ready for me to turn off the light?' he asked.

I scrambled under the covers. 'I am now,' I said.

Peter strode across the room and blew out the candle. The caravan plunged into instant darkness.

I closed my eyes, thinking of the lake and its numbing cocoon of water. I immersed myself, waiting to sink into peaceful oblivion, but all I could see was the Watch's face and the shape of his mouth as it formed the word 'Helen'. Despite my exhaustion I fought sleep, avoiding the dreams that I knew would come.

After a restless night I woke to the sound of groaning as Peter clambered off his mattress.

'Did you sleep well?' I asked.

'I suppose it was better than sleeping on the ground,' he replied. 'Marginally.'

I stretched out, luxuriating in the comfort of the bed.

'Are you not getting up?' he asked as he packed away his mattress. 'We should go find Nessa and Rory. I expect they'll want to leave as soon as possible.'

'Just a few more minutes,' I mumbled as I snuggled deeper into the covers.

'They might have a shower,' Peter coaxed.

I bolted upright. 'Really! Do you think so?'

Peter shrugged. 'You should go and ask Nessa.'

I leapt out of the bed and grabbed my rucksack. 'Come on,' I urged as I clambered down the caravan steps.

Outside the camp was a hive of activity as people dissembled tents and packed away crates. I searched the crowd of people and spotted Nessa in the midst of the chaos.

My heart leapt when she told me that the camp had a solar shower.

It was lukewarm, and certainly not the best shower I'd ever had, but it felt wonderful to be clean again.

I found Nessa waiting for me outside the makeshift shower block. 'Come with me,' she said. 'You need to look like circus folk.'

I followed Nessa back to the caravan and once inside she pulled out a chair and told me to take a seat. She unfolded a small table and busied herself mixing powder and water in a wooden bowl. 'You like purple?' she asked.

'Purple?' I queried.

'Purple hair,' she replied. 'I think it'll suit your colouring.'

I thought back to the time Georgina, my friend in the Neighbourhood, had persuaded me to have red highlights. She'd made a mistake with the colour mix and the result had been bright orange hair. I'd been forced to wear a hat for weeks until it faded.

Nessa must have sensed my hesitation because she gave me an encouraging pat on the shoulder. 'It'll look pretty. I promise.' I responded with a reluctant nod as Nessa set to work on my transformation. After she'd finished with the hair dye she opened a make-up bag. 'I'm going to give you traveller eyes,' she explained as she pulled out a black eyeliner pen.

All of the travellers had thick black-rimmed eyes and, combined with their bright hair and shimmering skin, it gave them a very dramatic look. Nessa displayed a steady hand as she showed me how to apply the eyeliner in thick broad strokes. Once she'd finished she stepped back to survey her handiwork and coughed nervously. 'Erm, we just need to…we should cover your…' she paused uncertainly.

'Scar,' I added helpfully. Now the bruising had disappeared my scar was visible once again.

'If the Watch are searching for you that's the first thing they're going to look for,' she replied.

'I've tried covering it with make-up but it doesn't work.'

'I think I can help with that,' she said as she pulled out a paint palette and an assortment of brushes.

She bent over my face and examined my scar so closely I had to resist the urge to pull away. She dipped the brush into the paint palette and set to work. When she'd finished she surveyed my face and then handed me a mirror.

I studied my reflection carefully. My head was threaded with strands of purple. It really did complement my colouring. More miraculous was my scar. It had completely vanished and in its place Nessa had painted a string of shimmering flowers. I touched them carefully and felt a lump in my throat. She'd turned something ugly, something I hated, into a thing of beauty.

'I love it,' I whispered.

'It's not permanent,' she replied. 'It'll wash off in a couple of weeks, but it should last until we get back to the caves.'

She exchanged the mirror for a bundle of clothes. 'You'd better put these on,' she said. 'They're Flo's,' she continued in a slightly choked voice. 'You're about the same size.'

I took the clothes and shook out a long purple skirt. It was laced with glimmering silver fibres. There was a matching waistcoat and soft cream shirt. I changed quickly and when I'd finished Nessa gave me an appraising look. 'You'll pass,' she said.

Peter was waiting outside. He'd also been given a makeover. His blonde hair was highlighted with slender strands of sapphire and his eyes were ringed with black. He was sporting brown cotton trousers, paired with a deep blue shirt that brought out the colour of his eyes and complemented his new hair.

'You look nice,' he said.

'You too,' I replied a little self-consciously as my hand flew to my scar.

'Come on, we're about to leave,' Nessa said. 'You can ride up front with Rory.'

The yellow caravan was hitched to a sturdy black horse sporting four white socks and a flash of white along its nose. 'Meet Mr Mumbles,' she said as the horse snickered into the palm of her hand. Peter stroked the horse enthusiastically while I gave it a reluctant pat on the nose.

We clambered up onto the bench beside Rory and as soon as we were comfortably seated he flicked the reins and the caravan lurched forward, taking us closer to the rendezvous.

The Show Must Go On

MARYANN:

'I think it's a roadblock.'

My eyes flew open at Peter's comment and I caught a flash of grey on the road ahead.

'It was only a matter of time,' Rory sighed as the caravan came to a halt. The Watch lined the road, blocking the way ahead.

A tall blonde woman extracted herself from the patrol and strode purposefully towards the train of caravans. 'I want everyone out now!' she boomed.

'You should go too,' Rory said as travellers spilled out onto the grass. 'Just try to blend in.'

With my heart pounding I climbed down from the caravan and hovered uncertainly at the edge of the group.

The Watch called for silence. 'We are searching for this girl,' she cried and held up a photograph. My stomach clenched in fear as I saw that it was my face that stared out from the picture. I felt a restraining hand on my shoulder. 'Stay calm,' Peter murmured quietly in my ear.

'The fugitive was last seen with the Union and is recognisable by a deep scar across her cheek. She may be going by the name of Beth Summers.'

The Watch paused and surveyed the crowd. 'The Director is offering a substantial reward for anyone who can give us details of her whereabouts. If you have information you should come forward now.'

I examined the crowd, anxiously waiting for one of the travellers to point me out to the Watch.

'Try not to draw attention to yourself,' Peter whispered.

His warning came too late! The Watch caught my eye and she frowned. She strode towards me, the crowd parting to let her pass. 'Do you have any information about the girl we're looking for? She's about the same age as you,' she asked. I shook my head, my mouth too dry to speak. I felt her eyes search my face, scrutinising the flower tattoo. She frowned.

'What's your name?' she asked.

My mouth opened but nothing came out.

'It's Bridget.' I glanced up at Peter. 'Her name's Bridget,' he said.

'And you are?'

'I'm Peter.'

'Well Peter and Bridget, tell me what you do?'

'I don't understand?' Peter frowned.

'What do you do in the circus?' she replied impatiently.

Peter hesitated for a heartbeat. 'We have a knife act,' he replied.

The Watch considered Peter for a moment. 'That sounds interesting. Maybe you can show me your knife act while the patrol searches the caravans.'

'You want us to perform our act now?' Peter queried.

'They can't perform out here. It's too dangerous,' Nessa protested.

'If it's inconvenient I can always take them away for further questioning.' Nessa threw Peter a panicked look.

His grip on my shoulder tightened for a brief second and then relaxed. 'We'll do it, but we'll need a few minutes to prepare.' Peter grabbed my arm, steering me away from the crowd.

'What are we going to do?' I whispered as soon as we were out of earshot.

'We're going to perform our knife act,' Peter replied calmly.

'No, really,' I protested. 'What are we going to do?'

'I just told you. We're going to perform our knife act.'

'But I don't know how to throw a knife.'

Peter's lips twitched and despite the seriousness of our situation he smiled. 'I'll throw the knife. You just have to stand very still.'

'Why do I have stand still…oh…you're going to throw the knife at me?' I shook my head vehemently. 'Absolutely not.'

'I don't see any other way out of this, do you?'

When I didn't respond he patted me on the shoulder. 'Trust me, it'll be fine.'

'Of course it's fine for you. No-one's throwing a knife at you.'

The Watch reappeared. 'Ready?' she queried.

'Yes, we're ready,' Peter replied. 'Trust me,' he whispered as he pushed me in the direction of the caravans.

I couldn't muster a response. All I could do was stare at him in horror.

'Bridget, go stand by the caravan,' he gave me a gentle shove. 'Just remember to stand very still,' he added quietly.

Heart sinking, I headed towards the caravan and leant back against its smooth wooden side.

'Arms out,' Peter called to me.

I stretched out my arms. They were trembling slightly.

'Ready,' Peter called as he pulled the knife from his belt and took a deep breath.

I tensed and waited for him to throw the knife. I prayed that he wouldn't damage any vital organs.

As he took aim he raised his eyebrows, his expression inviting me to trust him. I watched with horror as the knife hurtled towards me, lodging itself in the wood just below my right arm. There was a smattering of applause from the gathered crowd and Nessa and Rory shared a relieved glance.

'Very good,' the Watch observed. 'Now the other side.'

'I don't have another knife,' Peter protested.

'You can use mine.'

Peter accepted the knife she offered him and turned to face me. The last knife had missed, but I had a feeling that my luck was about to run out.

Peter took aim and I let out an involuntary squeak as the knife lodged into the wood just below my left arm. This time there was riotous applause from the gathered crowd.

As the applause died away the Watch turned to Peter. 'That was pretty good throwing. Maybe I'll come back and see your full act sometime.'

'If you've finished searching the caravans, we'd like to be on our way.' Nessa appeared beside the Watch. 'We've got a performance in a couple of days, and we don't want to be late.'

'We didn't find anything of interest. You're free to go,' the Watch confirmed.

Nessa responded with a curt nod.

'You can clear the roadblock,' the Watch called out as she headed back to the Watch. Before reaching the patrol she paused mid step and turned. I watched with horror as she made her way towards me. She'd been playing a cruel trick. She'd known who I was all along. As she drew close I held my breath. She leant towards me, grasped her knife and pulled it out of the side of the caravan. She tucked it into her belt, then turned and walked away.

'Alright everyone,' Nessa's voice rang out across the camp. 'We're back on the road in five minutes.'

Peter strode over to the caravan and grabbed his knife. 'Phew,' he whistled theatrically as he tucked it into his belt, 'that was lucky.'

I was shaking so hard I couldn't respond.

Peter peered at me. He frowned. 'Hey, don't worry. The Watch have gone.'

'The Director's never going to stop looking for me,' I murmured.

Peter glanced around to see if anyone had overheard my comment. 'Come on. We need to talk.' He grabbed my arm and steered me back towards the caravan. Once inside he guided me to the bed and then busied himself pouring a glass of water.

I took the glass from his outstretched hand and drank the water slowly, steeling myself for what was next. There was only one solution to my predicament and Peter wasn't going to like it. I was going to have to leave the Union and find somewhere to hide from the Watch.

'Feeling better?' Peter asked after I'd taken a few sips.

I placed the glass unsteadily on the bedside table. 'I need to talk to you,' I said.

Peter's eyes narrowed but he didn't respond.

'You have to listen to me. It's important.'

'I'm assuming you're going tell me about the noble sacrifice you want to make,' Peter replied.

'What do you mean?'

'That you plan to leave the protection of the Union,' Peter replied.

'How did you?…' I trailed off uncertainly. Sometimes it felt like Peter could read my mind.

'I've told you before you're not that difficult to read. It's an admirable sacrifice – but totally reckless.'

I bristled at his comment. 'It's not reckless,' I protested. 'The Director has patrols looking for me. If I stay with the Union I'm putting everyone in danger.'

'You seem to have forgotten that the Union have been fighting the Light for years. We're always in danger.'

'I don't care. I won't put the Union at risk,' I said, 'and you can't make me stay if I don't want to.'

Peter raised an eyebrow. 'Really! You think I can't make you stay?'

I glowered at him.

'Okay, so let's say you leave the Union. How will you survive? Where will you go?'

'I could find a Community, somewhere remote. I can work as a teacher to support myself.'

'...and what do you think will happen to the people living in the Community when the Watch find you?' Peter didn't wait for me to answer before continuing. 'The Watch will punish them.'

I gaped at him.

'Is that what you want?' he asked, 'for innocent people to die?'

'Of course not,' I replied.

'MaryAnn, the Union is the safest place for you to be. We have the training to protect you. The people in the Community don't.'

'What if I give myself up to the Watch?' I reasoned. 'Let them take me back to the Neighbourhood.'

'The Director will torture you and eventually you'll give up the location of the Union headquarters.'

With a sinking heart I realised that Peter was right. If the Director tortured me I would tell him everything.

Peter's face softened. 'I know it's a hard choice to make, but you have to stay with the Union. We can protect you.'

It was a hopeless situation. Whatever choice I made people were going to get hurt.

'This isn't just about you,' Peter added. 'The Director's using you as bait. We know where the LightHouse is. He wants to find a way to make sure we don't tell anyone about it. He wants us all dead.'

'So what do we do?' I asked.

'When the Director comes for you, and we know he will, he won't find you cowering in some remote Community. You'll have the power of the Union standing right beside you.'

'You really believe that,' I questioned, 'that the Unionists will stand beside me? They don't even like me.'

'It's not that they don't like you, they're just suspicious of you because you're from the Neighbourhood. It'll take time to gain their trust.'

'So why would they choose to fight with me if they don't trust me?'

'This fight has been building for a long time. Every year the Light demands more from us. They take our land and force us to grow worthless soya beans. They make our children work for them in the Neighbourhoods. The Union want a fair and just society and that's why I joined them. The Unionists will stand beside you because you're part of that fight now.'

I'd never heard Peter speak with such eloquence and passion before. It was clear that I had a choice. I could run and hide or I could stand and fight. There was only one option, I was done with hiding.

CHAPTER 29

Reunion

MARYANN:

It was dark when Nessa entered the caravan. She told me that we were close to the rendezvous and invited me to walk with her.

I welcomed the opportunity to stretch my legs and leapt out of the caravan behind her. Moonlight filtered through a break in the clouds, revealing a stone structure in the distance. 'I think that's the rendezvous,' Nessa said.

'It's an abandoned castle,' Peter said as he appeared by my side. 'The others should be waiting for us there.'

The castle was a ruin, its roof was missing and the ground around the walls was littered with fallen stones. As the caravans came to a halt I was overjoyed when Uncle Patrick strode out of the castle entrance. His face shone luminous in the moonlight. He covered the distance between us in a few short strides and pulled me into a hug. 'MaryAnn, you're safe!'

I caught a flash of pink and a high-pitched yell as Flo flew out of the entrance and threw herself at her parents. They responded with reciprocal cries of delight.

Will, Jake and Max followed Flo out of the castle and I was surprised when they pulled me into an enthusiastic hug.

'What about the others?' I asked. 'Is Daryl… ?' I was too scared to finish.

'He's coming,' Uncle Patrick said. 'I sent Murray to fetch him.' Daryl was alive! I threw Peter a relieved glance. His face broke into a grin.

A few moments later I spotted Daryl in the distance. He sprinted towards me and grabbed me in an embrace. 'MaryAnn,' he cried, 'I've been so worried about you.'

'I'm fine,' I wheezed as he squeezed the air out of my lungs.

Mr Murray appeared by his side. 'It's good to see you MaryAnn. You had us worried,' he said as he pulled me into a bear-like hug.

'The others are inside,' Uncle Patrick said as he waved us through the tumbledown castle entrance. 'Follow me.'

Charlotte let out a small cry of surprise as we approached the campfire. At the sound of her cry Dan and Ruth looked up. 'Peter, MaryAnn! What happened to you?' Dan exclaimed as he sprang to his feet.

'We made it to the cave,' Peter replied. 'We waited for you there, but when you didn't come back we decided to head to the rendezvous.'

'We tried to get to you,' Dan explained, 'but the place was crawling with Watch. It was too dangerous.'

'We thought you'd be here weeks ago,' Mr Murray said.

'The Watch found the trucks so we had to walk.'

'That's a long journey. It looks like you had a bit of trouble too.' Mr Murray indicated the faded bruises on Peter's face.

'We had a run in with the Watch,' Peter replied.

'Did they follow you?' Uncle Patrick's voice was sharp. Peter gave him a scornful glance. 'No, of course not.'

I surveyed the group. There was someone missing. 'Where's Bekka?' I asked. I was surprised when Charlotte let out an unexpected sob. Mr Murray and Dan sprang to her side.

'Bekka didn't make it,' Mr Murray replied.

'We had to leave her on the beach,' Flo said in a choked voice.

Daryl wrapped an arm around her shoulder.

'If it wasn't for Dan and the boys providing cover we'd never have got away,' Mr Murray said. 'We escaped in Dan's truck.'

I was shocked to hear about Bekka. I'd known her only a few days, but she'd helped me escape from the Director and had paid for it with her life.

Peter seemed distracted, only half listening to the conversation as he scanned the interior of the castle. I realised there was another member of the group still missing.

'What about Flash?' I asked quietly, giving voice to the question that was clearly on Peter's mind.

There was a long silence.

'He's dead!' Peter responded dully.

'He's not dead, but he was badly injured,' Daryl said. 'I'll take you to him.'

We followed Daryl to a dark corner of the castle where we found Flash curled up on a bed of grass. He raised his head as we approached and let out a low whimper. Peter ran to his side, gently lifting the dog's head onto his lap.

'He was shot,' Daryl said. 'He lost his tail. We patched him up as best we could. Ruth's been taking care of him.'

'Thank you,' Peter murmured as he stroked Flash's muzzle. Flash let out a high pitched whimper and licked Peter's hand.

Nessa approached the group. 'We're setting up camp outside. There's enough food for everyone if you want to join us.'

'Can I stay here with Peter and Flash?' Ruth asked as we all got up to leave.

'It's fine by me,' Peter replied.

'You don't want anything to eat?' Mr Murray asked.

'I'm not hungry,' she replied.

'I'll bring something back for you,' Mr Murray's tone was gentle. Ruth didn't respond.

'What's the matter with Ruth?' I asked Mr Murray as soon as we were out of earshot.

'She's not doing so well. We had to leave her mum behind. It was too dangerous to go back for her.'

'Oh no!' I replied. 'What if the Watch find her?'

'She can look after herself, she's hidden in the cellar for years. It's Ruth I'm worried about. She's been very withdrawn and spends most of her time with Flash. I can't get her to talk to me.'

CHAPTER 30

Nightmares and Dreams

CHARLOTTE:

The distant hum grew louder until it was almost deafening.

'Into the water,' a voice yelled.

Uncle Ethan dragged me to my feet. 'Over the side,' he cried as he pushed me towards the edge of the boat. He was so close I could make out deep lines of fear etched across his face. I jumped into the water and gasped as I sank beneath its surface. I was a strong swimmer and spent a lot of time playing in the lake at home but I struggled to push myself upwards, my arms and legs a frenzy of movement.

I burst through the surface to find myself alone in the water. In the distance the boat was ablaze, flames licking hungrily at the night sky. I could make out pinpricks of light from the helicopter.

'Uncle Ethan,' I cried out as I splashed around in the water, desperate to stay afloat.

'Uncle Ethan,' I screamed at the top of my lungs. I couldn't see him in the water. What if he hadn't made it off the boat? I didn't want to be alone at sea.

'Charlotte, I'm over here.' Relief washed over me at the sound of my uncle's voice and I struck out blindly towards him. 'Stay where you are,' he ordered, 'I'll swim to you.'

Uncle Ethan emerged out of the darkness, silhouetted against the burning boat. I clutched at him frantically. 'Charlotte,' his voice was stern. 'Charlotte, you have to calm down.'

'I thought you were dead,' I gasped.

'I'm fine,' he said, 'now let go of my arm. You're going to pull me under the water.'

I released my grip, paddling madly to stay afloat.

'We need to get to the beach before the helicopter comes back,' he said. 'You're going to have to swim to the shore.'

I nodded. 'I can do that,' I replied.

'Stay close to me,' he ordered. 'I don't want to lose you in the dark.'

Uncle Ethan struck out towards the shore and I followed in his wake.

We were buffeted by strong waves and soon I was exhausted and gasping for breath. 'We should rest for a while,' Uncle Ethan called out.

Grateful for the chance to catch my breath I rolled over onto my back, treading water.

The silence was split by a deafening yell, 'MaryAnn.' The voice cried out, 'MaryAnn.'

'Uncle Ethan, there's someone else in the water.'

'This way,' he said as we swam towards the voice.

The owner of the voice was Daryl, he was with Flo and Mr Hunter. Flo let out a cry of joy when she caught sight of us. 'Charlotte, I was so worried about you.'

'Is MaryAnn with you?' Daryl asked.

He was crestfallen when Uncle Ethan informed him that we hadn't seen her. 'She'll be alright,' Mr Hunter said. 'I've already told you that Peter was with her when she jumped out of the boat. I saw them in the water.'

In the darkness something bumped against my leg. I turned

to examine the thing that floated beside me in the water. It had the face and body of Bekka. The scream tore from my throat and shattered the darkness.

I bolted upright in my sleeping bag, my breath coming in ragged gasps. Every night I suffered through the same dream, reliving our nightmarish escape from the LightHouse, forced to remember the horrific events of that evening and to watch my friend die over and over again.

I recalled how Uncle Ethan had pushed me aside so he could check Bekka's pulse. It was weak, but she was still alive.

'We have to get to the beach,' Mr Hunter had yelled as we heard the sound of distant gunfire from the helicopter. Daryl had argued, refusing to swim back to the shore without MaryAnn. 'She's with Peter,' Mr Hunter had insisted. 'They'll head to the beach too.'

'We have to go now,' my uncle had urged as the lights of the helicopter turned towards us.

Exhausted, we'd staggered onto the beach, Mr Hunter and Daryl placing Bekka gently on the sand. Uncle Ethan had crouched beside her, tearing open her red shirt. I'd flinched at the ragged hole in her stomach. I caught the look that passed between Uncle Ethan and Mr Hunter, it was the same look my mum and dad had shared when my donkey had broken its leg. I couldn't accept what it meant.

'Uncle Ethan please, you have to help her.'

Flo had screamed when he shook his head. 'There isn't anything we can do. She needs a hospital.'

'She has a family, a grandma.' I wasn't sure why I'd told him that. Maybe I wanted him to understand that Bekka couldn't die. That she had a family waiting for her at home.

Uncle Ethan's face had scrunched up in the same way that Mum's used to when she was trying not to cry. He'd turned away so that I couldn't see.

Bekka had let out a sigh. A wisp of a noise that was barely audible. Flo grabbed her hand. 'We made it,' she'd said softly. 'We escaped.'

'Do you think she can hear you?' I'd whispered.

'Of course she can. She knows we're free.'

I thought I'd detected a slight tilt to the corner of Bekka's mouth. She sighed again and then her face went slack.

The memory of Flo yelling at Bekka to open her eyes forced me up and out of my sleeping bag. I wouldn't sleep again tonight.

I felt very alone as I wandered out of the castle and made my way along the cliffs. The ground underfoot was uneven but my feet followed the path instinctively; this was my regular nightly routine. I was surprised to find someone else sitting in my favourite spot. I was about to turn and walk away when the figure stirred. 'Charlotte, is that you?' It was MaryAnn.

'I couldn't sleep,' I said.

MaryAnn gave a laugh that was devoid of any humour. 'There seems to be a lot of that going around. I couldn't sleep either.'

'Do you want me to leave you alone?' I fidgeted, waiting for a response. Being in MaryAnn's company made me feel a little awkward. She was so confident and sure of herself.

'Why don't you sit with me for a while? It'd be nice to have some company.'

I studied her uncertainly, not sure if she was just being polite. Her offer seemed genuine so I took a seat beside her. We sat in silence and watched as the moonlight filtered through a break in the clouds. It was so different from the night of our escape. With no light to illuminate our path, the blackness had consumed us. I shivered, fighting the tug of memory, not wanting to be transported back to the horrors of that evening.

'You alright?' MaryAnn asked.

'I'm fine,' I replied as I gripped the front of my cardigan, wrapping it tightly around me.

'Do you want to talk about it?' she asked. 'Something's obviously upsetting you.'

'I can't stop thinking about everything that happened,' I paused awkwardly. 'I have dreams about it all the time,' I admitted.

'Have you told anyone?' she asked.

I shook my head. 'I can't.'

'It'll help if you talk about it,' she said. 'What about your dad or Uncle Ethan?'

'I can't,' I repeated. My dad and Uncle Ethan risked everything to rescue me. I didn't want to cause any more worry.

MaryAnn considered me for a moment. 'You can talk to me if you want to.'

I wasn't sure how to respond. MaryAnn was a Unionist; she was brave and confident. How could she ever understand how terrifying my nightmares were? There was a strained silence while I chewed on my thumbnail.

'The last time I saw you was when the helicopter fired on us,' MaryAnn said. 'Did you jump into the water with your uncle?'

'I was alone for a while,' I admitted.

'That must have been really scary,' she said. 'I had Peter with me the whole time and I was still terrified.'

I glanced at her, shocked that she'd admitted to being terrified. Bolstered by her confession I nodded. 'I was glad when Uncle Ethan found me,' I said. 'We were swimming back to the shore when we heard Daryl calling out for you. He was with Flo and Mr Hunter.'

'Was Bekka with you in the water?' MaryAnn asked

I suppressed a shudder. 'We found her floating in the water. She was unconscious. We took her back to the shore, but she died on the beach. We had to leave her. The Watch found us and started shooting.'

'I'm so sorry,' MaryAnn sympathised. 'She deserved better than that.'

'She did,' I replied. 'We shouldn't have left her.'

'You had no choice,' MaryAnn said. 'You couldn't take her with you.'

'It doesn't make me feel any better.'

'You were really brave,' MaryAnn said.

I hadn't felt brave. I'd been rooted to the spot with fear when I'd heard the sound of bullets. Uncle Ethan had grabbed my hand and yelled at me to run as he dragged me across the beach.

'Your dad said that he found you?' MaryAnn queried.

I nodded. 'He was in the lookout and saw the helicopter blow up the boat. He couldn't walk very far because of his sprained ankle so he sent the boys to get the truck. They searched the coast and found Ruth and Flash washed up on the rocks. They arrived at the beach just in time to rescue us,' I said. 'We tried to come for you and Peter,' I explained, 'but we ran into a Watch patrol and we couldn't get through.' I shuddered as I recollected our encounter with the Watch. Squashed into the back of the pick-up truck with Ruth, Flash, Will, Jake and Max, I'd thrown myself onto my stomach at the sound of the gunshots.

'That's when Flash lost his tail,' I continued. 'He was hit by a bullet.' I pushed aside the image of his tail as it flopped lifelessly onto the floor of the truck.

'So then you went to the rendezvous?' MaryAnn queried.

I nodded. 'Daryl didn't want to leave you, but Mr Hunter said that he'd seen you jump into the water with Peter so he knew you'd be together. We thought you'd follow us. We just didn't expect you to take so long.'

'We didn't have a vehicle,' MaryAnn said, 'so we had to walk.' The exhaustion was evident in her voice. When she'd arrived at the rendezvous I'd been shocked by her appearance. She was skinny to the point of being emaciated.

'Daryl's been out every day looking for you,' I said. 'He was convinced you'd broken down somewhere.'

'You didn't think about leaving and going back to the Union?' MaryAnn asked.

'Not at first,' I replied, 'but the longer you've been missing the more concerned Mr Hunter has been that…' I trailed off, not sure how to finish.

'Go on,' MaryAnn urged.

'Mr Hunter thought you might have been captured by the Watch and taken to the Neighbourhood. He was worried that you would give away the location of the headquarters.'

'He wanted to go back and warn the Stewards?' MaryAnn questioned.

'We were planning to leave at the end of the week,' I replied.

'You and Dan were going with them?' MaryAnn sounded surprised. 'I thought you'd want to go back to your farm.'

Misery washed over me. 'We can't go home. The Watch evicted us from the farm.'

'I'm really sorry,' MaryAnn said.

'It's strange knowing that I'll never go back,' I admitted. 'It feels like I've lost everything, my home, Mally, everything's gone.' I swallowed hard and blinked frantically as tears pricked the corner of my eyes.

MaryAnn patted my arm sympathetically. 'Mally was brave to stay behind and look for Eric.'

'I wish he'd come with us,' I said. 'Does that make me a horrible person?'

'Of course you're not a horrible person. Mally's your friend, you want to protect him.'

'I was hoping the Union would go back to the LightHouse to rescue him, but Mr Hunter said that he won't risk another trip north.'

MaryAnn chewed on her bottom lip. 'I don't understand. I thought that the Union would try to rescue everyone from the LightHouse now they know the location.'

'Your uncle thinks it's too dangerous.'

'That's not right!' MaryAnn sounded indignant. 'Does Mr Murray agree with him?'

'He tried to argue, but Mr Hunter is the leader of the Union. He has to do what he says.'

'If there's a way to save them Mr Murray will find it. He's one of the bravest people I know.'

'Before I tested Immune I didn't even know Uncle Ethan was in the Union,' I confessed.

'I suppose he couldn't tell you because he wanted to keep you safe,' MaryAnn replied.

'He doesn't have to worry about that now,' I replied. 'I'm Immune. I know the location of the LightHouse. I'm never going to be safe again.'

MaryAnn recoiled at my comment. 'You really think the Watch will keep looking for you?'

'Of course they will. Flo will have to go into hiding too.'

'You'll be safe with the Union,' MaryAnn said reassuringly, 'they'll protect you.'

CHAPTER 31

Somewhere I Belong

MaryAnn:

'MaryAnn! It's time to get up.' I felt a light pressure on my arm as Daryl gently shook me awake.

'It can't be morning already,' I murmured as I snuggled deeper into my sleeping bag. I'd stayed up late the previous evening talking to Charlotte and I was exhausted.

'Come on, everyone else is up already.'

I opened one eye and peered furtively over the top of my sleeping bag. 'It's still dark,' I groaned.

'We're going to travel with the circus and Nessa wants to be on the road by first light,' Daryl said.

I rolled away from him. 'I'll get up in a minute,' I replied as my eyes flickered closed.

'Come on,' he gave me a gentle nudge. 'You'll miss breakfast.'

When I opened my eyes again I was alone in the ruined castle. Feeling a little guilty for sleeping so late I slithered out of my sleeping bag. The grass was drenched with dew and it soaked through my socks. Shivering, I searched for my boots and found them hidden in the long grass. I dragged them on over wet socks and laced them tightly. Finally I packed away my sleeping bag and was ready to leave.

I headed out of the castle and found myself in the middle of a frenzy of activity. Charlotte hurried by carrying a box of pans. 'Do you need any help?' I offered. She responded with a shy smile, 'No I'm fine. It's not heavy.'

As Charlotte scurried away I observed the rest of the camp. Everyone seemed busy. I spotted the smouldering ashes of the campfire and suspected that I was too late for breakfast. My stomach responded with a low growl of disappointment.

With nothing to do and with everyone else occupied I went for a walk along the top of the cliff. I returned to the spot where I'd met with Charlotte the previous evening and sat down on the wet grass.

'You want some company,' I glanced up to find Daryl hovering uncertainly on the path, his eyebrows were knitted into a wary frown. I suspected that he'd followed me from the castle.

When I nodded he dropped down beside me. I could feel tension in the silence that followed.

'Are you alright?' he finally asked.

I picked anxiously at a broken nail. When I glanced up he scrutinised my face, searching for an answer.

'MaryAnn, I'm worried about you,' he said. 'Tell me what's wrong.'

I inhaled sharply, releasing the breath slowly until I found my voice. 'It's really bad,' I said.

'Whatever it is, you can tell me,' he said. 'I'm your brother.' He grabbed my hand.

'I killed someone.' I whispered the words so quietly that they almost seemed to disappear on the wind.

I peered through my hair, stealing a glance at his face, trying to gauge his reaction. I was desperate to confess everything. It was too much guilt to carry alone.

I saw shock ripple across his face. 'Who did you kill?' he asked. His tone was measured, but his grip on my hand tightened.

'It was the Watch,' I explained. 'He followed us from the island.

He would have killed us if I hadn't…' I swallowed, there was a bitter taste in my mouth and I couldn't continue.

Daryl released my hand, wrapping his arms around my shoulders. 'It's okay,' he murmured softly.

I rested my head against his shoulder. I'd been scared that when he heard my confession he would walk away in disgust. 'I killed someone.' A sob caught in the back of my throat. Daryl's grip on my shoulders tightened. 'It's not your fault. Sometimes you don't have a choice.' His voice had changed. His tone was rough. I pulled away from him, trying to get a better look at his face. 'Have you ever killed anyone?' I asked tentatively.

At first he wouldn't hold my gaze but focussed his attention on the horizon. Then he sighed and looked down at me. When he spoke his voice was raw. 'Some,' he replied.

'More than one?' He must have heard the shock in my voice, because when he answered there was a defensive tone. 'I've been a soldier for four years. Sometimes we don't have a choice. It's the only option.'

Only a few short weeks ago I would have argued that he did have a choice. That we were responsible for our own actions, but a lot had happened since then and now I wasn't so sure.

I paused uncertainly. 'Sometimes when I close my eyes all I can see is his face. I just want it to go away.'

Daryl shook his head. 'I don't think it ever goes away.'

'Then how do you make it stop?' I asked.

'You don't,' Daryl replied. 'After a while you just learn to live with it.'

'I don't think I can,' I whispered.

We were interrupted by the sound of someone calling our names. I spotted Uncle Patrick on the path, summoning us back to the castle.

'It must be time to leave,' Daryl said as he stood up and pulled me to my feet. He anxiously searched my face. 'Are you going to be alright?' he asked.

I nodded uncertainly. 'I just want to go home,' I said.

'I'm here for you if you need me,' he replied before we headed back up the path to meet Uncle Patrick.

Uncle Patrick had commandeered a wagon so that the Union could travel together. It would attract less attention than the truck and the circus would provide a good cover. As Daryl and I stowed our things in the back, Mr Murray approached. 'MaryAnn, can you go and get Ruth. I think she's still in the castle.'

I searched the castle and found Ruth curled up next to Flash in a tumble-down room.

'I'm looking after Flash for Peter,' she said in a voice that suggested she'd recently been crying.

'That was kind of you,' I replied.

She shrugged and tickled Flash under the chin. 'He's good company.'

'I'm sorry you had to leave your mother behind,' I said.

'I wanted to go back for her,' Ruth replied.

'I know you did,' I replied. 'It was too dangerous. The Watch would have captured you.'

'She'll be so worried about me,' Ruth sniffed.

'What if I never see her again?'

I wanted to reassure her that the Union would rescue her mother and that they would be reunited, but after my conversation with Charlotte I wasn't so sure.

'I left her alone in the cellar,' Ruth continued in a tremulous voice.

'You have to be strong,' I said. 'That's what she would want.'

Ruth wiped at her eyes with the sleeve of her shirt. 'Did you come to get me?' she asked.

I nodded. 'We're about to leave.'

'I'll take Flash with me,' she said as she shook him awake. Flash got to his feet and after giving me a friendly lick he trotted out of the room. Ruth quickly hurried after him. She seemed eager not to let him out of her sight. I followed at a more leisurely pace.

As I headed towards the castle exit I thought I heard someone call my name so I stopped and turned towards the source of the voice. To my surprise I caught sight of Daryl and Peter partially concealed behind a stone column. Peter held his hands aloft in what looked like a gesture of self-defence.

'There was nothing I could do,' I heard him say.

'I trusted you to look after her.' Daryl's tone sounded accusatory.

'I did my best,' Peter said.

'That was the best you could do?' Daryl challenged. 'She killed someone.'

'Don't you think I know that,' Peter replied. 'I found her with the knife, remember.'

'I don't understand how you could let her kill someone.'

'I didn't let her. I had no choice. I was unconscious the whole time. If I could go back and change things then I would.' Peter sounded so sincere that I had to resist the temptation to call out to Daryl and demand he leave him alone. It wasn't Peter's fault the Watch had found us. It was mine.

'She said it was the Watch from the island. That he followed you?' Daryl questioned.

'I made a mistake,' Peter said. 'I should have killed him when he pulled a gun on us.'

'He was a tracker, you must have known he could come after you?'

'MaryAnn begged me not to kill him.'

'Why would you listen to her? That wasn't her decision to make.'

'She stood in front of the gun.'

'You're a trained soldier…are you telling me you couldn't stop her? There has to be more to this than MaryAnn standing in front of the gun.'

'I'm not sure I understand,' Peter queried.

'I've noticed that you two seem to have grown very close,' Daryl replied.

Peter let out an exasperated sigh. 'What's that supposed to mean? We spent weeks travelling together to the rendezvous. We had to rely on each other. It requires a certain closeness.'

'I just want to know what your intentions are.'

Peter's face flushed a deep shade of red. 'We're friends. I don't have any intentions.'

'Well let's hope it stays that way,' Daryl said. I was surprised to hear the warning note in his voice. 'She's not like the other girls you're *friends* with. She's my sister.'

Peter threw his hands in the air, clearly irritated. 'Daryl, you're not making any sense. MaryAnn and I are friends. That's all.'

'I'm just saying that if you upset her I'll…'

'Daryl, you're being ridiculous. I haven't got time for this,' Peter declared angrily. 'I've got work to do,' he said as he turned away.

'Hold on,' Daryl called after him, 'we're not finished yet.'

'I think we're more than finished,' Peter replied icily as he stormed away across the grass.

I watched as Daryl followed Peter out of the castle and then hurried to the wagon. Uncle Patrick was already up front with Mr Murray. As I climbed into the back I ducked my head, my cheeks still burning with embarrassment at the conversation I'd overheard. Peter and I were just friends, and barely that most of the time. He wasn't the type of boy I could ever be attracted to. I couldn't imagine him dressed for dinner at a fine restaurant, or drinking cocktails at a charity ball. We were not a good fit at all.

I caught Dan's eye and he gave a nod in my direction. He was with Charlotte in the opposite corner of the wagon. She was fast asleep, her head resting against his shoulder. Ruth was also on board, with Flash sprawled out comfortably in her lap.

The wagon gave a judder as Jake vaulted on board. 'I'm starving,' he proclaimed loudly as Will and Max followed in his wake. Will rummaged around in his coat pocket. 'I have an apple,' he offered.

Jake grabbed it from his outstretched hand and took a bite. He nodded in my direction. 'You want some?' he asked as he held the half chewed apple towards me. I shook my head in disgust. 'No thanks. I'm fine.'

'Who are we still waiting for?' Mr Murray called out.

'Daryl and Flo are missing,' Dan replied.

'We're here,' Flo huffed as she ran towards us, pulling Daryl along behind her.

'It looks like it's just Peter then,' Dan replied.

'Has anyone seen him?' Mr Murray enquired. I studied my feet, not wanting to reply.

Will jumped to his feet and surveyed the camp. 'I can see him. He's heading this way,' he exclaimed. I watched as Peter strode towards the wagon. He leapt on board and without a word he sat down beside me. I felt a little uncomfortable having him so close after the conversation I'd just overheard.

Mr Murray flicked the reins and the wagon lumbered into life.

Charlotte gave a gentle snort and her eyes flickered open. 'Are we moving?' she mumbled sleepily as she yawned and stretched.

'Yes, we're on our way,' Dan replied.

'How long before we get back home...I mean the caves,' she corrected.

'It'll take couple of weeks,' Dan said.

'So we have a few weeks of freedom before we're trapped inside the caves forever,' Flo grumbled.

'You make it sound you're being held prisoner,' Daryl replied. 'It's for your own safety. The Light is still looking for you.'

Flo made a face.

'Maybe we can do something to cheer you up,' Daryl said.

'Like what?' Flo enquired.

'Well it's tradition to get a tattoo after an operation. Maybe we can all get a group tattoo?'

Flo's face broke into a wide grin. 'You have the best ideas.'

'Cool! A tattoo,' Jake interrupted excitedly. 'I have the perfect spot right here.' He indicated his chubby forearm.

'Our first group tattoo,' Max said as he exchanged a high five with Will.

Daryl frowned. 'I didn't mean you three twerps,' he said. 'I meant the rest of us.'

I turned to him in surprise. 'I don't want a tattoo.'

'You have to,' Daryl protested. 'It's a tradition for everyone to get one. Isn't it Peter?'

Peter nodded in response.

'And I don't get a say in it?' I queried.

Daryl shook his head. 'Nope. It's the rules.'

'I think we should get a lion,' Will cried excitedly.

'I already said you aren't getting a tattoo,' Daryl replied, then frowned. 'Anyway, what has a lion got to do with our trip to the North?'

Will blushed. 'I suppose it hasn't got anything to do with it,' he mumbled. 'I just think it would look cool.'

'Me too,' Max agreed. 'I think a lion would look cool.'

'I'm not having a lion tattoo,' I replied.

'Well what do you want?' Daryl asked. 'It's your first operation so you should choose the design, as long as that's okay with Flo.'

Flo nodded, 'I'm happy with that.'

I thought for a moment. If I really was going to get a tattoo I wanted something nice. 'I want some flowers like Flo.'

Peter and Daryl looked aghast.

'There's no way I'm tattooing flowers on my body.' Peter shook his head in disgust.

Daryl nodded in agreement. 'Me neither.'

A cold wind sliced through my thin jacket and I pulled it tighter around my shoulders, hugging my knees to my chest. As I listened to my friends and family bicker about the tattoo design I realised that everyone I cared about was in the wagon with me. When I thought of the danger they faced it terrified me, I couldn't bear to lose any of them, but we couldn't escape. The Director was determined to find me and take me back to the Neighbourhood. Given the resources at his command it was only a matter of time before our paths crossed again. When it happened I would have to face it head on. I would have to be ready to stand and fight.

END OF BOOK 2

Acknowledgments

There are many people who have helped and supported me in writing this book. Firstly Annwyl Port who has read every rough draft with unfailing enthusiasm and can always be relied on to ask the difficult questions that I need to go and find answers to. Michele Lemon a gifted writer and my sounding board. Bekka Kipling for reading rough drafts and providing intelligent feedback (looks like those 3 years at university where well spent). Andy Davies and his wife Sarah for their support and insight into the final draft.

To my research team: Lewis Beck for his insightful knowledge of Scottish hares, to Charlotte Baker for her technical knowledge of row boats. Brian Stevenson and Georgia Kipling who accompanied me on a wet but very fun research trip to the Scottish Highlands and the Isle of Skye (next time I'll write a story based in the Caribbean. It'll be a lot warmer).

Thanks to my family, Pip, Jamie, Ant, Will and David for all your support and to my friend Nikki Harris who not only provided feedback on rough drafts but also spent a weekend decorating my attic so I could free up time to meet writing deadlines.

Thanks to the enthusiastic and very supportive team at Cillian Press. It's a privilege to work with you.

Finally thanks to all the readers, bloggers and reviewers who have taken the time to read *Blinded by the Light* and provided great reviews and feedback. I love hearing from all of you.

About the Author

JOE KIPLING is a Hull born, west Yorkshire based young adult fiction writer with a lifelong passion for Sci-Fi, particularly the post apocalyptic variety. She currently lives in Holmfirth with her dog Rosie and is a full time consultant and part time writer. A lifetime of travelling and avoiding near catastrophe has provided endless inspiration for The Union Trilogy.

www.joekipling.co.uk

Join in on the discussion
www.facebook.com/theuniontrilogy

Lightning Source UK Ltd.
Milton Keynes UK
UKOW04f0926201115

263145UK00002B/24/P